Sanibel Tides

A Shellseeker Beach Novel
Book Five

HOPE HOLLOWAY

Hope Holloway

Shellseeker Beach Book 5

Sanibel Tides

Copyright © 2022 Hope Holloway

Cover designed by Sarah Brown (http://www.sarahdesigns.co/)

Introduction to Shellseeker Beach

Come to Shellseeker Beach and fall in love with a cast of unforgettable characters who face life's challenges with humor, heart, and hope. For lovers of riveting and inspirational sagas about sisters, secrets, romance, mothers, and daughters...and the moments that make life worth living.

For release dates, excerpts, news, and more, sign up to receive Hope Holloway's newsletter! Or visit www.hopeholloway.com and follow Hope on Facebook and BookBub!

Chapter One

Olivia

Control was the one thing Olivia Whitney couldn't live without. Also, a plan, a strategy, a profit-and-loss statement, a sales goal, a to-do list, a blueprint for the future, and the ability to solve a few problems.

She had all of those and more every afternoon at work. That's when she stepped into Sanibel Sisters and managed the women's clothing boutique she owned with her partner, Camille Durant. But for the last three months, that was the *only* time Olivia had control. The rest of her life was—

"More Cheerios!" Bash hollered from his child seat in the back, punctuating the demand by tossing a handful of dry cereal like confetti all over the car. It fell, joining yesterday's celebration.

Her life was *this*. Taking care of an F5 tornado of a toddler—a force of human nature, and an orphan who had landed in the lap of the man Olivia loved. Control was history.

"You've had enough, hon," she said brightly.

"More!"

His favorite word. Well, one of them. Right up there with no, up, down, now, and *Wibbieeee*, his personal pronunciation of her nickname, usually wailed at a decibel level that could be heard in the next county.

"No more for now," Olivia said in that simple, straightforward adult voice that Bash generally ignored. Still, she would not raise her voice. Not now, not ever.

Sebastian Thomas Royce, motherless, fatherless, and currently under guardianship, had been through enough in his few short years on Earth. Her job, whether she signed up for it or not, was just to love the kid. Surprisingly, that wasn't too difficult.

"Hungry, Wibbie!"

"Snacks soon. In the meantime, eat that thumb you like so much, little man."

Bash gave a crooked smile, smart enough even at not-quite-three to know sarcasm when he heard it. Popping his thumb in his mouth, he stared out the window.

There. She sighed with a millisecond of relief. Quiet. Plus, she got him to respond to a request. Yay. Why did this always seem so difficult?

She looked at him in the rear-view mirror, giving in to a smile. His blond curls fell like a mop over a baby face, his cheeks always rosy from the saliva that escaped when he sucked his thumb. His blue eyes were big and so effective, they could make the very concept of *bedtime* seem laughable.

And that's how he got away with stealing any semblance of control that Olivia hoped to have.

The fact was, Bash had sent her beloved control and her whole personal life spiraling into oblivion, or at least on a completely different trajectory than what she'd planned.

Three months ago, in October, less than a month from her thirtieth birthday, Olivia Whitney had finally put things together the way she wanted them. She'd moved from Seattle to Sanibel Island, Florida, where her mother had relocated to live and work. She'd left her corporate retail job and partnered with another woman to launch Sanibel Sisters, which showed every indication of being a massive success. And she'd finally given her heart to Connor Deeley, a former Navy SEAL who ran a popular beach accessories rental business, a man who was as good and strong and beautiful on the inside as he was on the outside.

She had a plan...ish. A strategy and a timeline, anyway. She'd begun nursing hopes that she could have the trifecta of "all" that she'd heard people talk about when they said a woman "had it all." That would be a successful business, a loving husband, and, someday, a darling baby.

And then...*wham*! Life threw a sad and shocking curveball and it hit her right between the eyes.

Sad, because Bash's mother, the widow of one of Deeley's fellow Navy SEALs, had been killed in a highway accident while ditching the kid and all her responsibilities to marry some loser named Eddie. Shocking, because Deeley had been appointed Bash's legal guardian until the child was eighteen years old.

So that changed the life plan for the next decade and

a half. Well, it changed his and, if they truly loved each other, it also changed hers.

Over the past ninety days or so, they'd explored every option. Bash had no close relatives, at least none who wanted the boy. His father had barely been on speaking terms with his family, and Marcie had no one.

Deeley and Olivia had talked to lawyers, met with judges, appeared at guardianship hearings, consulted child protective services, and even had a session with a shrink who specialized in orphans.

With texts from Bash's late father specifying that he wanted Deeley to be named guardian, the choices were limited. Deeley could continue as Bash's legal guardian, even possibly adopting him at some point, or he could put the little boy in foster care. That last option wasn't ever on the table, not for a moment.

Deeley had lived under the false belief that he'd been responsible for Tommy Royce's death, despite being cleared by the Navy. In that regard, he'd given his time and money and energy to helping Marcie Royce since she'd become a widow. Now, with Marcie's tragic death, assuming Bash's guardianship wasn't that much of a stretch.

Although it was quite a challenge for a thirty-three-year-old single man who knew less than nothing about raising a kid and had professed to never want one.

Without a moment's hesitation, Olivia had stepped in to help, already in love with both Deeley and Bash. The first thing she'd done was offer them a better home than

Deeley's apartment, and helped them move into her two-bedroom Sanibel Island rental house off Rabbit Road.

She hadn't planned on living with Deeley after dating him for less than six months, but it made sense for Bash, who had risen to their top priority.

Instead of feeling the new-love joy and basking in their budding romance, their deepest conversations were about discipline, education, religious beliefs, pediatricians, and bedtime. They'd become insta-parents, and cared deeply for Bash's well-being, but the entire thing was exhausting, confusing, and complicated.

And it was all exacerbated by the fact that Bash had not been well parented by his frequently negligent mother. To say he wasn't an easy child...well, that was an understatement.

So, yeah. Olivia had the business she wanted, but her focus was elsewhere. She had a man she loved, but no ring on her finger or commitment in her heart. And she had a child to raise with whom she didn't share a single gene.

Did Livvie Whitney finally "have it all"—or nothing of the sort?

"See 'Liza?" Bash asked as she made the turn to Shellseeker Beach. His baby-talk question reminded her of one important aspect of her currently out-of-control life: They weren't in this alone. Not by a long shot.

"Yep, going to see my mom, Eliza. And Teddy. I know you love them."

She and Deeley and Bash had a village—well, a beach

—full of babysitters, advice-givers, and hand-holders at the ready.

Which happened to be why Olivia was on her way to Shellseeker Cottages right now. Not to get help from them, for a change, but in answer to a cryptic text from her mother that said simply:

Please come over—we need you.

Finally, someone needed her instead of the other way around, so Olivia had left everything—the mashed bananas, laundry, and the latest episode of *Blue's Clues*—to run to her mother's assistance.

"What do you think Eliza wants, Bash?" she asked, musing aloud because everything she read said children engaged in dialogue were smarter and...better. So she did her best to keep a conversation going with Bash all the time.

"'Liza!"

Okay, not a sparkling conversationalist, but precious. "Yes, Eliza! She's your..." No, she wasn't really his *grand-mother*. Just like Bash wasn't Olivia's son, and Teddy wasn't Olivia's own grandmother. And Deeley wasn't her husband, and...*oh.*

"Here we are!" she announced as she turned on Roosevelt Road, peering at the parking lot behind the house where her mother now lived and worked with Teddy Blessing.

Together, Eliza and Teddy rented a small group of cottages, managed the tea hut business that seemed to be growing as fast as the lush garden around it, and also owned the shell shop at the opposite end of the property.

The whole thing was lovingly called "a resort," but it was really a refuge for the many people who visited or lived there.

No matter what you called the place, in January, this slice of paradise would be packed, so she focused on the challenge of finding a parking spot. Everyone who lived on Sanibel talked about "the season" that kicked off after the holidays, and this was Olivia's first one on the island.

From Thanksgiving to New Year's Day, it had been crowded, but Olivia had been so consumed with her new role as a shopkeeper and helping with Bash that she'd barely noticed the changes on the strip of land known as "the seashell capital of the world."

Now? Well, now she understood *crowded*. The main drag could be a parking lot at peak hours, the beaches were jammed with tourists and the snowbirds who lived here in the winter, and the wait for a table in most restaurants could be long even on a weeknight.

Was that why Mom and Teddy needed help today? One too many guests at Shellseeker Cottages?

Olivia snagged a spot when a van pulled out, and began the process of unlatching Bash while he chattered about what he would eat—was he ever *not* hungry? She managed to lift a massive bag full of junk—er, kid necessities—that somehow weighed more than the human who needed it all. Taking Bash's hand, they marched over the crunchy shells toward the turquoise water and wide sandy shore of Shellseeker Beach.

"See Jay-jay?" Bash asked, tugging at Olivia's hand.

"You'll see Jay-jay this afternoon," she assured him,

grateful for the brand new daycare center that had opened over the holidays exclusively for Shellseeker Cottage guests and staff.

Of course, it helped that "Jay-jay" was Jadyn Betten-court, daughter of a billionaire who financed the opera-tion, sister of the "head housekeeper" at Shellseeker.

More family-that-isn't-family, she mused.

"Extended family. Found family." She gave Bash's hand a squeeze and smiled down at him. "Even landed-in-your-lap family."

"Sand dollar!" He pounced on a broken shell, bliss-fully unaware of his own sad backstory.

Just thinking about it made her crouch down and take a moment to look at the shell with him. The poor baby wasn't even three years old and he'd experienced more tragedy and loss than some people ten times his age. She couldn't bear to let him hurt, ever.

"There you are, Livvie!"

Olivia looked up to see her mother rushing toward them, arms outstretched toward Bash. "Hey, big guy!"

Nope, Eliza Whitney might not be Bash's "real" grandmother, but she loved with the heart and soul of one.

"'Liza!" He popped up and let her lift him, rewarding her with a hug that was probably sticky and left a few Cheerios in her strawberry-blond hair.

"I got here as fast as I could, but..." Olivia gave Bash a look and tapped his nose. "We had a slight banana emer-gency this morning. As in someone smashed his all over the wall."

He smiled, as innocent as the day was long. "Naner mash-up."

But Mom didn't smile, just gave him a distracted kiss. "Katie and Noah are down at the tea hut waiting for him. They'll watch him for an hour so you can help us."

"Help? Do what?"

"We have an incredible opportunity, Liv," she said, hoisting Bash higher on her hip as they walked. "It could be absolutely life-changing for Shellseeker Cottages."

"I'm intrigued."

"Let me run Bash down to the beach, and meet me upstairs at Teddy's house." She started off, but Olivia snagged her arm.

"Hold up there, Grandma. Sunscreen? His bag? Some food in case famine hits?"

Eliza laughed. "Look at you, Mother of the Year."

Olivia lowered her sunglasses to let the full impact of her look hit the mark. "Don't."

"Whoa. Sarcasm or...what?"

"You know." She dug into the bag and found the baby sunscreen, slathering it on Bash as he squirmed and complained and darn near got it in his eyes. "Same old-same old."

"Livvie," her mother said. "You've got this."

"If by 'this,' you mean I have all the, uh, challenges, and none of the benefits, then, yeah." She slipped a tiny ballcap out of the side of the bag and tugged it over Bash's curls. "There you go, handsome." She kissed him on the nose, tasting sunscreen and...she didn't even want to think about what else. "I'll walk with you, Mom. Tell me about this opportunity."

"I will, I will." She slowly lowered Bash and he took off the second his feet hit the ground. Fortunately, his legs were tiny and he couldn't get too far ahead of them. "But are you okay? Having a time with the mashed bananas?"

"Having a time with life." She sighed. "I got everything I wanted and have nothing at all."

"No." Her mother put her arm around Olivia's shoulders. "You're in a storm, no doubt about it. But this is going to make you and Deeley stronger."

"It just didn't happen the way it was supposed to," she said, knowing she was whining just a little, but hadn't she earned it?

It had been a tough morning of potty training and banana mash-ups. Deeley had slipped out before the crack of dawn to take a group of tourists on a sunrise kayak trip, leaving her with the morning routine. Which didn't quite seem to be "routine" at all yet.

"Life doesn't always work out like you think it will," her mother said. "And if you don't believe me, go ask God about your dad."

At the reminder of her dearly departed father, the late and amazing Ben Whitney, and the hole his death left in all their hearts, Olivia closed her eyes. Who knew better about life's curveballs than her mother, who'd lost the love of her life not quite a year ago?

"You're right, Mom."

Lately, it seemed, Olivia said those words a lot.

"ARE you familiar with the website *The Last Resort*?" her mother asked after they'd dropped Bash off for some beach time and headed back to the main house.

Olivia thought about it, digging up what she knew. "It's a travel thing, right? A website, but more. They publish a magazine I've seen, and you can book trips through them, find timeshares, great deals, and off-the-grid places?"

"Yes to all of that. They also do lots and lots of property reviews and site visits, rating resorts all over the world. Their quarterly magazine goes to every travel agent on the face of the Earth, and getting in the pages of that is an absolute coup. No surprise, a recommendation from them means a lot to a hotel or inn. And a feature? It can put a resort on the map." Mom paused at the top of the boardwalk that led to Teddy's oversized beach house, looking out at Shellseeker Beach.

From this vantage point, they could see almost the whole stretch of waterfront that included the rental cottages, the gardens and sea grass, the sweet gazebo, the landmark shell shop that was once a boathouse, and the thatched roof of Deeley's beach rental business.

"Do you feel the difference, Liv? Smell it? Taste it?"

Olivia frowned, following her mother's gaze, but not her train of thought. "The difference?"

"Winter."

"Hard to actually call this winter," Olivia said on a

laugh. "Especially to someone who's been living in Seattle."

"And I'm from California. I know what a pretty winter is, but this is unlike anything I've ever experienced." She swept a hand toward the sky and sand. "Even the sunlight is different, like a warm hug rather than a kick in the stomach. Look at that sky. Have you ever seen anything quite that color of blue?"

"It's gorgeous," Olivia agreed, gazing up at the blinding azure sky dotted with the occasional puffy white cloud, then back at her mother. "Uh, are we writing advertising copy today, Elizabeth Mary?"

Mom laughed. "No, but I want you to know that I've finally realized the true potential of this place. I've been working here, what? Seven months now?"

"Is it official? Teddy pays you now?"

"Pay me?" she scoffed. "I live free and have never had so much fun in my life, Liv. Please. I was never cut out to be a talent agent."

"I think some of your happy clients, like Nick Frye and Pippa Jones, would disagree."

"This is my calling, Liv." She gestured again toward the world around them. "And I have ideas, you know? I can see a few additional cottages, and a way to really make each one unique and beautiful. We have that pop-up pizza night a few times a week at the tea hut, but what if we could turn that into a real restaurant or café or parlor? Even the shell shop could be...more."

Olivia frowned, taking all this in and not quite getting it. "I'm surprised, Mom. I honestly thought it was the 'less is more' element of Shellseeker Cottages that you found so enticing. I didn't know you were so interested in making money or getting on the map."

"I'm not motivated by money," her mother said quickly. "And I don't want to make this place all glitz and glam, but even with the upgrades and improvements we've done here and there, I feel like...well, like there's a fine line between understated elegance...and tired. This place could not only use a facelift, but also a kick into the new millennium."

"The millennium isn't that new anymore," Olivia joked. "We're well into the second decade."

"But Shellseeker Cottages isn't."

"I get that," Olivia agreed. "How does Teddy feel?" After all, Theodore Blessing had been born and raised on this land, and had worked in some capacity at the Cottages for her entire seventy-some years.

"She agrees. But she has only actually *owned* Shellseeker for a few months. Improvements were always in someone else's hands. So, yes, she likes a lot of my ideas but they seem a little overwhelming to her."

"Financially or logistically?" Olivia asked.

"Both. I have the money but she won't let me spend it. She agrees we could do a massive property overhaul, but she wants to earn the investment from the property. I completely understand, and that's where *The Last Resort* comes in."

"If they do a review, you'd book out for the foreseeable future and would easily be able to afford everything you want to do." Olivia nodded, her years of business training rising to the surface. "It's a phenomenal investment, Mom. You're smart to maintain and improve it for her."

"I knew you'd get it," Mom said with relief in her voice. "And that means we need to beconsidered a Hidden Gem."

"If Shellseeker Cottages isn't a hidden gem, I don't know what is."

"You would think." Eliza guided her toward the house. "But I mean we need to be officially named a Hidden Gem. *The Last Resort* is doing their next quarterly entirely on Florida, featuring ten off-the-beaten-path resorts in the state."

"Ooh, that would be good to get."

"No kidding, especially since only one will be selected in all of Southwest Florida, so that's Sanibel, Captiva, Naples, Marco. So much competition, but I think this place is special enough to be in the running."

"Absolutely! So what's the process?"

"Step one, get chosen for a walk-through, and I think they're doing dozens of them. After that, they pare it down to top contenders in each geographic area of the state, and send a contingent of reviewers you have to wow in a day. And then you find out if you made the top ten."

"Eesh. Okay, how do we get a walk-through?"

Her mother let out a noisy sigh as they walked up the steps to the main living level. "That, my darling daughter, is why you're here."

On the deck, Teddy waited for them, her silver white curls fluttering in the breeze.

"Livvie!" She reached out for a hug. "I don't think I've seen you without Bash for weeks and weeks."

"Unless I'm at the store, I'm not without Bash." She gave Teddy a loving squeeze, not surprised when the older woman held her close and tight for a few seconds longer than expected.

"Oh, honey." Teddy rubbed her back and took a deep inhale, and something told Olivia she wasn't merely enjoying the scent of her body wash. When Teddy inhaled and examined, the empath was about to make a pronouncement.

"Pretty sure you smell the scent of exhaustion, frustration, and overly ripe bananas," Olivia joked.

Teddy shook her head. "Confusion," she said softly, confirming that her freakish ability to read someone's mood was working as well as always. "And for a woman who knows exactly how to adapt, you're struggling now."

"Adapt? Me? I'm the most inflexible person on Earth."

"I don't agree," Teddy said simply, drawing her into the cool living area of her cheery coastal home, the array of crystals and aroma of lemon tea already a balm for Olivia's soul. "You're coping in ways mere mortals never could."

Olivia shrugged it off. She'd been called here for her business expertise, which was a far more comfortable zone for her than talking about her issues. "Okay, so what's the problem with *The Last Resort* thing? How to get on the short-list?"

"Oh, I know how," Teddy said, making a face. "The problem is that we're being kept off it!"

"What?" Olivia slid into a chair at the dining table, glancing at the pool of brochures, flyers, photos, and marketing materials spread over the surface. "What's keeping you off?"

"Not what, who." Teddy took the seat across from her. "And that would be Penny Conway."

Olivia curled her lip. "The insult-slinger who runs the Unwelcome Center?"

Her mother snorted. "Yup. Penny and her husband, Mayor Frank Conway, give *The Last Resort* their short-list of top-quality family-owned properties on Sanibel, which is one of the criteria. The website sends reviewers to every property on that list, and from there, will pick one, and only one, to represent Sanibel Island. We have to get on that list."

"So you need help persuading Penny to put your name on the list?" Olivia guessed, frowning. "I know she's a fan of the place. I've seen her at more than a few of our pop-up pizza events."

"I thought so, too," Teddy said. "But she didn't even tell us about it! Eliza unearthed the opportunity last night."

"I was on a Facebook group made up of Florida resort owners and someone was talking about it," her mother said, pushing a printout from the website toward Olivia. "I emailed *The Last Resort* this morning, of course, to submit our name and they wrote back that Sanibel Island was being exclusively handled through the mayor's office.

I called there, and they sent me to Penny, who announced it was too late. They're submitting a list at the end of the day."

"Why wouldn't she include Shellseeker?" Olivia asked. "What was her reason?"

Mom rolled her eyes. "She wouldn't say, but I pushed and finally got her to agree to meet with Teddy and me this afternoon so we could make one final pitch."

"We need all the help you can give us, Livvie," Teddy said.

"Me?"

"You know business and marketing," Mom insisted. "And you know what makes Shellseeker Cottages so special. We invited Claire, too, but she had a call with her law firm that she seemed a little worried about."

Olivia nodded, glancing at the website printout. "I'm happy to have an opinion, but geez." She tapped the page that listed the "must haves" to be considered a Hidden Gem. "They're looking for waterfront, family-owned, with a colorful history and unique features. I mean, they just described Shellseeker Cottages. Colorful? Unique? *History?* Your gazebo is built on a Calusa Indian sacred mound, for heaven's sake. And people get married there!"

"Not enough of them," her mother said. "Which is why we want to get this opportunity. More destination weddings!"

Teddy leaned forward, her blue eyes bright. "Not to mention seven spacious cottages touching the Gulf, the best shelling on the island, a landmark souvenir shop, homemade tea, and a family-run pop-up pizza business that has already been featured on the top pizza website in the world."

Olivia nodded as she perused the list again and couldn't find a single requirement Shellseeker Cottages didn't meet and master. "Plus, you have a message in a bottle from Teddy Roosevelt himself! Hello? What's wrong with her?"

"Well, she is one of the nastiest women to ever run a Welcome Center," Mom replied.

"She's not that nasty," Teddy said. "I mean, she wasn't always so...edgy. But she's had tragedy in her life." At their questioning looks, she added, "She lost her sister almost ten years ago. Very sad."

"There's a third sister?" Mom asked. "I figured it was just Penny and Patty, and no doubt which one is nice and which one is scary."

"Patty's a doll," Teddy agreed. "She was always the bubbly one. Penny was the brainy one, and Polly, the oldest?"

"Penny, Patty, and Polly?" Olivia groaned. "You can't be serious."

"As a heart attack, which was exactly what killed Polly, the most beautiful of all three McPherson sisters," Teddy said as she slipped into the kitchen and poured a cup of tea for Olivia. "She was voted Conch Queen at least five years running, maybe more, and rode in the front float every year of the Seashell Parade."

"Conch Queen?" Olivia asked, lifting her brows. "Please tell me this still exists."

"No, they stopped it years ago in response to noisy feminists," Teddy said.

"Then here's idea Number One," Olivia said. "Reinstate it right here on Shellseeker Beach when *The Last Resort* is visiting."

Teddy and Eliza looked at each other, eyes wide.

"Your daughter is a genius," Teddy said, setting the cup in front of her.

"Tell me something I don't know," Mom cracked.

"Okay, then, why don't you give me whatever pitch you planned?" Olivia suggested. "I'll give you feedback, and you'll be well-rehearsed."

As they walked through their presentation, Olivia sipped her tea and listened to what she thought was near perfection. *Why* would Penny Conway keep them off the short-list? She had no answer, but the distraction was quite pleasant, and for a time, she had all that control she craved.

Chapter Two

Claire

The Zoom call ended as abruptly as it had started, leaving Claire staring at the blank screen in her small home office, a tightness building in her chest.

Did she just get...*fired?*

"Call over?" The door popped open to reveal DJ, who looked a little disheveled, slightly unshaved, and utterly delicious to her.

"Call...and career," she whispered. "I think. I don't know."

"Claire." He walked in, a frown pulling his dark brows together. "Is everything okay?"

She looked up at him, taking a moment to just appreciate the man who'd stolen her heart twice in this lifetime. Once in college, but he'd left her—pregnant and alone—and another time a few months ago, when the twenty-six-year-old son she'd given up for adoption brought them back together.

"I don't know," she admitted. "On one level, I've never been more okay." She reached out her hand and he took it instantly, capturing her fingers in his much larger ones, the calluses and burns a testament to a man who worked hard in his pizza kitchen.

He crouched down in front of her office chair, the position forcing him to look up at her face through his thick lashes. Even at a few months shy of fifty, Dante Joseph Fortunato was one heck of a handsome man. He had eyes the color of the black olives he loved to pop into his mouth while he kneaded his dough, with just enough lines to show he'd laughed a decent amount in those fifty years.

But it was the soul that shone through those eyes that had drawn Claire back a second time, and the heart. Passionate about everything—pizza, wine, music, memories, and every tender kiss—Claire still wasn't used to the enormity of his personality, even though it had quite changed since the first time she'd fallen for him.

"So they're making it all too easy for you to say *adios* to the hell that is being a lawyer?"

It had never been hell to her, but then...this life was heavenly. Living with DJ and their son, Noah, was a dream she'd long ago given up. Now she had it, and would do anything to keep it.

"I'm not sure." She glanced at the blank screen, remembering the senior partner's parting shot: "We've got junior associates kicking your butt in the billing department, Claire."

"I've slacked for months," she admitted. "He didn't actually call me on it, but he did remind me that I had been on a nice, smooth track to senior partner sometime in the next few years. But that feels like it has come to a halt. All my fault, of course. I essentially moved to another state and have been hanging on to this remote-working situation well past the time they expected." She let out a sigh. "I'm not sure what I should do."

He searched her face, quiet for a long time. "You know how I feel. Those cases will be won or lost without you. Those hours will be billed and overpaid without you. Those blowhard lawyers will get their multimillion-dollar bonuses without you."

She gave a dry laugh. "Well, there goes law school, twenty years of practice, and a carefully constructed career right out the window."

"Right. Quitting isn't always the answer. It was for me, but..."

But? She frowned. "Are you having second thoughts about leaving life as an architect to become a world-class pizza...eye...whatever you call it?"

"*Pizzaiole.* No, I'm not having second thoughts about...that." He cast his gaze down, a rare break in his always-intense eye-contact.

She put her hand on his cheek, frowning. "What is it, Deej? Is something wrong?"

"It's Sophia. Trouble again."

"Really?" She sat forward, thinking of the last conversation they'd had about his seventeen-year-old daughter. "I thought she was doing so well since you went back to California over the holidays and spent time with her."

It had been a long two weeks without him in December, but he'd done the right thing by going. After his near-miss with a lightning bolt last summer, he needed to see his daughters, Sophia and Anna, and assure them he was fine.

And, she suspected, to assure himself that they were fine, too. Anna was in her second year at Stanford and far too involved in college life to care where her father lived, though she promised to visit at some point.

Sophia, a high school senior, was the more emotional of the two, with more teen angst and issues.

"She was actually really good, except for this way-too-serious boyfriend she has. She and her mother are at each other's throats, and it sounds like it's worse than usual. Not sure why."

"Any ideas? School? The fact that her mother has a new man in her life? Or...her father suddenly lives three thousand miles away?"

He winced. "I don't think this is about me, but indirectly? I'm not there and the kid only has one parent at the moment. If I had to put money on it, the problem is Sophia's boyfriend and that's what's causing the fights."

"Rachel doesn't like him?" she guessed, imagining how his ex-wife might feel about her seventeen-year-old daughter's "way too serious" boyfriend.

"Despises him."

"Do you like him?" Claire asked.

"I hardly know him, but I should. She told me over the holidays that she intends to marry him, and I was hoping that was just typical over-the-top Sophia. She never does anything...small."

Claire smiled. "Kinda like her dad."

He smiled back, but she could see some genuine anxiety in his eyes. And for a man who made an artform out of avoiding worry and stress, that was something.

"What does Rachel want you to do?" she asked.

"Drop everything and be Sophia's father."

Claire just angled her head, not sure what to say. He *was* Sophia's father, and she was a seventeen-year-old who was probably not thrilled that her father had moved three thousand miles away.

"It's hard for you," she said gently. "Hard for a man who just wants to live in the moment."

"Two different moments. Two different families." His dark eyes closed as he said the words. "But let's get back to your problems. If billing useless and meaningless hours and bowing down to soul-sucking law partners makes you happy..."

She chuckled softly. "Well, when you put it that way..."

"But if it doesn't, then..." He pushed up and, still holding her hand, brought her with him. "Noah and I are going to the mainland to do some kitchen equipment shopping, then we're going down to the beach to get ready for this week's pop-up. Come with us and have way more fun."

Fun was always on his agenda, and he offered it without hesitation. And Claire, who'd had a remarkably little amount of fun in her serious, quiet life as a single woman working in a law firm, usually took what he was offering with two hands.

But the conversation with her boss pressed on her heart.

"I'd love to, but..." She looked at the computer. "I've got to redact a document."

He bit his lip to keep from laughing.

"Stop it. That brief isn't going to redact itself."

And the laugh escaped. "Okay, Claire. It's your call. We'll miss you. Happy redacting." He inched away, but she grabbed his arm and pulled him closer, not wanting him to leave.

"DJ. I take my job very seriously."

He closed the space between them and gave her a kiss. "Do what makes you happy, sweet Claire." As they kissed again, they heard heavy footsteps in the hall, and barely separated before their son, Noah, appeared in the doorway.

Noah laughed and shook his head. "Don't jump apart on my account," he teased, his eyes, a carbon copy of the ones Claire had been looking into, only twenty-five or so years younger.

While Noah frequently embraced DJ's "live large because life's short" philosophy, he had a bit of Claire's practicality in him, too.

"How'd the call go, Mom?" he asked.

She still wasn't entirely used to the music of hearing him call her "Mom" but, in some regards, she didn't *want* to get used to it. She'd waited twenty-six years to reconnect with the son she gave up at birth, and every "Mom" was an unexpected gift from God.

"The call was...meh. They want me to come back to New York."

His shoulders sank. "For good? I hope you said no."

"I didn't say anything." And how could she even consider it when she mattered so much to him? Yes, she took her job seriously, but Noah? After a lifetime of wondering who and where he was, they now lived in the same house. That was everything to her.

DJ slipped an arm around her. "So, fun or work? Pick your poison, my love."

"Fun," she answered without a second's hesitation. "The redacting can wait."

SHOPPING WAS as fun as promised...until it all came to a halt.

DJ took a call while they were in a restaurant supply chain store, disappearing from sight. Twenty-five minutes later, Claire and Noah were still waiting and wondering.

"Let's go outside and sit in the sun," Noah suggested, tucking his hands in his pockets in a gesture Claire was starting to know meant he was feeling a little uptight about something.

Well, who could blame him? DJ had ditched them.

"Do you think it's Papa Luigi?" Claire mused as she followed him to a bench that faced the parking lot.

Noah's eyes flashed. "That would be...amazing. If Luigi decides to retire and DJ takes over his pizza parlor? Oh, man. Too good to be true."

"It would be," she agreed. "You and DJ could own and run the best pizza restaurant on Sanibel, possibly in the whole county."

"Then you couldn't go back to New York. You'd have to give up the lawyer life and be a pizza man's wife."

"Wife?" She lifted a brow. "Whoa, there, young man."

He laughed softly. "Hey, a kid can dream, right? Call me crazy, but the way you two look at each other?"

She just smiled, wrapping her arms around herself. "I will call you crazy. I haven't known him that long."

"Uh, twenty-seven years?"

"But for twenty-six of them, we didn't speak. We're good, but not there yet."

He nodded. "I get that, but I think it would be amazing. Don't you?"

"I think a man like your father needs time, especially after a rough divorce like he had and the blame he places on his own shoulders. I don't think he's..." How could she express her concerns to Noah? He was their son. "He's just not there yet," she said again. "And may never be. I don't know."

He nodded, glancing over his shoulder at the door. "Sometimes I think he uses all that...passion and bravado to cover the pain of that divorce."

She put a hand on his arm. "So wise for one so young."

That made him laugh. "I was a foster kid, you know. You get street-smart fast."

She gave him a squeeze, grateful he'd come out of that difficult upbringing with such a good head on his shoulders. She couldn't take any credit; it was truly a miracle. She thought about saying that, but he looked at the door again, his impatience obvious.

"Maybe he's talking to Sophia," Claire suggested. "Apparently she and her mother had another argument."

"Maybe." Noah stared straight ahead, a small vein in his neck beating in time with his pulse.

The truth was, she'd only known him for four or five months, so there were a million and a half things about her son that mystified her. But she knew the vein like she knew his tucked fingers and casual shrugs.

They were all a sign of old hurts in a boy who'd experienced a lifetime of them.

"I think he's starting to feel really torn," he finally said.

She couldn't argue with that. "It's not easy to have two families that are three thousand miles apart."

He turned to her, the look in his eyes reminding her of what she'd seen in DJ's a few hours ago when they'd talked about his daughter. True and deep worry.

"You think he'll leave us and go back there?" he asked. "I mean, they are his real family."

"Noah," Claire said softly. "We are *also* his real family."

"What if he has to choose? He'd have to go to them. Sophia's still a kid and we have each other."

She gave a tight smile, and tried not to think about her boss and his unsubtle efforts to get her back to New York. "I hope it doesn't come to that," she said softly.

"Because if we lose him, then we lose...this." Noah flicked a hand that she guessed was meant to encompass his whole life.

"I don't think that's going to happen." Although, truth be told, she had no idea.

"Last year, just a few months ago, I was a nomadic bartender carrying the weight of having no family and a life of foster homes," he said, almost to himself, as if he hadn't heard her. "Now, I'm living in a house on a canal with my real-live parents who are obviously falling in love with each other."

Were they? It wasn't exactly obvious to her, although sometimes she could feel herself slipping in that direction.

She put her hand on his arm. "Sometimes when life is really good, it feels too good to be true."

"And then it all changes." He let out a sigh. "You could even go back to New York."

She could, but deep inside, she doubted she would. "And you and your father could be running Dante's where Papa Luigi's is right now. You never know."

"DJ Fortunato doesn't want to own a restaurant," Noah said, sounding more glum with each minute his father was MIA. "He talks about it, but that means payroll and inventory and hours and staffing. That's not who he is. Not anymore."

She shifted on the bench, wanting to take the unhappiness out of his voice with a change of subject.

"So, how's Katie doing?"

It worked. His whole face lit up at the mention of the young housekeeper from Shellseeker Cottages who he'd been dating for several months.

"She's great. So great."

"Talk about two people who should be getting married," she said in a teasing voice, leaning into him.

He laughed softly. "Okay, okay, Mom. We're not there yet, either. But..." His smile widened. "I can't believe how crazy I am about her. And don't start on Harper. That kid is like..." He looked skyward. "I'm wrapped around her finger and I am one hundred percent here for it."

"Noah!" She pressed her hand on his arm, a little overwhelmed by the confession. "I'm so happy you have them. I liked Katie from the moment I first talked to her. I liked her strength—starting out on her own the way she did and building a life for herself and Harper."

He nodded. "When you think of the money she came from and how humble she is? God, I just love..." His voice trailed off. "I love that," he finished.

She smiled, knowing *that* wasn't what he loved. He loved Katie, and Claire could not be more excited with this news. "Another reason not to even think about leaving Sanibel Island," she sighed.

"I *knew* you were," he countered.

"Not thinking about it because I want to leave," she assured him. "But I'm going to have to figure out what to do about my job. I'm too senior in the law firm to work from a remote office indefinitely."

"It's a big firm," he said. "They have offices in Florida. What's the closest?"

"Miami and Jacksonville, so nothing around here."

"Then start one."

Now there was an idea. Actually, a good one. "Well, I

have to take the Florida bar to practice, but..." She angled her head, considering that option. "I like the way you think, Noah Hutchins. That isn't a bad idea at all. I'd have to hustle to bring in some clients, but you know? That's something to think about."

He grinned at her. "You said you'd stay or go where I stay or go, remember?"

"I'll never forget," she said, thinking of the moment they'd shared on the beach during a storm that nearly took DJ's life. "And I won't break that promise."

The door behind them suddenly popped open and DJ walked out, emotion etched on his features, but Claire couldn't quite read what those feelings were.

"Everything okay?" she asked.

"Yeah. No." He groaned and joined them on the bench. "I'm sorry, you two. I wrecked our shopping day with trouble from home."

At the word "home," she could have sworn she felt Noah stiffen, but his expression didn't change.

"Did you talk to Sophia?" she asked.

"No, that was Rachel." He shook his head and looked skyward, as he often did when he talked about his ex-wife. "I got the long version of the 'your daughter needs a father' lecture."

Noah still didn't say anything, but, whoa, that vein was thumping.

"What does she think you can do for Sophia?" Claire asked.

"Ground her for coming home at three a.m. on a school night."

Claire grimaced. "Ouch."

"She's almost eighteen years old, though. What exactly can I do? Other than, you know, be there." DJ threaded his fingers in his dark, thick hair, looking from one to the other. "The thing is, I lost that family in the first place because I was never there. I was at work with a singular focus on success in the world of architecture."

They didn't say anything, but looked at him, waiting as he processed this ache on his heart. While they did, Claire could practically feel Noah's whole body tense more with each passing second.

"And now I'm across the country with a singular focus on..." He let his voice trail off and then shook his head. "So, did you guys buy that pizza peel? The ultra-smooth one I loved?"

"No, we sat here and talked," Claire said.

His whole face softened. "About what?"

"Just life," Noah said quickly.

"Ah, my favorite subject," DJ quipped. "And life says that there's a peel in there that has my name on it and I'm going back to buy it. Who's with me?"

They stood and let the whole thing drop, but she couldn't help but notice that vein was still pulsing in Noah's neck. He was worried his newfound life could disappear at any time.

She wouldn't let that happen, at least not on her part.

Tomorrow, she'd call her boss and see if there was any interest at all in opening another Florida office. And if the answer was no? Then she'd start figuring out her next step.

Because if DJ decided to leave? Then she *had* to be here to pick up the pieces of Noah's broken heart. Yes, he was a grown man of twenty-six. Yes, he had a good woman at his side.

But he was still her son, and she'd protect him with everything she had.

Chapter Three

Camille

"Say something in French, Cami."

Camille looked right into Abner's warm hazel eyes, the ones that seemed to always be pinned on her lately.

She rattled off the first thing that came to mind, deepening her accent and emphasizing the absolute Frenchness of her words for maximum impact.

It worked. He slapped his hand on his chest, let out a moan, looked toward the heavens like she'd fallen from them. "My *stars*, woman." Then he frowned at her. "What'dya say?"

"I said, 'No one calls me *Cami* and lives to tell the tale.'" And they especially didn't draw it out in that slow, Southern accent that she used to think sounded inane but now was kind of...attractive.

"Well, no one calls me Abner." He lifted one bushy brow—did he ever think to trim those caterpillars?—and leaned a tad closer. He seemed blissfully unaware that he had the faintest odor of shrimp or whatever he sold in his bait store on his clothes. "'Cept you."

Camille didn't hate that scent. She didn't hate anything about this unexpected flirtation with the gentleman who owned the store next to hers. In fact, she secretly looked forward to their banter every day when she came to work at her upscale women's boutique.

Abner—there was no way she'd call him Buck, of all the atrocious names—was the one thing that made her feel alive again. Young, energetic, pretty, and spunky. All the things Camille Durant had been and longed to be again.

All the things, in fact, she thought she'd get from owning this store and dressing up every day and chatting with customers. She loved Sanibel Sisters, and had no regrets buying the business. But it had made her more tired, not less.

Until Abner came along. Then, his jokes, his compliments, and his unabashed crush on her were like an injection of Vitamin B. For Buck.

"C'mon, Cami. Teach me anything in French."

"Rein. Tout. Quelque chose."

"Ooh. Nice." His eyes flashed. "What does that mean?"

"Anything," she replied. "You said 'teach me anything' and I just did."

"That's a lot of words for one."

"There are several ways to say 'anything' in French. It depends on context." She glanced out of Sanibel Sisters' display window, catching sight of a few women chatting outside the store. The group of three talked and held to-go coffee cups, seemingly unable to commit to coming in or not. "You'd better go, Abner. You're scaring the customers away."

"You think I'm scary, Cami?"

"When you call me that, I do," she deadpanned.

But the truth was, she loved it when he showed up in the back office—using a secret door that had been built for the previous owner to connect their adjacent businesses—and lumbered onto the sales floor to play verbal volleyball and hint that he might ask her on a date soon.

Tall and lanky, silver-haired and crinkle-faced, he looked so out of place in this feminine store it was kind of funny. But then he'd drawl out a compliment and call her "Cami"—which was unthinkable and adorable—and basically look at her like she hung the moon.

Then, she was no longer a woman in her seventies who didn't sleep well and ran out of breath when she walked to her car and had to soak the swollen toes that didn't want to wear high heels anymore. Then, she was a sassy stewardess again, driving businessmen crazy in First Class.

Then, she was...immortal.

Was that so wrong? She didn't care. Maybe she should, but she didn't.

"Go." She flicked her fingers. "I want to sell these women oodles of overpriced clothes."

But he didn't move. He just stood there, more than six feet of quite nice manliness, wearing his seventy-five years like a soft article of clothing that fit like a dream.

"What about tonight?" He lifted a caterpillar again.

"Tonight?" she scoffed. "Tonight I'll be packing. I'm moving out of my cottage into a lovely little townhouse on Bowman's Beach tomorrow."

"I can help you pack. I can help you move."

"Thank you, but I have all the help in the world." She pointed toward the back and their connected offices. "Off with you, Abner. Olivia will be here any minute and I do not need my partner witnessing me dallying with the next-door neighbor."

"Livvie doesn't care, darlin'. She likes me."

She angled her head and let her lids shutter. "You have an inflated sense of yourself, Abner."

"Only around you, Cami." His wide mouth lifted in a smile that was just downright...delightful.

Wait a *second*. Who was falling under whose spell here?

"Buck." She rolled her eyes. "What kind of name is that anyway?"

"An American standard, just like me."

"How did you get that nickname? Horseback riding?"

He laughed, a deep rumble from his chest. "Someday I'll tell you." He leaned much closer. "And if you—"

At the sound of the door, Camille turned to greet the ladies from outside, except...it wasn't them. It *was* Olivia, even earlier than expected, and looking quite interested in the exchange going on at the cash register.

"Goodbye, Abner," Camille said, her voice rising as she stepped away and adopted the most casual attitude imaginable. "Thank you for checking on our Wi-Fi, which is working just fine. I hope you get yours fixed." She smiled at Olivia and walked across the store, praying Abner got the message and disappeared through the back. "You're early, Livvie!"

Olivia looked over Camille's shoulder, enough surprise and curiosity in her eyes to show she'd seen enough. *Mon Dieu!* Camille had done such a masterful job of hiding her chats with Abner, keeping their encounters limited to the morning hours when Camille was generally working alone.

It had been easy since Livvie and Deeley got the little boy—she was the one responsible for getting him to daycare and that meant she was always a few minutes late to arrive at the store for her afternoon shift.

"Hey, Buck," Olivia called. "Nice to see you again." She put just enough emphasis on "again" for Camille to wonder if maybe she hadn't done such a great job of hiding Buck's visits.

"Miz Livvie," he drawled. "How are you, ma'am?"

"I'm good. Do we have a Wi-Fi problem?" Olivia breezed past Camille, who turned to watch the exchange. "I thought we finally had that fixed with the router. Should I call someone?"

"No, ma'am. Your Wi-Fi is perfect, like everything else in this store." He underscored that by looking right at Camille and smiling. "And you remember, Miz Cami, if you need help moving into your new place, I'm your man."

"Thank you, Ab...Buck." It wouldn't do for Olivia to know they both had pet names for each other. Cami was bad enough. No one called this man anything but Buck.

'Cept you.

Ooh la la, she liked it when he said that.

He left them with a tip of an invisible hat, disappearing into the back.

"I love how he uses the secret door to come over here and flirt with you," Olivia joked.

Nope. She'd done a terrible job of hiding him. "Oh, he's harmless," Camille said, returning to the cash register. "He's a lonely old widower looking for someone to talk to."

Olivia's brows rose like she wasn't buying it. "Angler's Paradise is always packed. He has plenty of customers to talk to."

"His nephew—well, great-nephew—does all the heavy lifting," she said. "Buck's old."

"He doesn't seem old, though."

"No," Camille mused, glancing at the door to the back, thinking of how thick his hair was and how he didn't have a lot of age spots, only the lines of a life well-lived with sunshine and laughter. "He really doesn't."

"Miz Cami," Olivia teased, using a heavy fake Southern accent. "I do declare you have yourself an admirer."

"Don't be ridiculous, Livvie. He's desperately lonely since his precious Polly died."

"Polly?" Olivia looked up from the cash register, a slight frown on her face. "That's not a very common name."

"Neither is Abner."

"I mean because I've heard it twice today. Was he married to the sister of Penny and Patty, who work at the Welcome Center?"

"I have no idea, but his late wife was named Polly. Evidently she was famous for being the queen...of something around here."

"Conch Queen? The now-defunct beauty contest?"

"Yes," Camille said. "I think so. Have you heard of it?"

"Only today, which is bizarre and interesting and might explain a lot."

Camille frowned at her. "What does it explain?"

Olivia held up one finger to ask her to wait as she pulled out her phone and looked at the screen. "Yikes. I totally forgot this call with the merchandiser from Elan. She's working me a deal for their spring line." She started toward the back. "I have to negotiate this, because their resort wear flies out of here."

"Then definitely talk to her," Camille said as the three coffee-drinkers finally came in. "I've got this crew."

Olivia gave her a thumbs-up and slipped into the office while Camille fought exhaustion and the darn high heels, but made a few excellent sales.

⁂

It was more than an hour later when Olivia finished working in the back, and Camille was aching from head to toe. All she wanted to do was get her bag and head home with a speedy handoff of the two customers in the store.

With a quick goodbye to Olivia, Camille stepped outside just as the door to the bait shop opened, too. A young man Camille instantly recognized as Abner's great-nephew, Davis, stepped out.

His smile instantly disappeared. "Ma'am," he mumbled.

"Hello, Davis."

Right behind him, Abner came out onto the sidewalk, his gaze locked on Camille. "There you are. Leaving for the day, Cami?"

Did he have to call her that in front of other people? "My day is done, sir," she said, all cool and like a casual neighbor might.

"I'll walk to your car with you," he suggested, and she could have sworn she saw disapproval flash in Davis's eyes.

"That's not necessary," she said quickly. "I can see my car from here." And even still, she might be embarrassingly short of breath by the time she reached it.

But Abner didn't care. He strode along next to her, giving the quickest, most casual wave to his great-nephew.

"You stayed late today," he said, pulling a ballcap from his back pocket and tugging it over his white hair. "I thought you'd never leave."

"You were waiting for me?"

He slowed his step, and added a half smile that was so sweet, she almost forgot how her feet hurt. "Why do you sound surprised?"

"I'd think you have better things to do than stalk me."

He chuckled. "Not stalking anyone, Cami. Just determined to make you dinner. Tonight?"

"I told you—"

"I don't want to wait or hear any more of your confounded excuses. I'm seventy-five and the one thing you don't do at our age is procrastinate."

"*Your* age," she corrected. "I'm not seventy-five." Not far, but she'd die before she admitted it.

"Well, what do you say? Prove my nephew wrong?"

She glanced over his shoulder at the store where they'd left Davis. "How so?"

"He thinks you're going to turn me down. Told me I was actin' like an old fool, and you're...what's the expression? Out of my league. So I bet him five bucks you'd say yes."

She couldn't help laughing at that.

"Don't cost me a fiver, Cami. Just say yes."

Oh, it would be so easy. But would it be crazy?

She clicked her key fob to unlock the car, and chuckled again when he got between her and the car, blocking her way.

"Do you mind, Abner?"

He pushed up the bill of his cap and held her gaze. "I mind if you don't say you'll be at my place tonight at seven for the best fried catfish you ever ate."

"The *only* fried catfish I ever ate," she assured him.

"Is that a yes?" He seemed so hopeful, her heart sped up a bit.

She looked up at him, searching his face, enjoying the moment, the sunshine, the lovely feeling of being pursued.

"I'm moving tomorrow," she said slowly.

"See? All the more reason to have a nice dinner with me tonight."

Actually, he was right and...this was tempting.

"Where do you live?" she asked, knowing she was probably going to say yes. Then the chase would turn into something different. But what? She didn't know, but that was half the fun.

"Near the lighthouse, in the marina."

"*In* the marina?"

"I live on a boat, Cami. You'll love it."

"A *boat*? What kind of man lives on a boat?"

"One who doesn't need to be encumbered by grass that needs mowing or plumbing that ain't workin' right or neighbors that tick you off." He grinned. "And it's so pretty at night in the winter. Come on over, Cami."

"I don't know." But she did. She knew that this felt... exciting, and she didn't want that feeling to stop.

"Do you drink beer or wine?" he asked, then barked a laugh. "Nevermind, dumb question for a classy French babe like you."

"A French *babe*?" She nearly choked.

He leaned forward and for one insane second she thought he was going to kiss her, but he stepped to the side and opened her car door for her. "See you tonight at seven?"

She took a slow, deep breath. "All right."

"Yes!" He gave a little fist pump, which was just downright precious.

She looked up at him, the late afternoon sun showing his wrinkles and the fact that those caterpillar eyebrows were very, very gray. But there was a spark in his eyes, a light that came from deep down, a glimmer she hadn't seen in a man's eyes since...well, since Dutch.

It had been so very long since a man made her feel anything. She'd honestly thought those chemicals or hormones or whatever the heck they were had died years ago.

But from the way her heart was pounding, they apparently had just come back to life.

Chapter Four

Eliza

Years of working as a talent agent, of sitting in conference rooms and negotiating deals, should have prepared Eliza for a small-town meeting in the back room of the Welcome Center.

But Penny Conway was a worthy adversary, and the little building where visitors came to learn all about the island was clearly the royal court for this queen bee. She'd closed the door, taken the head seat at the table, and wore a blank expression behind her bifocals as Eliza kicked off the pitch.

She looked mildly interested all the way through Teddy's brief review of her family's history and connection with the property. She started glancing at her phone right around the time they talked about the renovations they'd accomplished over the summer. And she actually read two texts while Eliza waxed on about the growth of their tea hut and the success of DJ's pop-up pizza.

"*The Last Resort* isn't looking for the best pizza on Sanibel," she sniffed, brushing back her lifeless brown hair as she finally looked at them. "And if they were, I'd send them to Papa Luigi's."

"They're looking for color," Eliza said. "For something different and surprising. We have that."

Penny nodded and looked down at the new Shellseeker Cottages brochure they'd recently created, but her phone flashed again and she tapped it, reading another text. Then she looked up and sighed.

"It's so late to add another name to the list," she said. "We've been talking to the project coordinator at *The Last Resort* for quite some time, and I doubt they'll even consider another property at this point. Each one means a long walk-through and interviews, and they've got a tight schedule."

"They're still taking recommendations," Eliza replied. "I saw it on the website last night, so I know that we can get on the list if you add our name."

"But we can't inundate them with Sanibel properties," Penny said. "They asked us to be the gatekeepers of a very short list."

Teddy leaned forward, her eyes looking pained by the conversation "Why would you leave Shellseeker Cottages off that list, Penny? You had such a good relationship with Dutch, as I recall, and we've known each other for years. Didn't Dutch always call you 'Lucky Penny'?"

She winced. "I know, Teddy, he was very nice, but I'm sure you're booked for the season and, if you got chosen—which is a big if—you'd have to move a guest out. And you surely can't afford to do that." She pushed back from the table, suddenly ending the discussion. "Thanks for your time, ladies. If someone drops out, we'll certainly consider Shellseeker for a backup."

A backup? Was she serious?

"Camille is leaving Junonia," Eliza said quickly, refusing to give up. "That's our most spacious two-bedroom beachfront cottage and it is one hundred percent vacant. We will hold it for *The Last Resort* if we get chosen."

She froze and turned, lifting a brow with interest. "Is Camille moving away from Sanibel?"

"Oh no," Teddy said. "She purchased a townhouse in Bowman's Beach, in that new Mar Brisas complex. Like everyone else, she came and she's staying, because she fell in love—"

"She *what*?"

"With Shellseeker Beach," Teddy finished with a smile.

That story did nothing but make Penny scoop up her phone and empty notebook, ending the meeting. "I'm sorry, ladies. I appreciate your effort, but we can't add any more properties to the list. I have to get back to work."

As she stood, so did Teddy, who reached out and took Penny's hand, getting a wide-eyed look of surprise. "You could at least be honest," Teddy said softly.

"I am being honest."

Teddy raised their joined hands. "That's not what I feel, Penelope Conway." At Penny's surprised, Teddy took a step closer. "I've known you too long for this."

Penny managed to wrest her hand away, no doubt

knowing that the one thing someone couldn't do was lie to Teddy Blessing.

"C'mon, Teddy. You know what's going on."

"I'm not sure I do, but I'd like you to tell me."

"Just think about the timing seven or eight months ago when *The Last Resort* first contacted us for this feature. You...and your...*family?*" She dragged out the word as if there was something wrong with it. "I mean, if that's what you call each other."

Teddy blinked at her. "Yes," she said. "That's most certainly what we call each other."

"Eliza isn't your daughter-in-law, because Dutch wasn't really your husband, right?"

Of course, the rumors had traveled around this small town, and Penny was probably ground zero for town gossip.

"How could that possibly matter to the editors and reviewers at *The Last Resort?*" Eliza asked.

"Oh, it doesn't," Penny said quickly. "I mean, it might if it affected your management—"

"It doesn't," Eliza interjected.

"But when they came to us looking for small properties to review, you all were in the thick of it. That...that French woman—"

"Camille," Teddy supplied, frowning deeply. "Her name is Camille and she is my dear friend."

"And my daughter's business partner," Eliza added, pushing up to join the other two standing.

"Well, yes, I know. But stories were flying that she

was Dutch's real wife." Penny lifted a brow. "And it turns out those reports were true, weren't they?"

Teddy flinched but Eliza stepped closer, fury biting at her. "I fail to see what bearing that has on whether or not a resort is considered for this feature," she said stiffly.

"I'm sure you do, dear. He was your father and Teddy's...whatever. And Camille's husband. And there was another wife, if that business is to be believed."

"None of that *business* affected the resort," Eliza shot back. "We carried on, never missed a beat, and, as I said, have upgraded several of the cottages, continued to run at a profit, and added features to—"

"The answer is no," Penny said, crossing her arms. "We can't risk anything that would sully Sanibel Island's reputation as a family vacation place." She picked up her phone and read another text. "Excuse me, now I really have to go."

She sailed out of the small room, leaving them to stare at each other in shock.

"She can't be serious," Eliza muttered. "I get the timing, I get the vacancy issue, but...all that other stuff. If Dutch is her real reason for saying no, it's unbelievably unfair."

Teddy let out a sound of agreement. "I mean, Dutch had...some baggage."

Thinking about her father, Eliza fought a dry laugh. Baggage? Plenty. Aloysius Vanderveen was a bona fide bigamist. But that shouldn't come into play for this opportunity.

"He's not even the current owner," Eliza said,

glancing toward the door Penny had used. "What a complete—"

The door swung open, silencing her. Patty Burk-houser, Penny's sister, stood on the other side, her chubby, cheerful face set in a warm smile that was so different from her sister's sour expression.

"We'll be out of here in a moment," Teddy assured her.

"It's fine," Patty said. "Penny left to go to city hall and talk to her husband, Mayor Conway." With that, she closed the door until it latched and stepped into the room. "So I thought I'd use this opportunity to say I know she's not giving you a fair shake."

"It's fine," Eliza said. "You don't have to mop up your sister's mess."

"I think you should know what's going on and why... this is happening."

"Oh, we know," Teddy assured her. "Shellseeker Cottages has some, shall we say, dirty laundry? She's afraid it'll get aired."

Patty shook her head. "That's not it."

Eliza and Teddy exchanged a look.

"Then what is it?" Eliza asked. "What's keeping us off her list?"

Her shoulders dipped like the weight of the world was on them. "Buck."

"Buck?" They both asked the question at the same time, with the same level of surprise.

"Buck Underwood, your brother-in-law?" Teddy asked. "What does he have to do with the short-list?"

"Not a thing," Patty said, looking over her shoulder again like the wicked witch could swoop in at any moment. "But he apparently has a lot to do with Camille."

"Camille?" Again, the confused question came in unison.

"His bait shop is next door to Sanibel Sisters," Patty said, then leaned in. "And evidently, she's...making her move on him."

"Camille?" Eliza snorted the question. "Are you sure?"

Teddy slipped back into one of the chairs as the realization seemed to hit her. "Of course. That would make sense."

It would? Eliza certainly didn't think so. "What am I missing here? Camille isn't the kind of woman who makes...moves. Is she?"

"I have no idea," Teddy said. "But Polly, his late wife, was Penny and Patty's sister."

"*Oooh*," Eliza said. "I see."

"I don't have any issues with them as a couple," Patty said quickly. "But my sister thinks she's a gold-digging black widow who is about to take Buck down a forbidden path. And based on what Davis has said—that's Penny's grandson, who works at Angler's Paradise—Buck's ready to follow that woman down any path."

Was Camille an attractive older woman who enjoyed attention, Eliza asked herself. Absolutely. But a *gold-digging black widow*? That seemed extreme.

"How have I not heard about this?" Eliza asked. "My

daughter is with her every day. They're partners, you know."

"Oh, I know. Everyone knows." Patty looked like the confession pained her.

"So that's what's keeping Shellseeker Cottages off the short-list for *The Last Resort*?" Eliza heard her voice rise in disbelief. "How is that even fair? Camille has nothing to do with the resort. She's been living there for a few months since she sold it to Teddy—"

"For a dollar," Patty said. "What's that about?"

"That's none of your business," Teddy shot back, an unusual sharpness in her voice. "The ownership changed hands, as it has done many, many times in the decades since my father sold it for the first time in the 1950s. Eliza's right. What does Camille have to do with this opportunity? Not to mention that Buck Underwood is in his seventies and can do what he wants."

Patty sighed. "I don't disagree. But in my family, and in this town? Penny and her husband, Frank, call the shots. He's the mayor, as you know."

"When's election day?" Eliza murmured, tension stretching across her chest.

"Wouldn't matter," Patty said. "No one would have the nerve to run against him."

"Frank Conway's been on the school board, city council, election committee, historical society, shell festival board, and...you name it," Teddy explained. "Now he's mayor and quite enjoying this peak of power."

Eliza shook her head. "Whatever. This is really a shame. You know Shellseeker Cottages should be on that list, Patty. The only other property that's close is Tarpon Villas, and they don't have the rich family history and quirky adorableness of Teddy's property."

"They do have ghosts," Teddy said. At Eliza's surprised look, she shrugged. "It's a draw."

"I can't argue with any of this," Patty said. "I'm just telling you why it's not happening. Penny thinks you're all in cahoots, and as long as Camille has her claws in Buck, she won't change her mind."

"What if she didn't have her claws in him?" Teddy asked.

Patty lifted a shoulder. "I guess Penny might reconsider, but time is running out."

"We'll talk to her," Eliza said, closing her bag after putting everything away. "But Camille is...Camille. She does what she likes."

And apparently what she liked...was Buck Underwood. Which was news to Eliza.

CAMILLE WAS SIPPING some water on the deck of her cottage when Eliza and Teddy arrived later that afternoon.

"Hello, my friends," she called out with a wave as she spotted them on the path. "To what do I owe the honor of a visit from the owners?" She stood, brushing back some of her shiny black hair from an extraordinarily pretty face.

Camille Durant was in her seventies—no one really

dared guess what the actual number was—but her beauty
defied age. Her bone structure was timeless, her slender
figure was exquisite, and even her hint of a French accent
was nothing less than musical.

Poor Buck. He didn't stand a chance if she'd set her
sights on him.

"You seem rested and happy," Teddy said as she
greeted the other woman with a hug.

"I just napped, Teddy. You know that's my happiest
place. But you..." She drew back and searched Teddy's
face, then looked at Eliza. "Is something wrong? Oh, of
course. You want to know if I will be out of here on time.
I can only imagine how much you want to rent Junonia
again." She gestured toward the brightly colored two-
bedroom bungalow behind her, which was, without a
doubt, the jewel in Shellseeker Cottages' crown.

"We're not worried about that," Teddy said, although
Eliza knew they did need to get Junonia back into circula-
tion now that it was January and the high tourist season.

"I'm moving tomorrow, as you know. Now, can I offer
you two something to drink?"

"No, we just have to talk to you for a minute." Eliza
slid into one of the Adirondack chairs on the deck. "Is this
a good time?"

"Of course. I'm going...no, it's fine. I have time. Sit
down, Teddy." She gestured to one of the other chairs,
then took one of her own. "What exciting thing is
happening in Shellseeker Beach now?"

For a minute, neither one of them spoke, the beat of

silence making Camille sit up straighter. "Good heavens, ladies, spill what's on your mind."

Teddy nodded and took the lead. "Is there something going on with you and Buck Underwood?"

Camille just stared at her, the slightest flush rising on those stunning cheekbones, enough to let them know exactly what the truth was.

"*Mon Dieu*, I've heard about the rumor mill being overactive, but this is absurd," Camille scoffed. "I accepted his offer of a date less than two hours ago. Is it on the front page of the local paper already?"

"It might as well be," Teddy said. "Penny Conway has her teeth into this particular slice of juicy gossip and she's chomping down."

Camille's lip curled. "I don't like that woman."

The feeling was obviously mutual, but Eliza kept that to herself and rooted around for the right words.

"She's quite...vindictive," Eliza said. "As a matter of fact, she's decided that it's your, uh, relationship with her late sister's widower that will keep this resort off the short-list for an amazing publicity opportunity." She grimaced because that reasoning was so *dumb*. "So, yeah. It's kind of a big problem for us."

All that color that had risen to Camille's cheeks drained and her eyes widened. "Excuse me? A *relationship*? The man comes into my store, flirts his Southern heart out, and I have kept him at arm's distance—a stiff and unforgiving arm, I might add—for months!"

Eliza searched her face, seeing nothing but self-righteous fury, not the guilt of a woman who was leading the poor man down a "forbidden" path.

"You haven't encouraged him?" she asked.

"I've all but kicked him out until today," she said. "I've struggled greatly with this, to be honest. It seems a bit silly at my age. Silly but fun. Is that a crime now?"

Teddy inched forward, her blue eyes narrowing. "Penny seems to think you are the instigator, someone dragging poor Buck in the general direction of your bedroom against his will."

Camille gasped so noisily that she nearly choked. "Nothing, and I do mean *nothing* could be further from the truth! That horrible woman doesn't have any idea what she's talking about."

"Apparently, she's getting fed information from her grandson, who works for him."

"He's not a nice man, that Davis. He doesn't like me, I can tell. But Abner? He likes me. And he has absolutely pursued me for a dinner date and nothing more!" She huffed out a breath and fell back against the chair. "I shouldn't have accepted the invitation. I'm just feeding the beast. Should I cancel?"

Eliza was touched by the offer, which seemed deeply genuine, but Teddy shot forward.

"You will do no such thing, Camille."

"I could. It wouldn't be a big deal, merely a minor disappointment. If it helps the resort I've lived in for free all these months, then—"

"We are not going to fold to the imaginary power of Penelope McPherson Conway," Teddy insisted, slapping her palms on the armrests of her oversized Adirondack. "She's always had too much of it, if you ask me."

"But what is this publicity thing?" Camille asked. "What is she keeping you from?"

As Eliza explained the entire situation to Camille, Teddy practically squirmed in her seat. Her low-key anger was palpable, and by the time Eliza finished, she sensed Teddy was ready to burst.

"What an awful person she is," Camille said. "But I can easily—"

"If you want to go out with Buck Underwood, you should go," Teddy said. "If you want to have dinner, hold hands, stroll in the moonlight, and kiss the old coot, you should."

Eliza and Camille laughed softly, mostly because of Teddy's passion and high color.

"No one is kissing anyone," Camille said. "Not until he trims those brows and doesn't smell faintly of shell fish." She smiled and her dark eyes danced. "But how sweet of you to have such high hopes for me, Teddy."

"I have a good feeling," Teddy said, reaching for her. "I don't know why, I can't explain it."

"You never can," Camille teased, then looked at Eliza. "Do you agree?"

"I do," she said. "It's not fair to you or to us that she's doing this. You just go on your date, Camille, and forget we had this conversation."

"I doubt I will," she said, her gaze warm on both of them. "But you know what means the world to me? From you, Teddy, and you, Eliza?" She reached out and took each of their hands in hers. "That you believe me. I'm touched that you don't listen to that busybody and treasure our friendship."

"Of course," Teddy said.

"Not 'of course'," Camille added, squeezing their hands. "I was married to the man you nursed to his deathbed," she said softly, then turned to Eliza. "And we all know that it was me who broke up your parents' marriage."

Eliza couldn't argue either of those facts, but it all felt like so, so long ago. She knew Camille now, knew her quirks and her color, her rough edges and surprisingly smooth moments. And she couldn't forget that Camille's daughter, Claire, was the sister Eliza treasured.

"You're a good woman," Teddy said, putting all those thoughts into much more succinct words. "And I know you're not lying."

Camille nodded. "Someone is, though. Davis or Penny, maybe even Buck. I'm going to get to the bottom of it, and I'm going to help you.'"

"How?"

"I don't know yet," she admitted. "But I will. You can count on me."

They shared a long look and a smile and Eliza truly felt better than she had all afternoon.

Chapter Five

Olivia

The after-dinner shopping crowd was blessedly light at Sanibel Sisters, so Olivia was able to lock the door at seven-fifteen sharp and head home. The slow evening also gave her plenty of time to think and, being Olivia, plan.

When life felt out of control, Olivia Whitney took control, and this situation was no different. She'd made a list of ways to get ahold of her life, and at the top was to tend to a relationship that was suffering.

Tonight, Bash would go to bed by eight-thirty, and she and Deeley would have a quiet, adult dinner with a bottle of wine. They'd talk about something other than "the baby" and maybe get into the nitty-gritty of where they were as a couple...and where they were going.

They loved each other, that was certain.

Wait. Was it?

They'd only just told each other that for the first time the day they'd found Bash alone and abandoned by his mother. From that moment on, they never had another "normal" day. The "I love you's" were rare, but the feeling was still there. The intimacy was infrequent, but didn't that happen to couples who just had a child—whether they'd inherited it or had one together?

They never argued or felt terribly distant, but they had been denied a chance to just really be a couple.

Tonight, they would be.

A plan always made her feel better, so she arrived at her little house wearing a smile and carrying some beer-battered fish fry and shepherd's pie from Bailey's, ensuring that someone else did the cooking. The "witching hour," as Deeley called his few-hour window on Dad Duty, was never a good time to cook.

"Hello!" she called as she stepped inside. "I'm..." The next word was strangled in her throat at the sight of chaos —books, toys, clothes, junk—strewn all over the living room.

"Wibbieeee!" Bash came tearing into the living room, butt naked, soaking wet, arms outstretched, chocolate on his face. God, she hoped it was chocolate.

"Hey!" Deeley called from the back—the bathroom, she guessed. "Get back in here, you!" He marched out from the hall, his long hair looking as messy as Bash's, his cheeks almost as flushed, his eyes narrowed as he followed the child around the room. "Bath time is not over!"

"What's on his face?"

"He found a Hershey bar in my truck. That's why we went straight to the—hey!"

Bash jumped on the sofa and nearly tumbled to the floor, and they both dove to save him but Deeley got there first.

"Wibbieeee!" he protested, stretching his arms toward her. "Bath me! Bath me, Wibbie!"

"Okay, okay, I'll *bathe* you." She dropped the bags on the kitchen counter. "Why don't I take over and you can heat up the dinner I brought?"

"Thank you," Deeley said. "Bath's not my forte. None of this is."

Truer words were never spoken, and rarely with such bone-deep unhappiness. She could get rid of that, though. She had to stick to her plan.

She managed to corral Bash and get him back to the bathroom, which was dangerous, since the floor was soaked. Kneeling in the water, she got him in the tub, but he reached down and flung as much water at her as his little hands could muster.

"Bash!" Even for him, this was over the top. He was never a well-behaved child, but they had been making progress. He knew he was loved, he had boundaries, very little junk food, and a routine he was starting to follow.

"What's going on with you, buddy?"

She tried to ease him onto his backside, but he was having none of it, just splashing and kicking until she gave up, wrapped him in a towel, and finished cleaning his face with a washcloth.

The entire time, he screamed, "No!" and squirmed, flipping his face from side to side so the task was darn near impossible.

She cooed at him, cajoled and begged, and finally got him into his room, where the pajama battle ensued.

"Bottle!" he cried.

"No, sweet pea, you don't drink bottles anymore." Well, he had when he got here, but they'd just about won that battle. "I'll get you a sippy cup with water, then we're climbing into bed for night-night."

"No!" he screamed, but she got him up and over the side of the crib, praying he didn't yet figure out how to climb out of it. He would soon, then they'd have to get a toddler bed.

She rushed into the kitchen, expecting to smell the savory shepherd's pie warming in the oven, but Deeley was nowhere in sight. Without taking time to look for him, she filled a sippy cup and headed back, a little stunned to find Bash laying down, sucking his thumb, quiet.

"Okay, then, you're done for the day." She offered him the cup but his eyes fluttered closed, his cheeks bright red from the fight. "Oh, baby. You hit your wall. I feel you."

She reached down and touched his head, which felt warm, but hers probably did, too, after that bath.

"You go to sleep, angel. I'll put your sippy cup right here in the corner in case you get thirsty."

He didn't answer, didn't cry out or wail or fight when she turned the light out and quietly closed the door, leaving it open a crack as she did.

Now for the other man in her life. She still had a plan, remember?

Looking around, she saw the Bailey's bags hadn't even been opened. And Deeley was...outside on the patio?

Okay, a little wine might start things off nicely and they often shared a cocktail outside on a lovely evening. Or they used to, BB—Before Bash.

She pushed the slider open to step out and joined him, a little disappointed when she saw he held a cold beer when she'd been hoping to share that bottle of merlot. But okay. Not all plans go as expected.

"Hey."

He turned at the sound of her voice, nothing but agony in eyes just about the color of that brown bottle he held. "Hey."

"He sleeps."

He inched back. "Is that a joke?"

"Nope. He crashed hard."

"He hasn't had dinner yet," he said. "Unless you count that half a Hershey bar." He looked skyward. "Man, I was so unforgiving with Marcie, but that kid is a hot mess."

"He's just a child, Deeley." She approached him, searching his face, then wrapped her arms around his waist. "We'll figure it out. I'm starving."

He nodded, then dropped his chin on her head, nestling her in to where she fit so perfectly.

"I can't do this, Liv." His voice was so gruff and broken, she wasn't sure she understood him.

"Can't do...shepherd's pie? A hug? Life?" She eased back and looked up at him. "What can't you do, Connor Deeley?"

"Raise a kid until he's eighteen. I am not good at it."

Now? He decided this now after three months? "No

one is good at first. And he's had a challenging life. We just have to..." Her voice faded out as he closed his eyes and struggled to swallow. Good heavens, was Deeley about to cry?

"We? Liv, I can't drag you into this."

"It's a little late. I'm dragged."

"But it's not what you want."

"I'll be the judge of that."

"You might think you want this, and you care," he continued, as if she hadn't said anything. "God, you care so much, sometimes I can't even believe it. I never met a person who cares like you do. And I...I care about you. More than care. I cannot be so selfish as to just assume you're going to be my partner and help raise this child. I can't do that to you."

"You're not doing anything to me," she assured him. "I jumped in with both feet when you got him. I love Bash. And I love—"

He put his fingers on her lips. "Don't say it."

Her heart dropped as she stared at him, a new kind of hurt strangling her.

"Don't," he said again. "Because you're not going to like what I'm about to tell you."

She blinked at him, ice suddenly filling her chest. "What?"

"I talked to my sister."

She inched back at the statement, so far from anything she was expecting him to say. "Christine? Is everything okay? Is your dad good?"

"Pop's...okay. Slowing down a lot. Chris is great. My nephew got into NC State, so she's very proud of him."

"Why am I not going to like the fact that your nephew is going to college?" she asked, still hung up on the warning.

He searched her face, thinking before he spoke again. "Her great big house is going to be kind of empty."

"And?"

"And she said Bash and I could live with her. She could help me raise him."

What?

Olivia might have said the word, but probably she just mouthed it, because this announcement left her speechless. He would go live with his sister? In North Carolina?

"Doesn't your dad live with her?" It was a stupid question, one she already knew the answer to, but nothing made sense right then.

Not the buzzing in her head or the look in his eyes or the sound of...*she's going to help me raise him.*

"Yeah, he does. But she has a six-bedroom house and, honestly, she's depressed about Sean going to college. Chris is a natural nurturer, born to be a mother. With him gone, well...she's actually excited about the possibility of Bash and me living there. It was her idea, to be honest."

She was vaguely aware that she was taking tiny steps backwards, as if each word jabbed at her heart. Did he even realize what he was saying?

"Is...is this what you want?"

"I want you to be happy, and I want Bash to..." His whisper trailed off, his voice raspy with agony.

"I *am* happy," she said when he didn't finish.

He lifted a dubious brow. "Come on, Liv. I know you. I know you're struggling with all this. Having a three year-old is hard, and we're barely hanging on. This isn't what you want."

"Can't I decide that?"

"Yes, and you'll always decide to put everyone else first. Open up your home and take on my responsibility and give up any chance of having a kid of your own."

"Why am I giving that up?"

"Because I won't do it, as you know. I haven't changed my mind." He threaded his fingers in his hair and tugged it back in a classic Connor Deeley gesture that revealed all his inner turmoil on one handsome face. "I thought we could make this work. I thought we could do anything together—"

"We can," she insisted. "I know this is hard now, but it's only going to get easier when...when..." Her voice faded and he gave a bitter, dry laugh.

"Right. *When?*" he challenged. "When he's eight and needs to be taken to ball games and play dates? When he's twelve and turns into a middle school monster? When he's sixteen and we find pot in his room? When he's eighteen and...can leave?"

"Deeley. Is that what you think raising a child is going to be like?"

"I don't know what it is. I don't know anything except this: by the time we're *not* raising him, I'll be darn near fifty and you'll be a few years behind. And we'll have given our lives to Sebastian Royce. And I don't have a problem with that. It's the card life dealt me. But you didn't get that hand and you shouldn't have to hold it."

She stared at him, the ice in her chest starting to melt, as everything did when she looked long and hard at Deeley. "You can't give up on me."

"That's not what I'm doing!" he shot back. "Just the opposite, Liv. I care so much for you. I adore you. I admire you. I...I..."

She held her breath, waiting for the obvious next statement, even though he'd already stopped her from saying it.

"I can't ruin your life."

"You're not ruining my life. You've changed it and, yes, it's not quite what we thought might happen, but there's a child involved and he needs us both and you can't...you can't..."

But she knew from the look in his eyes that he could. And just might.

"*Wibbieeee!*" The cry was accompanied by a loud, long shriek.

"That doesn't sound good," she said, already pivoting to head in, but Deeley snagged her arm.

"I'll get him. I'll take care of him."

She didn't argue but took the beer he handed her and stood stone still as he disappeared into the house. The bottle was warm from his hand, but she pressed it against her face anyway, as if that could stem the tide of tears.

This so wasn't in her plan.

"Liv! Olivia!" The low-grade panic in Deeley's voice shot right through her, making her bolt into the house, barely aware that she put the bottle on the kitchen counter and flew back to the bedroom.

"What's wrong?"

"He's burning up," Deeley said, holding a limp but tearful Bash in his arms. "He has a fever. High."

She pressed her hand on Bash's head and gasped softly. "Oh my gosh, he does. Baby Tylenol? Emergency room? My mother? Let me think."

"Tylenol for sure. I don't think the ER, but we should take his temperature. I don't know what your mother will do, but..." He pressed his hand lightly on Bash's head, easing the blond curls to his chest. "I might call my sister."

"Oh, yeah, sure. Mother Theresa will know what to do."

"Livvie."

"I'm sorry," she said quickly. "I didn't mean that. I'm just hurt, Deeley. I'm really, really hurt."

He closed his eyes and walked to the rocking chair, easing into it with his strong arms holding Bash.

"I'll get the baby Tylenol and the thermometer," she said, walking toward the door.

The tears didn't fall until she was in the bathroom, where they spilled hard and fast.

Many hours later, the sun peeked over the horizon when Olivia opened her eyes the next morning, the long night and lack of sleep pressing on her heart like an anvil.

No, that wasn't what pressed.

This was not lack of sleep making her ache. Deeley was leaving. He was taking Bash and leaving her and Sanibel and...

She bit her lip to keep from letting out any sound—a moan of agony, a whimper of defeat. Instead, she angled her head to see Deeley next to her, eyes closed, his broad chest rising and falling with the peace of sleep.

The peace of a decision that he obviously wanted to make. And she had no right to stop him, but...

She put a hand on his arm, not to wake him and not to try and talk him out of this, but for the sheer pleasure of touching him. She never didn't enjoy that.

He let out a soft groan, turned, and wrapped her in his arms, pulling her close as he frequently did in his sleep, his mouth near her ear.

"If you love me..." She breathed the words. "You couldn't leave."

"I'd leave *because* I love you." His voice fluttered her hair and sent chills down her spine.

She held on to that—and him—letting the words ease a pain she knew would last a long, long time.

Chapter Six

Claire

E ven after she'd moved to a house a few miles away, Claire tried to start every day by walking Shellseeker Beach with Eliza. Occasionally, they missed their walks due to schedule conflicts, but those were rare at sunrise. The hour the sisters spent together was an absolute delight for both of them, and had become an almost daily ritual.

Noah frequently rode in with Claire to run the tea hut in the morning, serving drinks to the many shellseekers who came to discover what treasures the tide had brought. Today, after the rush, he'd be helping Camille move boxes into her new townhouse. And, of course, he met Katie, who was at the resort early to start the day of cleaning and caring for the cottages.

When Claire and Noah came through the gardens that morning, they spotted both Katie and Eliza on the boardwalk, watching Harper run along the sand with a bright red kite.

"Noah!" she called in her high-pitched mouse voice. "Look what I have! Look!"

He beamed at the little girl, breaking into a jog to go to her.

Claire slowed her step, watching him scoop up Harper and drop a kiss on Katie's cheek, the move so natural it sent a jolt of happiness through her. And, it was the first time she'd seen that bounce in his step since DJ had taken that call yesterday.

"Hey, you." Eliza bounded up the boardwalk, her reddish blond hair fluttering over her shoulders, the sun-dappled Gulf of Mexico providing the perfect backdrop for her sister.

"Hi," Claire called, reaching out for a hug. They might have spent all their lives apart, but now that they'd met, the bond was a strong one. Eliza had become Claire's closest confidante, due in no small part to these morning walks.

"Tide's low," Eliza said, gesturing toward the beach behind her. "Great walking this morning." She drew back and frowned a little. "You okay?"

"Yeah, I'm just..." She took a deep breath and drank in the morning vista, and then the concern in her sister's blue-gray eyes. "How do you always know when something's eating away at me?"

Eliza shrugged. "Just do." She put her arm around Claire and led her toward the sand. "Noah sure looks happy, though."

"He is, but sometimes that joy is hanging by a thread." She bounced as her sneakers hit the sand. "And that thread is named DJ Fortunato."

"Really? I thought they were like the dream team in the pizza kitchen, the best of friends, and a model father-son duo."

Claire considered that description, knowing in some ways it wasn't far from the truth. "They are, but DJ's daughter Sophia is having problems at home. He was on the phone with her and his ex-wife, Rachel last night for a long time." She blew out a breath, going right to the heart of the matter. "I think she's really pressuring him to go back to California."

"Oh, Claire. That's tough. What does he want to do?"

"The right thing. The only problem is, what is the right thing? Go back and try to be there for a girl who's turning eighteen and is carrying around a bunch of anger over her parents' divorce and her mother's new guy? Because if he does that, he's going to leave a kid who's never had a father but does now."

"Eeesh. Catch-22."

"More like *Sophie's Choice*. Which kid matters more?"

Eliza groaned. "Horrible position to be in."

"It is. Not much eats away at DJ, as you know. He takes what life throws and considers it a gift. But not this."

"Poor guy." She leaned in and gave Claire a look. "And what about you?"

"Me? I'm just along for the ride with the Fortunato men."

"But you must have an opinion on what he should do, even if you keep it to yourself. You can tell me."

"I know I can," Claire said. "But I don't know, Eliza. It's not my family."

"But it is," Eliza said. "Noah and DJ and you are as much a family as they are."

"That's true and I can tell you this," Claire said. "I can't bear to give up this unit we're creating. There's so much laughter and lively discussions and cooking and late nights on the patio sharing wine. I've been single for almost my whole adult life, with the exception of a short marriage in my twenties. I've *never* had anything like this and I want to keep it. I'm in love with the whole idea of it."

Eliza nodded, understanding that, but the statement begged another question. "Do you think you're in love with DJ...or the idea of this family?" she asked.

Claire considered the question for a moment, then said, "I think I could be in love with him. Easily. But that's a little scary. Yes, he's passionate and all in and intense in everything he does, but he's also...not a sure thing. The next tide could sweep him away to a new passion, a new place. It's a little daunting to fall in love with a man like that. And don't forget, I'm still an employee of a New York-based law firm. Or I think I am."

"What does that mean?"

Claire filled her in on the situation at work, including Noah's idea of persuading her law firm to open a local office.

"You should do that," Eliza said. "Cut the ties, move here, start a new life." She beamed and put her arm around Claire. "Never leave me, sister of mine!"

Claire laughed, letting Eliza's warmth pour over her. "You make it sound easy, but that's not a job you walk away from. Not for a man who could leave at any moment."

"For Noah?"

"Oh, yes. I want to stay where he is. I promised him I would, but..." She looked down the beach to where Noah was running with Harper, keeping that kite afloat. "I have a feeling he's about to make a family of his own and I'll just be...his mom. Not the Number One woman in his life, and that's as it should be." Claire let out a frustrated grunt. "I don't do well with turmoil and uncertainty."

"Then talk to DJ," Eliza said softly. "Communication is key in every relationship and you need to know what he's thinking and feeling."

Claire nodded, not really knowing how to say that even though DJ was a man who talked about feelings in general, he didn't always share his deepest, most personal emotional state.

"Enough about me," Claire said, longing for a change of subject. "What's happening around here? How did your meeting go with Penny yesterday?"

"Oh, boy. Long story. Let's start with another one. Your mother had a date with Buck Underwood last night." Eliza gave a light elbow jab to Claire's ribs, but that wasn't what made her nearly stumble on the sand.

"Excuse me?" she asked with a disbelieving laugh. "Talk about burying the real news."

"Hey, your relationship and job and family is the headline today. But this is kind of interesting."

"Kind of!" She crossed her arms and tipped her head, letting it sink in. "My mother? Camille Durant? Went on a date with that slow-talkin' Southern fish bait salesman? Wow, life can still surprise me."

Eliza laughed. "Right? Except it's way more complicated. That Southern fish bait salesman is the widow of Penny Conway's sister."

"Penny? That shrew who works at the Welcome Center?"

"The same. And that shrew is apparently certain that your mother has spun a web of lust around poor Buck. We've been surreptitiously informed by Patty, the other sister, that's the reason Penny is stonewalling our chances of getting that feature."

Claire practically sputtered with surprise. "Wait. What? And since when does my mother spin webs of lust?" She made a face. "I'm not sure I want to know this."

"Don't worry, she has denied that part wholeheartedly. She insists he's pursuing her, but she agreed to have dinner with him last night."

"How did I miss all this?" Claire asked, throwing up her hands in exasperation.

"You're kind of busy with the Fortunato men," Eliza teased. "But, whoa, that Penny. She's even more awful than I realized. And, in her defense, your mother offered to cancel, but Teddy and I talked her into going anyway."

Claire looked up at the cottages, glancing toward Junonia, where Camille had just spent her last night before moving. "Let's go talk to her and find out how it went."

"It's early for Camille."

"Then I'll wake her up..." She leaned closer and gave Eliza a playful look. "If she's alone and hasn't, you know, spun lust webs, not that I can even imagine what that would look like."

"Don't. It's your mother, after all."

Laughing at that, they ran up the boardwalk in a flash of fun that almost made up for the childhood they missed as sisters.

The cottage was quiet and locked when they got there, but Eliza dangled her master key, a question in her eyes.

"Of course open it," Claire said.

"What if..." Eliza waggled her brows.

"Not a chance."

"If you're sure..." Eliza unlocked the slider and inched it open.

"*Maman?*" Claire called, noticing the master bedroom door was closed. She wouldn't... Would she? She also noticed that the personal belongings Camille had collected in the past few months were packed up in bins all over the living room floor, which made sense, because she was moving today.

"Oh, Claire, hello!" The bedroom door opened and Claire was almost ashamed at how relieved she was to see her mother alone, in her dressing gown, sipping her morning coffee. "And Eliza! Just the person I wanted to see. Go look at that piece of paper on the counter and imagine all the ways you're going to thank me."

"Excuse me?" Eliza walked to the peninsula that separated the kitchen from the living area and picked up a slip of paper. "Who is Mia Watson? Have you already booked this cottage for us?"

"Only if you want the Coastal Reviews Editor of *The Last Resort* to stay here, which I think you do."

"What?" Claire came closer, looking at the paper over Eliza's shoulder. "That's who Mia Watson is?"

"It is, and you may call her directly, bypassing all the nonsense of getting on some list that Penny 'I'm in charge of the world' Conway is putting together. Abner gave that to me."

"How did that happen? Are you sure? How did he get this?" Eliza's questions came out in a staccato of surprise.

"He's quite resourceful, that Abner Underwood. And it turns out he somehow knows *everyone*." Camille breezed out of the bedroom to join them. "Sorry about the boxes. Sit, ladies. Do you want coffee?"

"And details," Claire said, glancing over Eliza's shoulder to look at the handwritten name and phone number. "How did he get this?"

"Turns out that about a year ago, a man came into his bait shop to sell ad space for *The Last Resort*. Abner made friends with him, as he does. They remained friends and last night, when I told him how utterly awful his sister-in-law was behaving—he agreed wholeheartedly she was acting like a monster, by the way—he picked up his phone, texted the man, *et voilà*! That is the woman who is making the final decisions for the whole feature. All you need to do is call her and convince her to include Shellseeker Cottages."

"Are you sure?" Eliza asked, staring at the name. "Penny insisted there was a process, a list that had to be submitted from the mayor's office, and—"

"Penny is full of...things a lady doesn't say in any language," Camille said with a cocked brow. "And you have nothing to lose by calling that Mia person."

"I certainly don't," Eliza agreed, using the paper to fan herself. "And I owe you one, Camille."

"I guess you do, but honestly, Abner was a gem."

"Speaking of," Claire said, leaning forward. "Since when does my mother go out on dates and not tell me?'"

"Since I became a grown woman with my own life," she said.

"Well?" Claire prodded. "How was it?"

"Nice." She smiled. "He lives on a boat and he cooked me dinner."

Claire blinked, still surprised by this turn of events. A boat? "How do you feel about him?"

She smiled. "Like my private life is private, *cherie*." She pushed up and glanced around. "We're almost done here. Noah should be here soon to start my move, then he and DJ are going to get my furniture out of storage."

"Oh, girls. I have to go." Eliza looked up from her phone, a frown on her face. "Olivia has to go open Sanibel Sisters and she wants me to stay with Bash, who had a fever last night."

"And Deeley has to work?" Claire guessed.

"And Deeley is...oh my God..." She frowned at the phone, then looked from one to the other, color draining from her cheeks.

"Deeley is what?" Claire prompted.

"He might be moving away. And taking Bash."

Claire and Camille gasped at exactly the same time.

"I don't know any more than that," Eliza said, rising. "But I better go. And thank you for this name, Camille. You're a godsend."

With a quick air kiss, Eliza disappeared out the sliders, leaving Claire and Camille with many unanswered questions.

"Leaving Shellseeker Beach?" Claire whispered. "With Bash? How can he do that?"

"I don't know," Camille said. "But I need to dress before Noah gets here. Now I wish I were going in to Sanibel Sisters today to support poor Livvie. She must be devastated."

Claire stared at her mother, angling her head as she processed the last few minutes.

"What?" Camille asked, touching her face. "Did I mess up my makeup or something? Why are you looking at me like that?"

"Because, you've...changed. Dating. Doing secret favors. And worried about helping Olivia."

"Well, I'm human and I care about these people, Claire."

"I know, but you are different." How could she not see it? Camille used to have an edge as sharp as that

Penny Conway, tempered by her beauty and French accent. "I think Shellseeker Beach is softening you."

"Stop it," Camille said on a laugh, heading back to the bedroom.

Claire stood, still smiling from the revelation, then stepped out to the deck to look at the Gulf. Change was in the air, some good, some not good. But she could feel it. Change was coming as sure as the next tide with another deposit of all new shells.

She couldn't do much about the changes in other people's lives, but she could do something about her own. She needed to talk openly and honestly with DJ.

That shouldn't worry her, but it did.

Chapter Seven

Eliza

The phone conversation she had with Olivia as she drove across Sanibel Island didn't give Eliza any of the answers she wanted. All her daughter would say was that Deeley announced he was moving to North Carolina with Bash so his sister, Christine, could help raise him.

The rest of it was a lot of crying and sniffing and the clipped answers Livvie gave when her life felt out of control.

When Eliza arrived at the small rental house, Deeley opened the door with Bash hanging on his arm.

"Thanks for coming," Deeley said gently, his big hands making Bash look very small. "I couldn't get anyone to cover for me at the beach, and Livvie had to open the store, so..." He stroked Bash's back as the child hung uncharacteristically quiet on Deeley's arm. "His fever broke but I think he could use a lot of rocking and... you know. That stuff."

Without a word, Eliza reached for Bash and brought him into her arms, his malleable little body a testament to how crappy he felt.

Deeley didn't look that much better.

"Livvie told me what you're thinking about doing,"

she said, trying not to sound cold or angry. This wasn't her fight, but her daughter's heart was broken, so if she had to take sides, it would be Olivia's.

Deeley let out a sigh and gestured her into the living room, which was dim and cool with all the blinds drawn.

"She's pretty upset," Eliza added when he didn't respond.

"I know," he finally said. "I know she is."

"And that's okay with you?" Eliza asked, carrying Bash to the big recliner where she expected she'd spend much of the day with him.

"Of course it's not okay, Eliza. I hate this." He glanced at Bash and shook his head, unwilling to say anything even though the child was half asleep. "I need to get dressed."

Without another word, he disappeared into the back of the small house, presumably to get out of his sleep pants and into the board shorts he wore to work at the beach.

Frustrated by the conversation, Eliza turned her attention to Bash, cooing and rocking him for a minute and before she knew it, he was asleep.

No, this wasn't her business and she didn't want to be the busybody mother-in-law—especially because she wasn't a mother-in-law or a grandmother or anything except Deeley's girlfriend's mother. Did that give her any clout?

She didn't know, but she wanted answers. She wanted his side of the situation, anyway.

When she heard his footsteps in the hall, she stood

very carefully and laid Bash down on the wide sectional, covering him with a soft blue blanket and stepping toward the hallway. She didn't want Deeley to slip out without some kind of explanation.

"He's asleep," she said as he walked into the living area.

"How did you do that?" he asked on a whisper, glancing at the sofa. "I couldn't get him to sleep for love or money." He walked to the kitchen counter, picking up his keys and wallet. "I never know what to do with that kid."

"So you're taking him away to share the responsibility with your sister?"

He looked up from the keys in his hand, a world of hurt in his golden-brown eyes, enough that she was sorry she'd asked the question that way. "I might. It's a good solution and I don't know what else to do, Eliza."

"How about you stay and let the people who love you here help you? They say it takes a village, and you have one."

He searched her face, thinking for a moment before answering. "I have a village up there, too. My sister is like the world's greatest mother." At her look, he flinched. "What I mean is there's nothing she loves more than kids and hers is leaving the nest. She's overjoyed at the chance to help me with Bash. My dad's retired, too, and has some serious health issues. Her husband is a little over-whelmed running a small winery on their property, and... it's just a better situation."

"Better for who? You? Bash? Livvie?"

"You think I *want* to leave her?" he croaked the question, the tone of his voice telling her it was a rhetorical question.

"I don't know what you want, Deeley," she said carefully. "I don't know if Livvie knows, either. But you're together. You're cohabitating. You're raising a child together, and—"

"Eliza, this isn't what she wants, and we both know it. She wants her husband and child, two-point-five of them if I had to guess, and a successful business. I'm just screwing up her life and her plans. If there's anything Livvie likes, it is plans."

"I don't think she sees it as though you're screwing it up, just coming at it from a new and different angle."

He shot her a "get real" look.

"Are you saying you could never be her husband?" Eliza asked. "Because, forgive me for overstepping, but I thought you two were pretty good together."

"We're *great* together," he corrected. "We're amazing. Livvie is the single most awesome, brilliant, beautiful, perfect woman I've ever met."

"Oh." The syllable slipped out like a whisper. "Well, I couldn't agree more."

"She deserves better than..." He shut his eyes. "She deserves better."

"Don't you think she should be the one to decide that?"

"She won't do it," he said. "She'll writhe around trying to make the best of it. She'll compromise because she's a giver like that, and she'll sacrifice, change, give up her dreams, and settle for what got dropped in her lap because she thinks she loves me."

"*Thinks?*"

He just looked at her. "Fine. She does. And, for the record, Eliza, I love her, too. So..." His voice grew ragged. "So stinkin' much."

Her whole heart folded in half, prompting her to go to him, pressing her hands to her chest even though what she wanted to do was take him in her arms and be his mother, too. "Then make it work, Deeley. You can, you both can."

"This isn't fair to her." He looked down, fighting his emotions. "It's just not fair to expect her to take on the responsibility of another person's child, and to get bits and pieces of me when there's a man out there who could give her his whole heart and soul and the children of her own she wants." He looked as if the very thought made him shudder. "I hate the guy, but I'm sure he's out there."

"Maybe you need to give this more time," Eliza said. "Another few months. Bash is getting better and you two are just finding your rhythm with each other. You're happy together."

"We *were* very happy together," he agreed. "But now, our whole world is that kid. And don't get me wrong, I love him. I do. But now..." He swallowed and hauled his fingers through his long hair. "I'm starting to resent him, which is wrong. I don't want him to sense that. I mean, talk about getting a bad hand in life."

"And landing in tall cotton with you and Livvie."

"He landed with me, not Livvie," he said. "It's not

fair to her. I don't know how else to say this, but I care too much for her to put her through this."

"Look, Deeley, on some level, some strange and complicated level, I get that," Eliza said. "Asking her to open her home and heart to a toddler and help you raise him is a huge request, and you think you're doing the right thing."

"I *am* doing the right thing—for them."

"But a change of life plan isn't the end of life," she said, pressing prayer hands to her lips, practically begging him to understand that. "That's how life is sometimes. It isn't what you expect, it's the opposite. You get a hand that isn't the one you thought you'd get." She gave a tight smile. "Trust me, when you look across the desk and a doctor tells you, privately, that your husband isn't going to see sixty? When all the 'golden years' go up in smoke and you have nothing but nursing, tears, and a funeral?"

"God, Eliza. It had to be so hard for you," he whispered.

"It was wretched," she said. "But look where I am. I found a way, a family, a home, and a purpose. You can't just run away when you don't like what you have. And this isn't death, Deeley." She gestured toward the little boy asleep on the sofa. "This is life and hope and a child who will bring you so much joy. And Livvie..." She sighed. "She could bring you both joy."

He stared at her for a few heartbeats, the sound of them pulsing in her head as she waited and hoped that she'd gotten through to him.

"I'm leaving, Eliza," he finally said.

"For work? Or for North Carolina?"

"Work." He slipped his wallet and his keys into his pocket and took a step closer to the door. "And most likely North Carolina, after I figure out what to do with the business."

She gave a soft, sad moan, and he reached out his hand and touched her shoulder. "Believe me, if there were any better solution, I'd take it. I love your daughter, Eliza, and I want her to have everything she deserves and desires. This isn't fair to her."

With that, he walked over to the sofa and looked down at the sleeping child. "Be good, Sebastian Royce." He blew a kiss and walked out the door, closing it with a click of finality.

And Eliza sat down on the rocker and cried, because he wasn't wrong, but he wasn't right, and she didn't know how to fix it for them.

Two hours later, Eliza still hadn't made the phone call to Mia Watson. She'd tried a few times, but Bash woke up and he needed...something. A trip to the potty, food, a toy, a rock on her lap, a big drink of water, and all the attention Eliza had.

He seemed to feel better, and had enough energy to play. She couldn't make such an important call while he was toddling around with his little hands holding two cars each while she tried to keep up.

At the sound of a car door—a real one—she pushed

up from the floor, hoping that maybe Olivia got away from the store and they could talk. It wasn't her daughter's familiar face that greeted her when she opened the front door, but Miles Anderson's, and that was almost as good.

"The cavalry is here," he called out as he opened the back door of his truck and Tinkerbell came bounding out. "And the canine crew."

"Hello!" She stepped out to get greeted by the Boston terrier mix who had decided long ago that she loved Eliza, and loved her hard. Tink shot forward, tongue out, tail wagging, eyes gleaming with joy.

"All I had to do was say your name, and she was in the truck," Miles said on a laugh.

"How did you know I was here?" she asked, bending over to give and get some sloppy Tink love.

She never knew what she'd done to deserve Tinkerbell's undying affection, but she had it. And from the look in Miles's green eyes as he gazed down at her, she was reminded that she had his affection, too. Never sure what she'd done to get that, either, but she liked it. And him.

More with each passing day, in fact.

"I stopped by Shellseeker and saw Deeley. Man, he's a wreck."

She stood slowly, knowing the two men were very close friends. "Did he tell you why?"

"I've known he was thinking about this for a while."

"And didn't tell me?" She lifted her brows, a little disappointed.

"I was trying to talk him out of it, E." He reached her,

wrapping his arms around her. "How's Bash? I heard he was sick."

"On the mend. Come on in."

She led Miles and Tinkerbell into the house and Bash instantly abandoned his cars for the dog.

"Pupp*ieeeee!*" He tore toward Tinkerbell, rewarded with a lick on the face, which made him giggle.

"Hey, buddy." Miles ruffled the little boy's curls. "Heard you're not feeling well."

"All better!" he announced, pulling Miles's hand. "Play cars?"

"Oh, sure." Miles gave Eliza a quick look. "And maybe you need a break?"

"That's very kind of you, Miles. I actually need to make an important work call, if you wouldn't mind playing cars for a few minutes?"

"I'm a great car player," he said, folding right onto the floor with ease and picking up one of the tiny toys. "Is this a Porsche? My dream car. *Vrrrroooom* goes your money right out the door!"

He rolled the car playfully up Bash's belly, making him giggle.

"Go make your call," he said, smiling up at her. "I got this."

"Awesome. I won't be long." She grabbed her bag with the phone number Camille had given her and started off to Bash's bedroom, but stopped and turned to watch a grown man on the floor with a two year-old, explaining why that Porsche was so awesome.

For a moment, she couldn't move, struck by how

sweet and considerate he was, and handsome, and funny, and...Miles.

Without a word, she went back to him, bent over, and planted a kiss on his head. "Thank you," she whispered.

He looked up at her, so much warmth in his eyes. So much caring. "Anything for you, E."

And she knew he meant that.

Next month it would be one year since Ben died. For no real reason, she'd put that arbitrary timeline in place when she met Miles. They'd started as friends, and now were "dating"—if that was the correct term these days—and he was patiently waiting for more.

A lot more, if he was to be believed. He'd told her he hoped to make their relationship permanent and official, but he was letting Eliza dictate the pace of everything.

For her part, she never planned to marry again. But right now, watching him play with a child that for all intents and purposes was like a grandchild to her...she wasn't sure what she wanted to do.

He winked at her, holding up the car. "Probably the closest I'll ever get to owning one of these," he said with a laugh.

She suspected that wasn't true, considering he was a former JAG attorney who'd used his "retirement" to start a lucrative PI business. He had a beautiful home on Sanibel with a sizeable boat in the back.

But here he was—not boating, not working, not fishing or relaxing or living his life—but rescuing her when she hadn't even asked.

"You're a good man, Miles Anderson," she whispered.

His smile widened as Bash climbed onto his lap, rolling a car on Miles's cheek and begging for attention.

"And my secret's out, Bash!" He took the car from the laughing boy and started to make the motor sound again.

Laughing, she headed toward the room that was going to be a guest room/office when Livvie moved in but now had a crib with toys, books, and a rocking chair.

Taking a seat in that, she fished out the paper and stared at Mia Watson's name. While Bash had slept earlier, she'd Googled the woman and searched *The Last Resort*'s main website for information about her. She was indeed a high-ranking editor and property reviewer, and it made sense that she'd have a say over this project.

But would she be furious that Eliza had bypassed Penny and the mayor and whatever "system" they'd set in place?

Too bad. Eliza had to try. Taking a breath, she punched in the number and closed her eyes while it rang.

"Hello, this is Mia." The greeting was so cheery, it instantly wiped away Eliza's misgivings.

"Hello, Ms. Watson. My name is Eliza Whitney, and I'm calling about a small property on Sanibel Island called Shellseeker—"

"Cottages!" she finished with a little laugh in her throat. "Please tell me you've changed your mind. You will make my day."

Eliza sat a little straighter. Changed her mind? "Uh...

I guess it depends," she replied with a confused laugh. "Although I don't think we've ever talked before."

"Oh, no we haven't. But my family stayed at those cottages one Christmas when I was a kid, and I have such fond memories. I had the project coordinator beg the Sanibel people to put it on the list, but they said you weren't interested in being considered for the Hidden Gems feature. We have you listed as 'declined to participate.'"

Declined to participate? "Honestly, I only learned about the Hidden Gems feature a few days ago."

The other woman was quiet for a beat, long enough for Eliza to wonder if Penny Conway had declined for them. Just how deep did her issues with Camille really run?

"I was told by someone in the Sanibel mayor's office that Shellseeker Cottages didn't want to participate."

Deep, Eliza thought. Very deep. "Well, we've had a breakdown in communication then," Eliza said, still not willing to throw Penny all the way under the bus. "So I hope you don't mind that I've taken the initiative and called you."

"Not a bit. I'm scheduling walk-throughs in south-west Florida over the next week or so. I'd love to do one for your property. I have Thursday or Friday open. Will either work?"

"Absolutely. Take your pick and we'll make it happen."

"Friday. I'd love a full tour, maybe talk to a few guests and staff, and get a sense of the place. We'll narrow it down to a few contenders in each of the ten areas around the state, and then we bring a team in and give you an afternoon and evening to knock our socks off."

"We love to knock socks off," Eliza said, "and send you straight to the sand to find shells."

Mia let out a musical laugh. "Perfect. After that, we will choose the Top Ten Hidden Gems in the state, but only one in southwest Florida, so competition is tight. If you're chosen, then we arrange for our reviewer to spend a week at the resort writing the feature that will most likely guarantee you won't have a vacancy for a long, long time. Does that sound doable?"

"Yes, yes, and so very much yes," Eliza replied on a soft laugh. "All doable."

As they chatted and made some plans, Eliza stepped out into the hall to check on Bash, grinning when she saw Miles on his hands and knees while the little boy rode him like a horse, complete with cries of, "Giddy up, cowboy!"

Once again, her heart just melted and she finished the conversation with a huge smile on her face.

Things were still...challenging. But in the last half hour, they'd taken a turn for the happy and surprising, and she decided to hold on to that for a while.

Chapter Eight

Olivia

Sanibel Sisters enjoyed a steady stream of non-stop customers that day, which was a blessing and a curse. Without a minute to wallow in self-pity, Olivia managed to keep her mind off her problems. But without that minute, she didn't make any progress on the process of coming to terms with what Deeley was thinking about doing.

That left her feeling out of sorts and stressed and even more miserable than she'd been—which was pretty miserable.

Early in the afternoon, though, there was a lull, long enough for her to run to the bathroom, fight her tears, text her mother, and grab half a cup of coffee. She'd barely had a sip when she heard the front bell and she stepped out, ready to greet a new customer.

"Oh, it's only you," she said on a sigh when she caught sight of Asia Turner's long black braids as she pushed her baby into the store in a stroller.

"And you sound so excited about it," Asia teased, breaking into a wide smile.

"Relieved to see someone I can talk to." She came around a display of new shorts and T-shirts, peeking at the nearly six-month old baby snoozing in the stroller. "Hello, Zane," she whispered, leaning over. "You're looking more beautiful than ever."

Olivia smiled at Asia, who looked a bit more tired than breathtakingly beautiful today. "How goes the mommy wars, Asia?" she asked with a sympathetic smile.

"Losing the battles, winning the war."

Olivia laughed for the first time all day. No surprise, since she and Asia had become friends over the past few months. Asia had arrived after having a baby on her own up in Ohio. She was the daughter of Roz and George Turner, who managed Sanibel Treasures, Shellseeker's souvenir shop. Close to Olivia's age, Asia had worked in corporate, too, as an executive recruiter, which gave them an automatic connection.

Asia had vented to Olivia about her conflicts with her uber-controlling mother, and their friendship had blossomed as they created a little "Mommy and Me" group of two.

Zane was obviously too young for real playdates, but a few months ago, they'd found a park that Bash loved and had spent many mornings there. While Zane snoozed in the stroller and Bash climbed the play equipment like his life depended on it, the two women talked and discovered how much they had in common.

Olivia bit her lip, thinking how much she'd miss those mornings when...when...

"And it looks like you're losing the battle *and* the war." A statuesque five-nine, Asia had to dip her head down a bit to get closer to Olivia's face. "What's wrong, Liv?"

Was it so obvious?

She glanced at the door, grateful for the lull in business, and in the next five minutes, poured out her heart, soul, and woes.

Asia listened to every word, nodding, asking a few questions, and then Olivia braced for the cascade of sympathy she so richly deserved.

"Well, good for him," she said simply. "You should be deeply grateful."

"Asia!" She blinked at her friend, aching for a different answer, but knowing that this woman was nothing if not honest and pragmatic. Maybe Olivia should have expected this response.

"I mean it," she said. "How easy would it be for Deeley to just lean on you, to use your obviously soft heart and caring nature as an auto-mom and a solution to problems of his own making? I hate to say this, because you don't want to hear it, but I respect the heck out of him for this."

Olivia just stared at her, trying—and failing—to see it that way. "But then I lose him," she said. "And I love him."

She rolled her big brown eyes. "Love is for fools, Liv."

"Spoken like a woman who got her baby from a sperm bank and avoided the mess of love."

Asia's eyes flickered. "I stand by my position that Deeley's doing you a favor."

"Wow, I knew you were, you know, not a fan of the whole traditional relationship thing, but..."

"I'm sorry," Asia said, her voice softening. "I know you need an understanding friend, and I *do* understand that this is a huge heartache for you. But, Liv, you love your control and you don't have any with this child. It's only going to get worse as Bash gets older. He's gotta be the center, and he's not yours. He's not Deeley's, either. Resentment will grow. Your sadness will come out. And you'd never know if Deeley stayed with you because he needed to or wanted to."

She stared at Asia for a long minute, finally hearing the words and...yeah. She never would know that, would she?

"I guess that's true, but it doesn't make the idea of him leaving hurt any less."

Asia put an arm around her and gave a hug. "I know, sister. I know. What does World's Greatest Mom say?"

Olivia smiled at the reference to Eliza, who Asia openly adored. Asia frequently waxed on about the glories of Eliza Whitney and how she treated Olivia like an adult with a brain, unlike overbearing Roz Turner, who tried to micromanage everything Asia did.

"We haven't even talked about it yet," Olivia said. "My mom jumped in to watch Bash— who ran a fever last night—because Deeley and I both had to work."

"But Eliza will be in your corner."

"I hope so," Olivia said on a soft laugh. "'Specially since you're not."

"I'm totally in your corner, Liv. Which is why I think Deeley's doing you a favor."

"But what if I don't want him to leave? What if I don't care that Bash is part of the package now? What if I really do love him? I should be glad to lose him?" She heard her voice rise and didn't care. This mattered to her.

Asia didn't answer right away, but looked down at Zane, her whole expression softening as it always did when she looked at her baby.

"You don't need a man to be happy and whole," she said softly.

Olivia crossed her arms. "But I *want* this man. He makes me happy and whole."

Asia sighed. "He has you in a prison and just handed you the key. Take it and be grateful he's not using you."

"Is he using his sister?" Olivia countered.

"That's different. That's family. And, heck, maybe he is. Because most men..." She made a face. "Well, you know how I feel about them."

Bitter, Olivia thought. Whatever had happened to Asia—she didn't say, but it had to be something—had left her just about as bitter as a woman could be about relationships.

"You're raising a man," Olivia said, trying to keep it light, because she knew it was a tender subject. "So at least there's one you love."

"Yes, and I'm going to raise him to be better than the rest." She leaned over the stroller and stared at the sleeping baby. "Isn't that right, Zee?" She straightened and smiled. "My mother wants to cut my tongue out when I call him that," she added on a laugh. "Which only makes me want to do it more."

"You're bad, Asia Turner."

She grinned. "And I'm sorry I didn't give you the soft place to fall that you needed, but I hope you'll look at this from both sides. Give Deeley some props for thinking about you more than himself. I would hope Zee would do the same thing for his woman someday."

Olivia made a face as a few women came into the store, ending the conversation but leaving her with lots to think about.

⁂

LATER THAT AFTERNOON, Olivia read a text from her mother and nearly cried with relief. The sympathy she needed was on its way. Mom was swinging by the resort to get Teddy and they would both be in the store shortly. Deeley, apparently, found someone to cover the cabana and had come home to take over with Bash, who was doing much better.

And there was a picture of Miles carrying Bash on his back, which did exactly what Eliza wanted it to do— made Olivia smile.

The smile wavered when she looked up from the cash register, fully expecting her mother but seeing the young man who worked next door instead.

David? No, Davis. Buck's nephew, she believed, although they didn't speak that frequently.

"Hello," she said, coming around the cash register

table to greet him. "Taking a break from bait to buy a new dress for the lady in your life?"

He didn't smile, and that was her first clue this wasn't a neighborly visit. "Is Camille here?" he asked.

She shook her head. "Not today. She's moving into a new place. Is there something I can help you with?"

"So that's where Buck is. Helping her move."

She actually didn't think so, since Camille said Noah and DJ were doing the work, but who knew? They had a date last night, if the Shellseeker Beach rumor mill—AKA Eliza Whitney—was to be believed. And that was an issue with this guy's...grandmother, Penny?

Gosh, she'd been so wrapped up in the Bash and Deeley saga she hadn't paid attention to this other drama unfolding, which had been delivered to her in bits and pieces of conversation and texts.

"I'm not sure who's helping," she said vaguely. "But if you need something—"

"We need your help."

We? She lifted a brow, somehow surprised by that pronoun. The family we? The corporate we? The bait shop we? What we was he talking about?

"How can I help, Davis?" she asked. "It is Davis, right?"

He nodded and blew out a breath, brushing back very short hair. He was about her age, maybe a year or two younger, but had the posture and expression of someone much older. It reminded her of Dane, her younger brother, who always acted like he was the older, more mature one.

"You can put the kibosh on this budding romance."

She blinked at him. "Not sure what word in that sentence throws me more. Kibosh? Seriously? And by budding romance, I take it you mean my business partner and your—"

"Uncle. Technically, my great-uncle, and he really was. Great, I mean."

"Was? Did something happen to him to make him not great anymore?" She was only kind of kidding. She was pretty certain she knew what—or who—happened to old Buck. Hurricane Camille hit him hard.

But was that this guy's business?

"Nothing happened...yet. But your, uh, partner? She needs to cool it. We don't know how to tell her this, so maybe you can."

"Who's we, Davis?"

"My grandmother, Penny Conway."

"Ahh. The kind and lovely maven of the Welcome Center."

"And my mother, who is the head of the historical society," he added, just in case Penny didn't carry enough clout. "And my father, who is the head of the City Council."

"And your grandfather, who I believe is the mayor."

He gave her a tight smile and nodded again.

"Quite the power family you come from," she said, only half kidding.

"We're a close family, that's for sure," he added. "And all of us, every last one, is concerned about Uncle Buck. I'm here to ask you to please have that woman stop whatever she's doing, because...because it's not good for him."

"How so?"

"And it's wrong."

"Excuse me?" A whole bunch of irritation marched all over her, and it was frankly a welcome respite from her day of feeling sorry for herself. Mad was so much more her style than self-pity, and right now? She was furious. "What is wrong about a man and a woman going out on a date?"

"It won't stop at that."

"You think they're going to have sex? How is that your business?"

He paled as if the very word "sex" had thrown him. "That's what we're worried about."

She shook her head, trying not to laugh at how ridiculous this conversation really was. "He's a widower and so is she, and both consenting adults. They're close in age, although she'll kill you if you say that out loud, and they seem to like each other. What is the problem?"

"The problem is my great-uncle's heart!"

"You think the French vixen might break it?" she challenged.

"I think she might give him a heart attack, which is what killed my great-aunt Polly. He has a pacemaker in there, plus a stent. And Camille...she gets him going."

She bit her lip at the expression, and the image of old Buck getting riled up over Camille and her French wiles.

"I'm sure he's seen a doctor and has medical permission," she said.

"Oh, he has. And got the little blue pills to prove what a seductress she is."

Seductress? That was hilarious on so many levels.

She managed not to laugh, but then remembered a text she got from her mother last night, shortly before she got home and found Bash sick and Deeley...ready to bolt. She'd forgotten all about her mother saying that Shellseeker Cottages was being kept out of the running for a big tourism feature because of Penny and her issues with Camille.

She'd said Camille was flirting with Buck and "hitting on him," and Mom had asked if Olivia had noticed that.

She'd never answered, but if she had, it would have been to say it was definitely the other way around.

"I don't know where you or your family is getting their info, Davis, but Camille is not the aggressive one here. Buck's hanging out in this store every time I turn around, and using that secret passageway between your place and this one in the back."

"I've got to close that off."

"No," she said, a little surprised at how vehemently the word came out.

"I have every right to."

"You might, but you have no right to interfere with two people who are older, lonely, and enjoying each other's company. So I'm not putting the *kibosh*—whatever that is—on anything or anyone. Talk to your uncle your own if you are worried about his health. And maybe give the guy a break. There's nothing wrong with falling in love, at any age."

Not that she'd know, but—

"*Love?*" He gasped like a pearl-clutching little old lady. "He *was* in love. With my great-aunt Polly, and he'll never be in love again."

"Not if you and your syndicate family have anything to do with it."

His eyes narrowed. "We're watching out for his health. It's all that matters to us."

"Happiness and joy and socializing with people his own age are part of his health, too, you know." She gave a gesture toward the door. "You better get back to the bait shop. Or use the convenient door in the back before someone heartless closes it off."

"Just talk to her. Because this is going no further. We'll see to that."

She lifted a brow. "Is that a threat?"

"It's a fact." With that, he walked out, leaving Olivia to stare at the door, realizing that for the first time in hours, she was thinking about someone other than herself. And that was a baby step in the right direction.

Chapter Nine

Camille

The townhouse on Sea Bell Road seemed huge after all those months of living in a two-bedroom cottage, and Camille found herself a little overwhelmed the fourth time she had to go up the stairs to find something.

This whole getting old thing was not for the faint of heart, and hers was pounding.

"You okay, *Grandmère*?" Noah asked as he carted two massive storage bins like they weighed next to nothing, avoiding a collision with her on the landing. "You look a little winded."

"I'm fine," she assured him, smiling at the French name, which he used religiously and always pronounced correctly. "I'm not twenty-six and strong like you are."

"Let me put these in the second bedroom and get whatever you need."

What she needed was the energy of youth, but she'd never find that again. "I'm going to have something cold to drink," she said. "And so should you. Meet me in the kitchen after you carry those up."

"Will do. And do you have a Band-Aid?" Bracing the bins on his thigh, he held up a thumb wrapped in the bandana he'd been wearing. "I cut this on a staple sticking out from the bottom of that ottoman."

"Oh, dear. Yes, I can find one. Just put those down."

"I'll be fine. I'll put them where they belong and meet you for first aid in a sec."

By the time he came back, she'd found the box with bandages and antiseptic ointment, and had a tall glass of iced tea poured for him.

"Wash it first," she instructed, turning on the faucet. "Then we'll dress it."

He grinned at her, looking down as he took the bandana off and slipped his thumb under the flow. "You don't strike me as the Florence Nightingale type," he teased. "But I appreciate it."

"Isn't that what grandmothers are supposed to do? Fix boo-boos?"

"I dunno. I never had a grandmother before. Just you."

"And I've never been a grandmother before, so I'm probably doing it all wrong," she joked. "No chocolate chip cookies baking, no quilts being made, and no garden full of tomatoes and flowers. I'm a grandmother fail."

He cracked up at that as he shook the water off his hand and accepted the wad of paper towels she held. "Not in the least. I think you're perfect at the job."

"Thank you, Noah. And you're a perfect grandson, especially for carting all this stuff to my new place." She took his hand in hers and slowly revealed the cut, making a face. "That's kind of deep, but I know how to fix it with a butterfly bandage."

"Where'd you learn that?"

"Being a stewardess." She looked up with narrowed eyes. "And, yes, I know they are called flight attendants now, but you can't imagine how much I hate that."

"Why?"

She patted the cut and squeezed some Neosporin on it. "Because in my day, being a stewardess was like a badge of honor. It meant you were beautiful and smart and glamorous and young." She sighed on the last word.

"You're still beautiful and smart and glamorous and—"

"If you say 'young,' I'm going to rip this cut open wider."

He barked a laugh. "Hilarious. You are definitely a funny grandma."

"Thank you." She opened the bandage and smoothed it on right as it should go, no bumps or creases. "And there you have it. Stewardess Nursing 101."

He held the thumb up and examined it. "Nice work, ma'am. Thank you."

"*De rien,*" she whispered. "Now sit and have your tea...except there are no chairs. No wonder I'm tired."

"There's a bench outside on the back patio." He moved to the kitchen slider and pushed it open. "And as soon as I finish bringing in this stuff, I can get DJ and we can hit your storage unit for the furniture. Mom is ready to help, too."

"Thank you, Noah," she said, stepping outside to the shady side of the bench, his words echoing in her head as she sat. "Can I ask you a personal question?"

"What are grandmothers for, if not meddling?" he teased as he took a sip of his iced tea.

"Why do you call Claire 'Mom' and DJ...not 'Dad'?" She lifted her brows. "Or is that none of my business?"

"Would you care if I said it wasn't?"

"No," she said. "Like you said, meddling is in the job description."

He laughed softly and sat next to her, quiet for a minute, then he said, "I think I'll regret it if I call him 'Dad' too often."

Camille drew back, surprised at not just the answer, but the sheer candor of it. "Why would you regret it?"

He stared straight ahead. "I don't know if I can count on him," he said. "Claire? Solid as a rock."

"That's my daughter," she agreed.

"But DJ?" He shrugged. "He's fun, he's brilliant, he's untethered and unpredictable and awesome."

"But you can't call him 'Dad.'"

"He hasn't quite earned that yet," he said slowly. "But you?" He held up his thumb. "*Grandmère*, with or without the cookies, quilt, or...whatever you think grandmothers are supposed to supply."

She studied him for a moment, looking at every feature in his profile and seeing...the past. Her own grandparents, bits of Dutch, Claire as a child, and even a piece of herself. Yes, he favored DJ, there was no doubt of that. But he was also a Durant and a Vanderveen.

"What?" he asked, turning when her gaze became too intent.

"I'm thinking of all the DNA that got combined and

shared and passed on to make you."

He chuckled. "I think about that a lot."

"Do you?"

"I have since I was old enough to understand I had it."

"Did you ever do one of those DNA tests?"

He shook his head. "I was too scared, if I'm going to be real. I searched out my birth mother and records, and that was all I needed. And, obviously, it was enough. Now I know I'm French and Italian."

"And Dutch, from your maternal grandfather. And my grandparents were actually born in Switzerland."

"Really?"

She nodded. "I have pictures of them, old ones in sepia tones. They're in that bin you just carried upstairs."

He sat up straight. "Really?"

"Yes. Do you want to see them?"

"More than anything." He put his hand over hers in a rare act of affection. "As far as grandmothers go, Camille? You're rocking it."

She just smiled at him and nodded her thanks, putting her hand on her chest because she still felt winded. Or maybe she was just completely full of love for one thing she never thought she'd have, but realized was one of life's great treasures—a grandson.

By the time DJ, Claire, and Noah left late that afternoon, Camille was aching for her nap. Although they'd done the heavy lifting, literally and figuratively, exhaustion pressed on her.

But a nap would have to wait, because the doorbell rang its unfamiliar chime as she was facing the stairs to climb one more time. Turning with a sigh, she headed to the front door and peeked through the glass...and suddenly the exhaustion lifted when she saw Abner Underwood holding a huge plant.

"Aren't you the sweetest man alive?" she asked as she opened the door with a smile she didn't need to force.

"I'm just here to help you get settled in your new home, Cami."

She laughed at the nickname and welcomed him in. "Still kind of a mess, but the furniture I had in storage has been delivered, so progress is made. What a beautiful plant, Abner."

He placed it in a corner in the entry and beamed at her.

"I can't stop thinking about you," he said, his directness always such a surprise to her. It made her feel... lighter. Younger. And forget about being tired.

"I had a lovely dinner on your boat," she said. "Thank you, again. Come in and see the place."

She ushered him into the small living area, which was open to the kitchen, all bathed in late-afternoon light. "I can't offer you much, because I haven't unpacked the kitchen yet. I was just about to."

"Let me help you."

"That's not necessary, Ab—"

"I want to." He hoisted a box labeled "dishes" from

the floor to the counter as easily as Noah had. "Let's do this."

She sighed. "Well, I was just about to take a break."

"Breaks are for the lazy," he said, tearing the tape off the box in one long strip. "Or you just sit right there and tell me where you want everything to go."

"You're a determined man, aren't you?"

He grinned at her. "Determined to make you like me."

Well, it was working, she thought, but held back the assurance. Being chased was fun—it made her feel alive again—and she had no intention of getting caught *that* easily.

"All right," she said, opening one of the cabinets. "Plates here, soup bowls there."

They worked together, talking easily, sharing stories, and before she knew it, the kitchen was put away. Abner broke down the boxes with ease, and made three separate trips to the outdoor recycling bins to keep the place tidy.

While he was gone the third time, Camille sat down at the table and exhaled. Good heavens, she might have trouble keeping up with this man!

A minute later, he came back in, made them both a glass of iced tea, and started naming restaurants nearby.

"So, what'll it be? Seafood? Italian? Or can I surprise you?"

She slowly shook her head. "I'm taking a pass, Abner. Moving has worn me out. I'm going to have a cup of soup and call it a day for me."

"I can make you some—"

She held out her hand. "No, thank you."

"Okay, okay. I know when to back off." He chuckled. "Usually. Will I see you tomorrow?"

"At work, in the morning. I promised Livvie I'd be at my post bright and early at nine a.m."

"Then I'll be at mine, with coffee, and meet you in the back at 8:45."

"Abner," she said on a sigh.

"Cami," he teased with a laugh.

"Have you never heard of taking things slow?"

"At my age? No. If you want me to go away, back off, or leave you alone, I will, but—"

"No." She laughed at how easy it was to interject that. "I really don't. I just don't want to go full-steam ahead." It was grueling, for one thing, but she was a little ashamed to admit that to this fireball of energy.

He grinned at her. "I like full steam, Cami."

"I can tell."

"And I like you." He bent over and planted a kiss on her head. "Get your beauty rest, not that you need it, and I'll see you for coffee in the morning." He put two hands on her shoulders, strong and secure. "Stay right there. I'll show myself out."

She sat for a few minutes after she heard the front door close, smiling.

It had been a long, long time since a man made her feel like this.

Mon Dieu, she liked it.

Chapter Ten

Claire

For the first time since they'd started the pop-up pizza nights at the tea hut, Claire got the feeling that DJ wasn't excited about the evening ahead. He'd been a tad withdrawn for the last few days, in fact, ever since the last call with Rachel.

But they were alone in the car, meeting Noah, who'd gone early to start the pizza ovens and set up the tables. The pop-up pizza nights had grown extremely popular in the past few months, transforming from a one-time experiment to a crowd pleaser and revenue generator.

DJ had a magical touch with pizza, and had done in Shellseeker what he'd already done in Northern California. He not only had a recipe and formula for world-class pizza, he brought a passion and light to the project that was simply infectious.

But that passion seemed subdued and he certainly wasn't shedding his usual light.

Claire reached over the console and put her hand on his arm, knowing it was time to follow her sister's advice. "Want to talk about it?"

He slid a smile in her direction, and a warm look that

never failed to make her feel closer to him. "No hiding my mood swings from you, huh?"

"Mood swings?" She considered the expression. "I'm not sure that's what I'm getting from you, a man whose mood generally swings from happy to happier."

His eyes shuttered. "And sometimes to unhappy."

But that was so rare. "What's wrong, DJ? Just tell me everything that's on your heart, please."

"What's on my heart is that Anna is telling me that Sophia needs a father."

"Anna said that, too?" She'd thought it was only Rachel making that assertion. If his older daughter thought the same thing, then maybe it was true. Although, his conversations with her were rare, and usually tense. Anna Fortunato, from what Claire had gleaned, was much, much closer to her mother.

"We've been texting, which is the closest thing to a conversation I have with her. She's twenty and busy at school, but not too busy to worry about her little sister." He shook his head. "And she said something rather upsetting, and I'm not sure what to do about it."

"What is it?"

He turned to her, sadness in his glance. "Apparently, Sophia never sent in a single college application in the fall. Not one. It's January and she hasn't even applied."

Claire knew that was late, especially if Sophia wanted to get into a school the quality of Stanford, like Anna. "It's not a bad idea to take a gap year," she said. "She's not even eighteen yet, right?"

"Yeah, she's a young senior with a summer birthday,

but she's not taking a gap year. It's way worse than that."
He grunted as if he didn't even want to say the rest.
"She's talking about *marrying* Kyle Truitt."

"What? Now?"

"She thinks they're going to graduate and get married
right away, and she doesn't have to go to college because
Kyle's going to slide right into his father's uber-successful
car dealership business. By the time he's twenty-five, he'll
be a multimillionaire, like his dad, and Sophia doesn't
need a college degree to be a rich man's wife." He shuttered his eyes with an even louder groan. "I don't even
know what to say to that."

"Do you think she's really in love, or just rebelling?"
she asked.

"I'm going with the latter, because this boy? Loser
with a capital L and I don't care how much money his
family has. That doesn't make him good enough for
Sophia."

"Have you talked to her about it?" Claire asked. "Or
is this Rachel's conjecture? Maybe it's not that serious."

"She's not answering my calls or texts. And all Rachel
does is scream that I should at least *be* in California to
talk some sense into her."

Claire's heart slipped a little at that. Well, she'd
wanted to really talk to him about this, but that was no
guarantee she'd like what he said.

"I guess it's really hard for the family to be split up
after a divorce," she said.

"Actually, we made it work," he replied softly. "Even
after I sold my business and moved to Carmel, I was

within driving distance and Sophia loved to spend time
with me. And now I'm gone and Kyle is...filling her head
with nonsense like getting married at eighteen and skipping college."

"What do *you* think you should do?" she asked, trying
not to fist her hands as she waited and hoped he didn't
say that he should go back. But who needed him more?
The troubled daughter who had him her whole life, or
the son he never knew he had?

It would crush Noah if he left, and Claire wouldn't
be too happy, either.

"I don't know," he answered, giving her an honest
look. "But Anna thinks I need to end my little 'Florida
escapade,' as she calls it, and let Sophia move in with me,
but that would mean my living in San Leandro so she can
stay in that school until she graduates."

"I guess she wouldn't consider coming here, maybe
transferring schools?" Even as she suggested it, she knew
it was a long shot.

"She doesn't want to come to Sanibel Island," he
said, confirming that. "She's seventeen and is finishing
her senior year. I mean, yeah, I do want her to spend
spring break here, and I thought she would, but Anna
said I'm dreaming. Her rich boyfriend wants to go to
Cancun."

"Oh." That was going to be another disappointment
for Noah, who really wanted to meet his sisters. "No
wonder you've been a little blue."

He threaded his fingers through hers. "Hard to be
blue with you and my son," he said. "But I am...worried."

"And that's not like my 'live in the moment and make the best of life' man at all."

He gave her fingers a squeeze. "Your man, huh?"

"Well, there were several words between 'my' and 'man,' but how else would you describe this?"

"I don't like to label things, as you know." He lifted their joined hands and pressed his lips to her knuckles. "But I would describe it as the best thing I've had since..." He laughed softly. "Since the last time I was your man, oh so many years ago."

"DJ, that's sweet, but you did fall in love, marry, and raise a family with Rachel. I'm sure she was the best thing you ever had. And that's not fishing for a compliment," she added quickly. "Just reminding you that you did have a good thing."

"Until I didn't."

When they'd talked about it, DJ had given her the "big picture" of his divorce—he had been obsessed with his career and ignored his family, Rachel got sick of it and left him after begging him to change—but Claire didn't know much in the way of details.

The subject pained him, and reminded him of choices he'd made that left him ashamed and sad. A year after the divorce, he'd sold his business, left the corporate world, and pursued a new passion.

But maybe she needed to know the details. Maybe it would help offer advice with this dilemma.

"But you and Rachel are on speaking terms..." she said, trying to give him the opportunity to share more.

"Speaking-about-the-kids terms." He turned toward

the beach, quiet for a moment. "I have to get my soul in the pizza game now. Gotta forget that..." He winced. "But that's how I got into this position," he added, almost as if he were talking to himself. "By putting my head into work and taking my heart from my family."

She waited a beat, then eased her hand out of his, trying not to let the hurt of that statement hit too hard. But he turned to her instantly.

"I know, you and Noah are family, too."

She was touched that he could read her non-verbals so well, but really didn't know what to say. "We are, but we also come...after the fact. The second family."

"But you were first, long before Rachel, Anna, and Sophia."

"You didn't know we existed."

Silent, he slid the car into a parking spot and turned off the ignition, staring straight ahead for a long time.

"What am I going to do, Claire?" he finally asked.

"You? What you want to do, DJ. The moment, the decision, the *life* that feels right." She swallowed hard. "Selfishly, I hope that's us, but remember, I have my own problems with someone who wants me back. Work. Not as emotional a tug as your family, but it's real."

He turned to her, the sadness visible in his eyes. "I'm so torn. I don't want to make the same mistake with this family that I made with that one, but I don't want to abandon Sophia if she needs me. Whatever I do, I lose something, or someone, I love."

"You won't lose us," she assured him. "Not emotionally, anyway."

He leaned closer and kissed her lightly. "I left you once before, Claire. It might have been the stupidest thing I ever did, and, man, I've done a lot of stupid things. I don't want to do it again."

"It's not just me. It's Noah I'm worried about. Have you talked to him about this?"

"No. I know I should, but I feel like he's starting to get his hopes up that the pizza business could be...I don't know. Something we share. Maybe we *could* buy Luigi's place, or open one of our own, or even work with Teddy and Eliza to get the business licenses necessary to transform the tea hut into a real pizza joint on the beach."

"But none of those pipe dreams could come true if you go back to California."

"Not for a while, anyway."

Well, she had her answer—he was torn and didn't know. Not exactly the declaration of love or commitment she might have hoped for, yet it was the truth. But hers wasn't the only heart he could break.

"DJ, you better talk to Noah. At least tell him what's going on with Sophia and that you might..." She didn't even want to utter the word *leave*. "Have to change things."

"I will. Tonight, maybe, after we close up." He closed his eyes and sighed deeply.

ONCE THE POP-UP event got well underway, Claire didn't have a lot to do but eat, socialize, and have fun. But after the conversation in the car, she didn't feel like doing any of that. Instead, she found herself at the top of the boardwalk, looking down at the beach as the sun dipped for another glorious sunset. The tide was going out, and it seemed like each wave was just a little less aggressive than the one before.

With every new wave, there was an infinitesimal change on the beach. Some new shells, a shift in the sands, a slightly different color on the shore, and fresh prints from the sandpipers and gulls. A constant reminder from Mother Nature that change was inevitable.

"You look deep in thought, my darling sister."

Claire turned to meet Eliza's concerned gaze with a wistful smile. "Just thinking about the tides and change and how much we don't control."

"Whoa. Deeper than I even imagined. I thought you might be contemplating how you're going to quit your job and move down here, but here you are, going all existential on me." She tucked her arm around Claire's waist. "I know it's late for us, but would you like to take a walk and talk?"

"I would, but..." Claire jutted her chin over Eliza's shoulder. "I think there's someone who needs you more."

Olivia walked toward them, wiping her eyes under the sunglasses she really didn't need in the waning light, her shoulders slumped from the weight of unhappiness.

Claire knew why, and right this minute, she could truly relate to the fear of losing someone dear.

"We're just about to take a walk," Claire called to her niece. "Join us?"

"Yeah." She reached them and slid her sunglasses up, and both her mother and aunt tried not to react to her red-rimmed eyes. "Deeley took Bash home."

"Is he sick again?" Eliza asked.

"No, he's fine. Just a runny nose, but he was getting cranky and I wanted to go but..." She closed her eyes. "I think if we have another long, emotional night of talking, I'll just break. We just go 'round and 'round with how we're each trying to make the other one happy, but neither one of us is. I'd rather stay here and watch the sunset with two of my favorite ladies."

"Oh, honey." Eliza hugged her and patted her back.

"It's okay, Mom. I'm okay." She smiled at Claire over her mother's shoulder. "I know I don't look it, but we've talked and I understand why he wants to do this...sort of. I think he's waiting for me to say 'Go,' which I don't intend to do. Come on. Let's walk."

The three of them headed down the long boardwalk that cut through the sea oats and led to the sand, silent but for the sound of their sandals on the wood. At the bottom, they kicked those off and walked on the sand barefoot.

"I'm worried I'm about to be in your same situation, Olivia," Claire admitted.

The other two women froze mid-step, turning to her.

"What do you mean?" Olivia asked. "DJ is leaving?"

"Or you are? Back to New York?" There was a trace

of panic in Eliza's voice that made Claire smile and hug her.

"You'd miss me, huh?"

"Duh. What's going on?"

"Well, I talked to him like you suggested, and this is what I learned." She shared the Sophia situation with them and explained how torn DJ felt right now, how mistakes of the past haunted him, and how having two families on two different coasts was taking its toll.

"He wants to be with us, to make a family here," she added after they'd reacted with understanding and sympathy. "But he can't ignore the one he left behind. If his seventeen-year-old daughter is struggling, then he needs to help."

"Could he somehow divide his time?" Olivia asked. "Live in both places?"

"Or maybe you and Noah could..." Eliza squished up her face. "Nevermind, I hate that idea."

"I suppose I could work remotely from California," Claire replied, following Eliza's logic. "But I hate that idea, too. For one thing, my mother isn't getting any younger and we finally live in the same place. I don't relish the idea of leaving her. For another, Noah. He is really my priority, and he's very happy here. I couldn't bear to tear him away from Katie and Harper."

"Oh, no," Eliza agreed. "I think those two have a real future together. And Noah's never really had a home."

"And your long-lost sister and niece are here," Olivia added with a playful hug.

"That goes without saying," she agreed. "But if DJ

pulls out of here and leaves us? What would Noah do? He's starting to count on the pizza life for his future."

"Is that what he really wants to do?" Olivia asked.

"He wants to write novels," Claire said. "But he also is crazy about his father and will do anything to be with him, including become a pizza restaurant owner. And, I don't think he wants to get too serious with Katie until he's in a stronger financial position."

"Maybe he can run Deeley's rental business," Olivia said with a dry snort of sarcasm, then she wrinkled her nose. "No, scratch that. I shouldn't be trying to help him leave sooner. Finding someone to take over that business is the only thing keeping him on Sanibel Island. And that includes me."

"Livvie." Eliza put her arm around her daughter. "I don't think this is an easy decision for him at all. He just wants to do the right thing for you and Bash."

"Then he should stay. Don't you think, Claire?"

"Of course I do, but we aren't walking in his shoes, just like we're not in DJ's. And from what I've heard, Deeley is making this decision because he doesn't think forcing you to raise Bash is really fair. Is it what you want?"

"No one is forcing me." She sighed and slowed long enough to pick up a shell, studying it while she thought. "I've fallen for the kid. Yeah, he's a handful, but he's part of the deal now. And I'm crazy about Deeley, that's no secret. But, in some sense, on some level, I sort of get his thinking. We haven't been together that long, truly less than six months, which seems soon to be raising a child together. This is a huge responsibility for him. His sister is apparently dying to have them both back in North Carolina, and family is a powerful pull and..." Her voice cracked. "I don't know what to do."

They stopped for a group hug, getting support from the physical contact.

"All I know is I want both of you here," Eliza said. "And I guess that's selfish, but I'm not going to lie."

"I'm not leaving, Mom," Olivia assured her. "I just started my dream business and I like it here."

They all pulled apart, the other two women looking at Claire and waiting for her declaration.

"I promised Noah that I'd be where he'd be," she said. "I haven't made that promise to DJ, and he hasn't made it to me. Not sure he ever will, but that's the price of a man like DJ. If Noah's here, I'll be here." She took a deep breath and put her hand on Olivia's shoulder. "I don't want to push Deeley out the door, and I don't know if you were kidding or not, but I don't think Noah would hate the idea of taking over Deeley's business."

"He's running the tea hut," Eliza said. "And has plans for it, but he's capable of running both of those as ancillary businesses at Shellseeker—"

"Whoa, ladies." Olivia stepped back. "You really *are* pushing Deeley out the door."

"No, no," Eliza said quickly. "Just talking out loud and thinking and trying to make everyone happy."

"Good luck with that," Olivia said glumly. "This change is coming and I can't stop it."

Claire nodded, turning to the tide, which was even

lower than when she first stepped on the boardwalk, remembering her earlier thoughts.

"Life ebbs and flows, Liv. And sometimes all you can do is..." She looked up and down the beach with a sigh. "Appreciate the beauty of that."

Olivia answered by flicking her shell out to the water.

Chapter Eleven

Eliza

Mia Watson arrived an hour late, which had been just enough time for Teddy and Eliza to convince themselves that somehow Penny Conway had inserted her nose into things and actually stopped them from getting the walk-through.

But the editor and reviewer from *The Last Resort* assured them she'd just been delayed by a longer-than-expected tour of Tarpon Villas, the property they sensed might be the strongest competition for them.

That stress was gone within ten minutes of meeting Mia, a lovely young woman in her late thirties or early forties. She moved with the grace and power of an athlete, her caramel-colored waves barely held back with a clip. When she took a moment to use the restroom, Teddy excitedly whispered that her energy was positive and her aura was yellow.

Eliza took that as a good sign, confident by now in Teddy's vibe-reading skills.

"I'm so sorry to be late," Mia said a few minutes later as they started the tour in the gardens bursting with herbs and flowering hibiscus.

"Traffic is a bit heavier this time of year," Eliza said, wanting to give her an easy out.

"I planned on traffic, but I didn't plan on a ghost tour at Tarpon Villas."

"They have a ghost there?" Eliza asked, brows up in surprise.

"So they say," Teddy chimed in. "It's quite the tourist draw."

Mia laughed. "They definitely like to build up the old smuggling stories from the pirate ship days."

"Pirates and smuggling?" Eliza glanced at Teddy and stage-whispered with a laugh, "Can we compete with that?"

Teddy responded with a secret eye-roll that Mia didn't see.

"I won't lie," Mia said. "It's a point in their favor, but only because they've made the most of it to appeal to guests."

"How so?" Eliza asked.

"Oh, they've set up a boat tour to the spot allegedly favored by pirates for illegal drop-offs—and the tour includes rum," she added with a laugh. "The folklore says that two pirates died in a duel on the beach and haunt the villas."

Eliza frowned, not at all sure she'd want a ghost lurking in her villa. "That's...different."

"They make it fun and the whole pirate thing really appeals to the kids and adds a lot of color to a background story." She paused for a moment as they reached the top of one of three boardwalks that took guests from the property to the sand. "Oh, my, yes. Some things never change. Shellseeker Beach." She let out a long, sweet sigh. "I remember it well."

"That's right," Teddy said. "Eliza told me you'd stayed here as a girl."

"I did, over Christmas in 1995."

"I was here," Teddy said. "The Swain family owned the property then, and they maintained it well enough, but it's improved with every owner since."

"I'm sorry I don't remember you, but I was thirteen and...distracted."

"Did you return?"

"No, sadly. The Watson family never went to the same beach twice, which might be where I got my talent for visiting and reviewing resorts. Not that I'm complaining," she added. "I'm single and have no ties, so it's a dream job for me. And speaking of dreams, this garden is every bit as beautiful as I remember."

"Then you remember Teddy, whether you realize it or not," Eliza told her. "She's the green thumb that makes this place so gorgeous." She gestured toward a huge blossom of pink and yellow lantanas, which were doing their work of attracting butterflies. "And just about every flowering plant and herb can be—and is—dried and brewed as Teddy's very highly regarded tea."

Mia looked impressed, slowing her step. She brushed back some hair from her face, taking a long look from Teddy's house to the beach, letting her gaze linger on a few of the brightly painted cottages, the palms that shaded the boardwalk, and, of course, the blue horizon.

"Wow." Her single syllable held a lot of high praise.

"We're rather proud of it," Teddy said, beaming with something that superseded pride. She truly loved Shellseeker Beach and longed for everyone who visited to feel the same.

"I bet you are," Mia said. "And I can tell you that Shellseeker Cottages meets my Number One criteria for the Hidden Gems feature."

Eliza and Teddy shared a look, waiting for the rest.

"It's authentic," she said. "Don't get me wrong, there's a place for marble floors and pool boys at the cabana and a spa that costs a fortune and makes you feel like a queen. We're considering a few of those, too."

Teddy put a hand on the woman's back and guided her into the sweet-smelling herb section. "If that's what you're looking for, you aren't going to find any of that here."

"I know," Mia said. "I just love the vibe here. And that you've been part of the property for...how long, Teddy?"

"Ever," Teddy joked, then explained how her father had started the resort in the 1950s, then sold all but the main house in the 1970s. She and her family had been the only on-site managers Shellseeker Cottages had ever had.

"I've lived in that house"—she pointed to the multi-story beach house as they passed it—"my entire life. I've worked at Shellseeker Cottages in every imaginable capacity, but now I'm the owner." She gestured to Eliza. "With a lot of help from Eliza."

It wasn't clear how much of the recent history this woman knew, which was as complicated as it was colorful —and Eliza wasn't sure how much to share. Mia did seem interested in history, but would the whole story of Dutch, the last owner, and his many wives help or hurt the cause?

"Do you remember which cottage your family stayed in?" Teddy asked as they passed Slipper Snail and nodded in greeting at the family hanging out on the porch there.

"It was further down this path," she said, frowning. "Named after a seashell."

"They all are," Teddy told her. "Would you remember it if you heard it?"

"All I remember is that everyone said it was the rarest of all shells."

"Junonia!" Teddy and Eliza said together.

"Yes!" She clapped her hands and laughed. "That was it. Junonia. Is it still here?"

"Absolutely," Teddy assured her. "In fact, it's vacant today. You could stay there tonight if you want to extend your trip."

Mia's big brown eyes widened. "Really? I wish I could, but I have a few other stops today. But, wow. Tempting."

"Well, the offer stands. You can be our guest," Teddy said, rushing a little to get them to Junonia. "I'd love to see if it brings back any memories."

"So would I," Mia said. "Oh, is that the cottage? I do remember it!"

She pointed to the teal and yellow bungalow that Eliza had come to think of as Camille's house for the months she'd been here. It was empty now, and she'd stopped in earlier. Katie had worked her magic to make it look warm, welcoming, clean, and cozy.

Four bright blue Adirondack chairs were lined up on the wooden deck in front of the sliding glass doors, each looking like they were just made for an afternoon of gazing at the water.

Teddy unlocked the doors and led Mia inside, where the sun reflected off the shiny tile floor and the shiplap-covered walls. Overhead, a paddle-shaped fan cooled the area and spread the fragrance of the fresh flowers Katie had placed on an end table.

"Oh, how lovely," Mia cooed, giving Eliza and Teddy a chance to slip each other an optimistic look.

"Do you recognize it from 1995?" Teddy asked.

"It's the same but different," Mia said, walking to the giant graphic of a Junonia, admiring the giraffe-print that made the snail shell famous. "There was a different painting here, but the same shell. And the kitchen was much smaller," she said, making her way to the counter. "The furniture was older and the walls weren't wood, but...yes. It was as special then as it is today."

"You must have had quite the family vacation," Teddy said. "That warms my heart to know the memories have lasted."

She gave a sly smile. "Well, there was this boy visiting from Indiana."

"Ahhh!" Teddy laughed. "Now *that* I can't supply to

every guest, but romance is always in the air at Shellseeker Beach."

"It was for me," Mia said on a laugh, her dark eyes dancing. "In fact, I got my first kiss right out there on that beach, standing in a darling gazebo that I doubt is still there."

"Oh, it most certainly is," Teddy assured her. "That gazebo will be part of this property for as long as I am, and I hope for many years past that."

"See what I mean?" Mia beamed at them. "Authentic."

"Do you remember his name?" Eliza asked. At Mia's look, she added. "The boy from Indiana."

"Alec Dornenberg," she said with the sigh of a girl who once had a very deep crush. "Blond hair, blue eyes, and the sweetest smile I'd ever seen."

"Dornenberg? From Lebanon, Indiana?" Teddy asked.

Mia just stared at her. "If you tell me he's still coming here with his own family, I might cry."

"If his parents are Jeff and Valerie Dornenberg? They're regulars who've come just about every winter for decades. And they do have a son named Alec, as I recall."

"Really? Well, that's a point in your favor." She pointed to Teddy, then her cheeks deepened with the faintest blush "You know, because you keep regulars for so long."

"I try to do that," Teddy said with a sly smile. "And wait until you see the gazebo. It's as romantic today as it was then."

Mia gave a self-conscious laugh. "That sounds wonderful."

"We'll end the tour there," Eliza said. "Would you like to take a walk to Sanibel Treasures first? That's the shell and souvenir shop on the property where we have a message in a bottle from—"

"Teddy Roosevelt," Mia finished. "I remember that, too. Yes, let's do walk there, but can I look around this cottage first?"

"Absolutely."

She stepped away to the master bedroom and Eliza and Teddy shared another quick and hopeful look.

"She loves it!" Teddy mouthed.

Eliza responded with a thumbs-up as Mia came out of the room, smiling. "Like I said, the same but different, and utterly lovely. Now, let's go see Teddy Roosevelt's message in a bottle. And I'd like to hear more about your father, who started the resort."

"Actually, my grandfather first bought the land..." As Teddy spun her family's tale, Eliza locked the sliders to Junonia, optimistic that they had a really good shot at being selected for the feature.

And if Mia was on the fence, maybe they could call the Dornenbergs and find out if sweet, blue-eyed Alec was still available for the pretty and single Ms. Watson.

AN HOUR LATER, after a long and lively lecture from George about Teddy's bottle, and a few gifts of shell art from Roz, Teddy went back to her house to make some fresh tea. While she did, Eliza took Mia to the gazebo, thrilled that it was empty and that God had provided a picture-perfect beach day with sapphire skies, a few puffy clouds, and a sun-dappled Gulf of Mexico.

"Someone needs to get married here," Mia said as they stepped inside the structure that sat on a slight rise overlooking the water.

"I think quite a few people have," Eliza said. "I'd love to beef up the wedding business here." Not that she wanted Mia to think the wedding business wasn't great, but it was definitely something she wanted Shellseeker Cottages to get more of.

But Mia didn't have her "reviewer and editor" cap on as she slowly strolled the perimeter of the gazebo, letting her fingers brush over the carved posts, and perched on one of the worn wooden benches that lined the structure.

"There's quite a story with this gazebo," Eliza said.

Mia looked at her with a spark in her eyes. "I was thinking of my own."

"Ah, yes, the first kiss."

She flicked her wrist like it was a silly topic. "Tell me some others."

"Teddy is the one to share some of the history and folklore," Eliza said, taking a seat on another bench. "I believe it was her mother who had it built and chose the site because she found hundreds of arrowheads buried deep in the sand and in the surrounding shrubs."

"This was Native American land?"

"The Calusa Indians lived all over this area until the

1600s, but Sanibel was believed to be the home of at least one of their kings, and the story goes that he lived here. This was his lookout for invaders, but now it's just the perfect place to watch the sunset. In fact,"—Eliza gestured toward the horizon—"because Sanibel runs east to west, the sun sets up that way, but it moves, of course, throughout the year. Each of the benches offer a direct view, depending on the time of year. Right now, that's where you'd sit. Six months from now, over there." She pointed from one bench to the other. "And to top it all off, Teddy calls this an 'honesty house.'"

Mia's brows lifted. "An honesty house? That's intriguing."

"When you're in here, she says, you never lie. You get to the real truth and revelations." Eliza smiled. "I know a few people who swear that's true."

"Ahh," Mia said. "Well, that makes sense now. There was some honesty when I had that first kiss."

Eliza smiled, imagining that. "Do you want to tell me about him?" she asked.

"Do you?"

She inched back, confused by the question. "I haven't met his parents, but Teddy—"

"I meant this famous, or should I say *infamous*, man named Dutch."

"Dutch?" Her voice lifted in surprise, the non sequitur throwing her. "My father?"

"Oh, so the rumor mill had that much right."

The rumor mill named Penny Conway? Eliza didn't respond, considering all the ways she could handle this, and what would be best. This was still a pitch for a very important opportunity.

But she was in a gazebo famous for honesty, so there could only be one way to address this conversation. With the truth.

"I'm happy to answer any questions you have about Dutch Vanderveen, Mia. As you likely already know, he was the owner of Shellseeker Cottages before Teddy, and they lived together until he died."

"And that he was, uh…"

"Married to two other women at the same time." Eliza gave a tight smile.

"Was one your mother?" she asked.

"No, she was his first wife, and they divorced when I was young. But the two women, well…one is currently dealing with some legal issues, and could actually be behind bars, I'm not sure. The other, Camille Durant, lived in Junonia until a few days ago. She currently runs a boutique with my daughter called Sanibel Sisters. Did you get all that from the rumor mill, too?"

She swallowed and looked more than a little guilty. "It's a dark story, Eliza, you have to admit."

"Dark? I don't see it that way. It's not like two pirates died on the property and left their ghosts behind. Frankly, that all feels a lot darker than the personal lives of former owners."

"Yes, those stories are from the ancient past. This… this business with Dutch happened a few months ago. And while that doesn't have a bearing on the experience a guest would have here, knowing that the current owner was living with a man who was married to two other women—"

Eliza stood as annoyance shot up her back and left the hairs on the nape of her neck standing tall. "You met her," she ground out. "Theodora Blessing is—"

"Lovely," Mia interjected, holding up her hand. "But her involvement with a biga—"

"Is not relevant," Eliza said. "What matters is that she has created an oasis that gives friends, family, and guests a whole new perspective on life. If you don't believe me, stick around and you might get one, too."

The other woman studied her for a long moment, giving in to a smile. "It *is* an honesty house," she said softly. "And it's clear your love and respect for her is genuine."

"Deeply," Eliza agreed.

"Oh, excuse me a moment." Mia pulled out her phone and angled it. "This is about my next appointment."

"I'll go help Teddy with the tea," Eliza said quickly to offer privacy.

As she turned, she saw Teddy coming down the boardwalk with a tray of iced tea. Her silver curls fluttered in the breeze and her warm smile could be seen from here. Just looking at her made Eliza's heart melt, and gave her a feeling she could barely put into words.

She did give people new lives and perspectives, but Eliza didn't know how to explain that to this reviewer, or if it mattered to her.

Well, it mattered to Eliza, she thought as she crossed the sand to meet Teddy halfway.

"Eliza," she whispered as Eliza took the tray. "Are you okay?" She put a hand on Eliza's cheek.

"I'm fine."

"But you're so..." She stroked Eliza's face, her blue eyes searching as if she might find a clue. "Oh, my dear! You're full of love. Bursting with it."

Eliza relaxed into her touch and smiled. "And the person I love is you, Teddy Blessing. Come on, let's have tea with our guest. But brace yourself. She's still, at her core, a reporter of sorts and she may be looking for your story."

Teddy just gave a scoffing laugh. "I fear nothing."

"Another thing I love about you."

When they turned to go back to the gazebo, Mia was standing, phone to her ear, talking quietly.

Teddy set the tray down and they both started to back away to give her privacy, but the other woman turned and held up a finger, asking for just a second.

"I understand that, Penny," she said into the phone, her brows flicking as she looked from Eliza to Teddy, a hint of a smile pulling. "But I don't need another resort on the list. Yes, yes, I know you want to keep sending me more names, but I have found all that I need."

Penny was still sending her candidates? The lying snake. Eliza glanced at Teddy and could see she was thinking the same thing.

"Goodbye, Penny, and thank you." She slipped her

phone into her bag and gave in to that smile as she took the tea Teddy offered.

"I know you have a lot of work to do before you make a decision," Teddy said. "But I'm curious. If we were to make the final cut, would you be the person who stayed and wrote the feature?"

"I guess the answer is, it depends. Why do you ask?"

"Would that review possibly happen at the end of February?"

"Yes, it could. Is that when you have a cottage available?"

"That's when the Dornenbergs are going to be here, and they stay for well over a month."

Mia blushed just enough to let them know Teddy had hit her mark. "Interesting."

"Isn't it," Teddy agreed, lifting her glass. "What should we toast?"

They both looked at Mia, whose dark eyes danced. "How about...to new lives and fresh perspectives?" She winked at Eliza, who just smiled and dinged her glass.

After they all took a sip, Eliza leaned in to whisper, "Be careful what you wish for, Mia. Stranger things have happened around here."

Chapter Twelve

Olivia

Olivia read the text five times. And then a sixth.

When you have a moment, can you please call me? I would like to talk with you privately.

Christine Paige wanted to talk to her? Deeley's sister? Why?

She had no idea, but it wasn't a request she'd ignore. She'd never met Christine, but they'd said hello on a video call over the holidays and Olivia had only heard good things about her. She was, by all reports, a wonderful mother of one son, caretaker to their father, and even though she was ten years older than Deeley, a very close and loving big sister.

"Are you okay to work one more hour?" Olivia asked, looking up from her phone to Camille, who was organizing some new beach coverup arrivals.

For a split second, she thought Camille would say no. Not that she looked unhappy at work that day, but she seemed tired and like she didn't have her usual coloring. Still, she managed a bright smile and a nod.

"Of course, *cherie*. Inventory? Purchasing? Hunt down that missing Claiborne delivery?"

"I wish," Olivia muttered, glancing at the phone. "Deeley's sister has summoned me to a call."

"Oh? Are you scared of her?"

"Not scared of her," she said. "But of what she's going to say."

"Telling you why you have to let go?" Camille cocked a brow. "Not her place, if you ask me."

Well, she hadn't asked, but Olivia was in no mood to spar with Camille. She'd save her witty comebacks for the sister, if she needed them.

"Just give me fifteen or twenty minutes in the back," she said, searching Camille's face. "Unless you want to go home."

"I'm fine," she said, flicking her hand to send Olivia to the back. "I might have to shatter my personal standards and wear flats, though." She glanced at her stilettos. "Breaks my heart to be that old that I can't work in heels."

"Flats rock, Camille." She held out her foot, which looked so much more comfy in sandals. "And we're getting some new ballet-style shoes in here next week. I can save you a size...seven?" she guessed.

"Six," Camille corrected. "And ballet slippers are for dancers. I'm a former stewardess who should be able to stand on stilts if I have to."

"You don't have to, that's just the point." Olivia said on a laugh. "But since you insist on it, and no one is in the store shopping, why don't you sit in one of the chairs and take a load off?"

"Take a load off." She rolled her eyes. "Some English expressions need to simply go away."

Olivia smiled. "Well, *merci beaucoup, Madame.* I'll be back in a jiffy." She zipped to the back office and slid into her desk chair, reading the text a few more times. Wishing she had some idea of what Christine was going to say, she took a deep breath and dialed.

"Livvie," she answered in a soft, sweet voice. "How sweet of you to call so quickly. Thank you so much."

The kind greeting put Olivia at ease, so she leaned back and exhaled. "No problem at all, Christine. I was surprised by your text and wanted to get right back to you. Is everything okay?"

"Here? It's wonderful. It's your life I'm worried about, and, of course, my little brother."

Funny to think of Deeley as anyone's "little" anything, since he was tall and broad and, well, Deeley. But Olivia had a "little" brother, too. And she'd do anything for Dane, just as she imagined Christine Paige would for her brother.

"I understand your concern about Dee...Connor," she corrected, knowing that this woman didn't call her brother by his last name, which would also be Christine's maiden name. "These are really challenging days for him."

"And for you, I imagine."

"I'm trying—and, I think, succeeding—to make the best of it."

"Oh, you are succeeding," Christine said in a gentle voice. "Everything Connor has told me, well, I just can't believe the goodness in your heart, Livvie. It takes faith and strength and something very few people have to step into a motherhood role when you didn't want or ask for it. I truly admire you."

Olivia smiled, even though the other woman couldn't see it. The compliment warmed her. "Thank you, Chris. I know we joke about Bash being a handful, but he's honestly a great kid who's just stealing more and more of my heart every day." Not to mention your brother...but she opted not to add that. "Um, is that why you called?" she asked, anxious to know the reason.

"Not exactly," Christine said. "I have to ask you something and I don't know how you're going to take it. I hope you understand."

Olivia stayed quiet, waiting for whatever curveball was about to hit her.

"We need Connor here, Olivia. We really, really need him."

That curveball. "I know he's seriously considering going there," Olivia replied carefully. "But I didn't think the move was imminent." Especially because she hoped every day that he'd reconsider the idea. "I didn't actually think it was a done deal."

The other woman was quiet for a moment. The only thing Olivia could hear was a soft sigh. "My father's not doing well," she whispered.

Olivia nodded, knowing that "Pop," as they called him, was nearly eighty, since Deeley had been a late-in-life surprise, and that he had some health issues. Working side by side with Camille, who made seventy look like twenty, it was hard for her to imagine what Deeley's father was like, but she respected that he'd been sick with a variety of problems, some serious.

"He's never fully recovered from the loss of our mother," Christine continued. "And he retired a few years ago, as you know. All Pop talks about is Connor, and Bash. He's living for the day they walk in the door. And, honestly, that's *all* he's living for."

Olivia just closed her eyes. She could hardly fight a sick and dying father, too.

"I know you're in a tough position," Christine continued. "I know you have feelings for Connor—"

"I love him," she interjected, because "feelings" wasn't good enough.

Christine waited a beat. "I respect that," she finally said. "And I know Connor has deep feelings for you, as well."

Feelings again. This time, Olivia let it go.

"But he needs us at this time in his life, Livvie, and we really need him. I'm longing for Bash to live here, and am totally prepared to be a full-time mother...well, aunt, to him. I know he's an, um, exuberant child, but I don't work and he'd never be in daycare where they get so sick."

Silent, Olivia made a face at that. Bash was benefitting from the structure and discipline at Jadyn's daycare, and except for that one cold, he'd been super healthy.

"Livvie, I've been deep in prayer over this and it wasn't a suggestion my husband and I made lightly," she added. "We feel this is the right thing to do, for my father, and for my brother. Bash will be loved and cared for. We will put him in private schools, raise him with faith and love, and do everything to ease Connor's burden every single day."

All things Olivia wasn't doing at all, and might not ever do.

"I think you know we own a small winery and my husband is just aching for a business partner, because he's expanding. You know that was what Connor wanted to do when he got out of the Navy?"

"Yes," she said softly. "He's told me that." Deeley had planned to leave the Navy and turn his father's farm in the Blue Ridge Mountains into a vineyard. He wanted to grow grapes and make a wine he'd call Carolina Seal.

He gave up the dream to stay in Florida and help Marcie and Bash. He didn't talk much about it, but when he did—usually at the tail end of a nice merlot—she'd heard the longing in his voice. She knew that dream hadn't died.

"Sammy said he'd pay for Connor to get an MBA in Wine Business. And while he does that and helps with our vineyard, I could take care of Bash. And my father? Well, if he knew his Con Man was about to walk through that door and stay? I think he'd jump out of that wheelchair and dance."

Olivia just hung her head in defeat. "I understand, Chris. You're asking me to let him go, and soon."

"I guess I am," she acknowledged. "Although, please know that you are more than welcome to move here, too! We can have the wedding right here at this house, it's so big. And the vineyard grounds are beautiful."

Wedding? They weren't there yet. They weren't even close, and that's when her heart thudded right to the ground and shattered.

It was like she was force-fitting Deeley into her dreams, and that wasn't quite working. And he was force-fitting her into his kind of messy life situation, and that wasn't working, either. But if they gave each other up? Then...well, at least one of them might be happy.

And Bash? Her chest tightened at the thought of him being loved morning, noon, and night. With a routine he craved, and a beautiful home, and a woman who wanted nothing in the world but to raise him.

"Thank you, Christine," she said haltingly. "Thank you for being honest and for giving me additional perspective."

"Thank you for listening," the other woman replied. "You know, sometimes God does give us more than we can handle. But He always gives us the right solution, too. We all feel like this is the right solution. When you accept that, I promise you will have peace in your heart."

"And if I don't?"

She sighed again. "I think you will, Livvie. And I know Connor will. And Bash? He will have everything a boy would ever need."

And Deeley's father might live longer. There really was no downside to this...except her poor broken heart.

"I know what to do," she said, as much to herself as to Christine. "And I promise you it'll be the right thing."

"Thank you so much. You're changing our lives for

the better. It's a very unselfish decision, Livvie. No wonder Connor thinks so highly of you."

Highly. Right there with...*feelings.* Two things that were a long way from that other word she used...*wedding.*

"I only have one other thing to ask," Christine said, making Olivia smile humorlessly.

What else could she want? A kidney? "What's that?"

"Please don't tell him we talked," she said. "It's important that he thinks he has your whole support. It's gutting him to let you down and I just...I just think this would be better for everyone."

"Sure," she agreed, because what else could she say?

"And my offer stands, Livvie," Christine added. "You are welcome into our home and family anytime. It's beautiful here and, like I said, we could host the wedding."

"Thanks again, Christine. But to be honest, we're a long way from...anything like that."

They said goodbye and Olivia sat stone still for the longest time, vaguely aware of voices in the store, but lacking the energy or spirit to get up and see if Camille needed help.

How could she stand in the way of what was right for the man she loved, or the child? Even old Pop Deeley would benefit from her unselfishness.

She knew what she had to do. The decision didn't give her any of that peace Christine mentioned, but maybe that would come later. Maybe.

CAMILLE GOT A SECOND WIND—WHICH might have had something to do with Buck Underwood coming into the store for a visit—and graciously offered to close for Olivia so she could leave a little early.

Instead of going home and preparing for what she had to do, Olivia went straight to the small daycare center less than half a mile from Shellseeker Beach. Jay-jay's Sunshine and Funtime Preschool was the brainchild of Jadyn Bettencourt, who'd come to Sanibel last fall to reconcile with Katie, her long-lost sister. Over the holidays, Jadyn had found a thousand-square-foot former photographer's studio in the strip center closest to Shellseeker Beach.

Buying and transforming the space had taken imagination and money, but Jadyn had both—thanks to her uber-wealthy father—and started a very small business that catered only to Shellseeker Cottages patrons and staff. She had plans to grow it, but while she was finishing the last of her certification, she'd hired one highly qualified person and now ran a dear little center that was full of love and joy and toys and fun.

Bash loved going to see Jay-jay, as the kids all called her.

But wouldn't he be better off in a loving home with his Aunt Christine? Cruising around a vineyard with Deeley on a tractor? Going to private schools, being raised with the best possible foundation, and fully loved?

"*Wibbieeee!*" He tore across the floor with his arms out, his cheeks pink, his hair looking like it had been through a blender, his Thomas the Tank Engine T-shirt stained from whatever they had for snacks today, one shoe untied, and his face coated with a sheen of sweat and grime that would take a good long bath to get rid of.

The image of a neatly groomed Bash wearing plaid shorts and a crisp white shirt with the emblem of a private school on his chest flashed in her head. Was that the life that Bash would have? And wouldn't some faith-filled academy designed to get him into Harvard be better than...Jay-jay's Sunshine and Funtime Preschool?

She scooped him into her arms, lifted him, and squeezed harder than ever before.

"Bashman!" She nestled him close, sticking her nose in his slightly damp neck and getting a whiff of hard play on a sweet boy. "I missed you today!"

"Where Deeley?" he asked, leaning back and looking around.

"I beat him here today, big guy." She lowered him to the ground. "I'll text him and he can meet us at home. What do you want for dinner?"

"Ice cream!"

"Oh, really? I don't know about that. Why don't you get your bag from your cubby?" As he took off, Jadyn stepped closer, looking remarkably unruffled for having had four kids all afternoon.

"Look at that, Mom," Jadyn teased.

Mom? Hardly. She just smiled at Jadyn. "Look at what?"

"How he did exactly what you asked him to do, no argument, no discussion. Sebastian Royce!" she called out his name, loud enough to be heard over anything else, and with enough force that Bash stopped in his tracks and turned, eyes wide.

"I caught you being good!" she announced.

His whole face lit up like a Christmas tree. "Prize, Jay-jay?"

"You pick it, buddy. Get thee to the Good Kid Prize Bin! Congratulations!"

He shot off to a huge bin in the front, reaching in with his eyes closed and pulling out a little rubber ball, looking at it with the expression of someone who'd just found a diamond.

"What do you say, Bash?" Jadyn prompted.

"Thank you!"

"Thank you for being good. Now get your backpack, love." She turned to Olivia, her eyes bright. "That kid."

"He's a handful, right?"

"Of love and joy and energy. When he's in this place, it's like we turned the power on. When he leaves?" She pushed her hands to the ground. "All the light shuts off."

"Wow, Jadyn. I love that you feel that way." And would any teacher at that imaginary private school feel the same?

"Oh, look who's here." Jadyn's brows lifted as her gaze moved past Olivia. "You guys did double duty tonight."

Olivia turned and caught sight of Deeley coming into the building. With his weathered T-shirt, board shorts, and wild long hair, he looked like he really could be Bash's father. Same vibe.

Would *he* fit in when he walked into that private school?

"Hey, you." He came right up to her and pulled her in for a hug. "This is a surprise."

"I left a little early and decided to get him. I should have texted you."

"It's fine. It's great, in fact." He glanced toward Bash. "How'd he do?"

"Apparently, he's the light and joy and power in the classroom."

His smile grew and then he beamed as Bash came tearing across the room to him.

"That's my boy!" he exclaimed, lifting him much the same as Olivia had but with so much more strength and control in his mighty arms. "Whoa, you look like you had fun today."

"So much fun!" he said, his chubby legs kicking like he was ready to run in the air.

"Did you learn anything?"

Bash looked at him like he didn't understand the question, and then he laughed. "Tractors make noise!"

"You went on a tractor?" Olivia asked, stunned that the answer had echoed her own thoughts.

"We played tractors," he explained. "Can I go on one?" His eyes grew huge at the very idea.

If he lived on a vineyard in the Blue Ridge Mountains he could, Olivia thought sadly. But she just smiled and took his bag.

"Bash wants ice cream for dinner, Deeley. How 'bout you?"

He screwed up his face. "Ice cream? Nah. Let's go out for burgers and fries." He gave Bash a squeeze. "Want to?"

"Fries!" he hollered in response.

All that energy waned, though, when they pulled up to one of their favorite beach hangouts in Deeley's truck after dropping her car at home first. With the time on the road back and forth, Bash had crashed in his car seat.

"And now he'll be up until ten," Deeley said with a grunt when he turned around to look at him.

"We can wake him. He wakes for fries."

But Deeley just sighed and shook his head. "He's tired from all that fun. It's not a great schedule for a kid."

Not like it would be when Aunt Christine picked him up after school and helped him with homework and set up a play date and fed him a healthy dinner at five that didn't include fries or ice cream, only a scoop before bed at eight on the nose.

"What's wrong, Livvie?" he asked, studying her face and letting her know those thoughts might be very easy to read.

"All of this," she whispered.

"I know. That's why I think I should—"

"You *should*."

He stared at her. "You agree?"

Not one single bit, she thought, but managed to nod. "He needs...all that your sister can offer."

She could have sworn Deeley's shoulders dropped in defeat.

"Have you changed your mind?" she asked. "You still want to go, right?"

"I don't *want* to go, Liv. It just feels like the best solution for him. And for you." He touched her face. "You deserve so much more than running to daycare at five o'clock and squeezing in dinner between a nap and bath and bed for a kid who isn't yours."

"Forget that part, Deeley," she said, glancing in the back. "I love him and if you'd quit reminding me that he isn't, I'd think of him as mine."

He didn't answer, but held her gaze.

"The one who isn't mine," she whispered. "Is you."

His eyes flickered with confusion. "What do you mean?"

"You know what I mean. If this was forever for you, if this was *it*...then none of this would be a problem."

"I don't know what you—"

She stopped him with a finger to the lips. "I just realized that today. When I..." She swallowed the next phrase in her head, because she had promised Christine she'd keep their conversation private. "I just know that if this was the ultimate love of your life, then you and I and Bash...we'd be a family."

He didn't argue, but huffed out a breath.

"I think you should go, Deeley."

"Yeah, I figured you'd come around. I still have to do something with the rental business, but—"

"Noah can run it."

"Noah? He's doing the tea hut."

"He can do both, and I honestly don't think a life of

serving tea and pop-up pizzas will be enough for him. He wants to save money and get financially stable so he can..." She gave a dry smile.

"So he can what?"

"Marry Katie."

"Oh."

The irony of that was not lost on him, she could tell.

"So, you should ask him if he's interested in taking over the beach rental business. Maybe combining it with the tea hut and folding it back into Teddy's whole business."

"That's a really good idea. I guess you've been thinking about how to help me get out of here."

She angled her head and gave him a "get real" look. "It was Claire's idea," she said, "not mine. But I have been thinking and...I guess this would be..." *Say it, Livvie. Say it.* "Best," she managed.

She took a slow breath, dreaming of him hotly denying that, pulling her in for a kiss and pronouncing her crazy for going along with his dumb idea, because they belonged together forever and if she didn't—

"You're right," he whispered instead. "I'll talk to Noah tomorrow and get this show on the road."

Thinking of his ailing father, she nodded. "The sooner, the better, I guess."

He just closed his eyes like he wanted a different response, too.

Chapter Thirteen

Camille

Bath. Wine. Salad. Sleep.

Camille repeated the mantra all the way home, practically singing it as she pulled into her parking space at the townhouse and turned off the ignition.

Bath. Wine. Salad. *Sleep.*

She nearly moaned at the thought of the last one. Enough that she actually considered skipping the first three and falling onto her bed for the night.

Why was she so tired all the time? She climbed out of the car, cursing the ache of her high heels.

Yes, she was working at an age when most people were well into retirement. But age had only ever been a number to her. Yes, she had some aches and pains, like that heartburn after lunch and a bit of an upset stomach that came and went so often. But who cared? Discomfort never bothered her. And, yes, she'd added a few hours to her schedule to help Olivia, who was obviously very upset after her phone call, and unwilling to even talk about it.

But this was a different kind of tired and it worried her.

Until she reached her front door, came to a halt, and

suddenly didn't feel tired, old, or worried. How did he do that?

"Hello, gorgeous." Abner was leaning against the door, holding a single rose, looking...well, awfully darn good. "You had a very, very long day."

"Abner." She sighed his name and gave in to a smile. "You're a...I believe the expression in English is 'a sight for sore eyes.'"

"Say it in French. You know I love that."

She laughed, her heart light instead of burning for the first time since lunch. "I think it would translate into something like...you make my eyes hurt less." She took a step closer. "To be honest, you make everything hurt less."

His whole face lit up at that, and he held out the rose. "Have dinner with me."

"Oh, I don't know. I was thinking about wine and bed."

He lifted one bushy brow, saying nothing, but the sly look in his eyes said it all. And made her laugh again.

"Stop it," she said, finding the house key on her chain.

"You have to eat dinner, Cami."

She smiled at the name, which was starting to grow on her. Oh, who was she kidding? She loved it.

"I don't have to," she said, dropping her keys and bag on the entryway table inside. She started to walk into the living area when he surprised her by putting a light hand on her shoulder, easing her around to face him. Well, to face his chest. She had to look up—way up, even in heels —to meet Abner's gaze.

"Let me take you to dinner," he said. "If we leave right now, I have a surprise for you."

"A surprise?"

"Have you ever heard of a green flash?"

She frowned. "Isn't there a restaurant on Captiva by that name?"

"There is, and it's where you see it. Hurry. It's a perfect night for it. You can tell me about your day, take in the beautiful view, drink from an exclusive wine list, and let me kiss you goodnight at the door."

She felt a frown pull. "You know, this romance was not what I expected from the man who goes by the name Buck."

"Or we could fish off my dock and eat what we catch. Your call."

"Please. I want the...flash." She looked at him for a long time, that fluttery, flirty feeling in her chest again, along with something that felt like hope and a second chance and youth.

All so...intoxicating to her.

"I am about to say something I never dreamed would come out of my mouth, Abner Underwood."

"I hope it's yes."

"Let me change into flat shoes." She put her fingers to her lips, kissed, and transferred her touch to his. "Then I'll have to get way up on my tiptoes to kiss you goodnight."

He grinned like the Cheshire cat and let her go. She fairly flew up the stairs and kicked off the heels and suddenly felt like dancing.

She had a crush on Abner "Buck" Underwood and she could not remember feeling so good. Whatever medicine he was doling out with his caterpillar brows and Southern drawl and long-stemmed red roses at her door... she was taking extra doses and it was working.

Not an hour later, he introduced her to Greenflash, his favorite restaurant on Captiva, a sister island to Sanibel. The minute they sat down, Camille forgot about the long day. She was exactly where she belonged—at a linen-covered table with a water view, sipping a stunningly delicious Châteauneuf-du-Pape from the vineyards of her homeland.

"Watch carefully now," the waiter said as he topped off her wine, and nodded toward the window. "Green flash should be any minute."

On the way over, Abner had told her about the light phenomenon that occurred under certain conditions just seconds before and after the sun fully disappeared over the watery horizon. He explained that it had to do with the light spectrum, but the science of it didn't really interest Camille.

She just wanted to experience it.

Abner sat kitty-corner at the small square table, so both of them could see each other and the view. In this lovely light and atmosphere, he seemed different tonight. Not the bait store owner who amused her, and not the slow-talking Southerner who flirted with her.

Here, he seemed...sophisticated. Like the upscale date had worked like brass polish on his rough and tarnished exterior, making him shine.

She liked it.

"There, Cami. Look."

She took her eyes off him and studied the horizon, staring hard at the tiny sliver of disappearing orange sun. Then, sure enough, there was a flash of chartreuse light, flickering over the water. The entire restaurant seemed to react in unison, with oohs and ahhs and, "There it is!"

Caught up in the moment, she inched closer to him and lifted her glass. "To whatever it is I'm seeing," she whispered, looking into his eyes. "I like it."

He laughed. "I'm not sure what that means, but I like it, too."

"It means..." She sipped the wine, rooting for a way to describe it. "You seem different tonight. Not what I'm used to."

"Not everyone is exactly what they seem to be on the surface, Cami. You have a lot of layers, too."

"You think?" She felt a smile pull just because it was so dang fun to be on this date, talking about each other to each other like a couple of teenagers. She couldn't even imagine that an hour and a half ago, she was ready to collapse. Abner was just so good for her.

"I don't think, little lady. I know," he said. "Oh so many layers."

"Like what?"

"Like when I met you, you were like that rose I gave you."

"Sweet smelling and pretty?" she guessed.

"But whoa—there be thorns."

She lifted both brows, not sure how to respond.

"Oh, I saw all the judgment in those big brown eyes when I came sneakin' in from the back."

"I didn't...okay, I judged."

He chuckled. "Then each conversation, I learned how to hold you—figuratively speaking—and how to avoid getting...wounded. Now, all I see are the petals and the beauty."

Lifting her glass, she touched the rim of his again. "Quite poetic, Abner, if I may call you that."

"Ma'am, you can call me anything you like, just call."

She laughed and took a sip, then studied him again. "You still haven't told me exactly how you got that nickname, you know. How about now?"

"Oh..." He kind of shook his head. "I barely remember."

"Really?"

"Well, I remember, but it ain't worth talkin' about."

"I'd like to know."

Quiet for a moment, he took a deep drink of his wine then shifted his gaze to the view, and it was almost as if he had let his mind and memory go out there, too.

"Polly," he finally said, his voice low. "She called me Buck."

"Oh, I see." She nodded, noticing that he rarely mentioned his late wife much in their conversations anymore. "What was the, uh, impetus?"

He gave a slow smile. "Now *that* is personal."

Her eyes widened as her brain went to all the possible reasons a woman would call a man Buck, most of them...well, yes. Way too personal.

"Why don't we pick our dinner?" he suggested, the change of subject clear as he handed her an oversized menu.

"Of course, I—"

"Buck!"

They both looked up to see a gentleman walking toward their table, a portly man with a receding hairline and dark-rimmed glasses. He looked vaguely familiar to Camille, and she knew he was a local she should remember. But her mind, heart, and soul were so deep into this conversation that she couldn't remember what town she was in, let alone a virtual stranger who lived there.

"Frank, you son of a gun." He put his drink down and stood, reaching out both hands for a manly embrace. "What are you doing here?"

Frank looked past Abner at Camille, his smile wavering just a bit. "Oh, hello. Camille, is it?"

"I'm sorry, have we met?" She straightened in her seat but didn't stand, not wanting to get into a long conversation with an acquaintance. She was having the time of her life and resented the intrusion.

"Cami, this is Frank Conway, better known as The Mayor around these parts."

"Oh, Mayor Conway. Of course." She started to push back her chair to stand, but Frank held up both hands, stopping her.

"No need, ma'am. I don't want to interrupt your dinner."

"It's fine," she said, even though it wasn't.

"Well, then, I'll stop a bit while I wait for Penny to stop yackin' with whoever she met in the ladies' room."

The next thing she knew, he was pulling out one of the empty chairs, blocking her beautiful view of the last rays of sunset, and ruining her romantic dinner.

"How's that new store of yours going?" he asked. "As good as Sarah Beth? She was a mighty fine businesswoman."

"Sanibel Sisters is doing well," she said, coolly enough to convey that she didn't want him to settle in for a long, unwanted exchange.

"And have you—"

"There you are!" a woman practically shrieked, marching over. "I thought you left without me, Frank."

Now this woman? Yes, Camille recognized Penny Conway. They'd met the day Camille and Claire stopped into the Welcome Center looking for Shellseeker Beach. She'd run into her now and again, and remembered her stopping into Sanibel Sisters during the grand opening, but not since then.

And she happened to know Penny had tried to keep Shellseeker Cottages from being included in that big feature on a website—the name of which she couldn't remember for the life of her. All she knew was this woman was foe, not friend.

Camille sat straighter and gave Penny a smile that she, as a stewardess, had reserved for the most annoying of Pan Am customers.

"Hello, Camille," Penny said, the corners of her

mouth turning down to accentuate the deep lines around her lips. "Hey, Bucky."

Once again, Camille's date stood, but this time, the hug Abner offered was much cooler. "Penny," he said. "How's it going?"

"It's...going." She looked from one to the other as she spoke with enough vitriol in her voice to let them know it wasn't going *well*. "Are we interrupting a romantic dinner for two?"

"Yes." Abner said.

"No." Camille said at the exact same moment, making Frank laugh and elbow Abner.

"Hah! Better let this lovely lady know what you have in mind tonight, you sneaky devil."

Abner didn't say a word, but Camille shot Frank a withering look.

"Have you eaten yet?" Penny asked, pulling out the last chair to sit, utterly uninvited and unwelcome.

Camille just stared at her.

"We haven't even ordered," Buck said. "So don't get comfortable, Penny."

Thank you, Camille thought with a silent sigh.

"Oh, shut it, Buck. I want to get to know your lady friend." She pushed back her drab blond hair and Camille resisted the urge to suggest she get her roots done to make that mess all one color.

But that would make Camille as mean as the woman staring at her, and hadn't Abner just said he'd discovered the sweet layer under her prickly exterior? She didn't want to ruin that, but this was ridiculous.

"Why don't you chat while I powder my nose?" Camille suggested, pushing up. Abner politely stood one more time and nodded to her.

"We'll order when you get back." He leaned very close to hug her, putting his lips next to her ear. "Alone, I promise."

She thanked him with a smile and started away when she heard Penny say, "I'll go with you."

Closing her eyes in disgust, Camille continued walking, pretending not to hear.

"You just went!" Frank said.

"Oh, you know my bladder."

Classless, rude, and nasty, Camille thought as she strode through the restaurant, moving quickly thanks to the flat sandals she'd chosen.

But not quickly enough. As she reached for the heavy handle of the ladies' room door, Penny was right next to her.

"Camille," she said, getting much too close. "I want to talk to you."

"Really." She rolled her eyes. "I can't imagine what you have to say, Penny."

"No need to be mean about it," Penny shot back.

Camille yanked the door open, making a snap decision. Two could play this game and whatever the other woman's was—probably to dissuade Camille from seeing Buck—offense was the best defense.

Or was it the other way around? She didn't care. She knew what she was going to say to Penny.

Happy to see the bathroom empty, Camille took a

stealthy check for feet under the stalls. No one was here, so she spun around and looked hard at the other woman.

"Why did you try to keep Shellseeker Cottages from that magazine feature, Penny?" she demanded.

The question had its intended effect, making Penny draw back with a soft intake of breath. "I...I...I don't even remember now. It was a complicated process and happened a long time ago."

"The walk-through was a few days ago."

"What?" she gasped. "They walked through Shellseeker Cottages? How did that—"

"Why?" Camille demanded. "What do you have against Teddy and Eliza?"

For a few heartbeats, she didn't answer, but searched Camille's face with a slicing gaze. "Nothing," she said.

"Your beef is with me, isn't it?"

She inched closer to Camille, narrowing her eyes. "You need to stay away from my brother-in-law."

"Former brother-in-law," Camille corrected. "He's a widower."

"He is part of my family. Was, is, and always will be. You can't change that."

Camille shook her head. "First of all, I am just getting to know the man, not planning a wedding. Second of all, I don't have any interest in taking him away from your family. Why would you even suggest that?"

"Don't take me for a fool, honey. You know and I know that you know and you know that I know."

What? Camille nearly laughed. "What are you talking about? His health? I know your grandson marched into my store and tried to tell my business partner that I'm going to give Abner a heart attack." She snorted. "That really takes a lot of nerve."

Silent again for a long moment, Penny's forehead wrinkles deepened as she frowned. "You don't *know*?"

"Know *what*?" she demanded.

Her nostrils flared with the next breath. "Nothing," she said, which was actually laughable. "Just let me be clear about something. You will never, ever, and I mean *ever* replace my sister, who was ten times the woman you are. She was...special. Perfect. Like no other woman who ever walked this Earth, and Buck will never love anyone else. Do not even try, because you will lose."

Camille blinked at her, speechless at the warning.

"Listen to me," Penny continued. "We have the power in this town. We can wreck your business, stop customers from going to your friend's resort, and make sure everyone on Sanibel knows you were married to a bigamist. Don't put anything past me. *Anything.*"

"Why?" She barely breathed the question. "Are you *that* opposed to his happiness?"

Penny dipped her head and narrowed already beady eyes. "You really don't know, do you?"

"Know *what*?"

"If I were you, I'd keep it that way."

With that, she pivoted and waltzed out of the bathroom, leaving Camille alone and a little frightened and, once again, very, very tired.

She washed her hands, patted her face with a damp towel, and didn't bother to touch up her lipstick.

The uninvited company was gone when she returned, but so was the sunset and the spark and the special moment she'd been enjoying. Her chest burned again, her stomach was in nauseous knots, and as much as she hated to, she asked Abner if they could call it a night and go home.

Of course he agreed, paying the bill for the wine and leaving the restaurant. They drove back to Sanibel, silent until they turned toward Bowman's Beach and her townhouse.

"So," he said with a mirthless laugh. "She got to ya, huh?"

She must have, because Camille was too scared to admit he was right, or ask for more information.

"Not at all," she said with false brightness. "I just..."

"'Sokay, Cami. It comes with the territory and you wouldn't be the first one she scared off. I was just hopin' you were different."

He pulled right in front of the entrance to her townhouse, stopping his car but not turning it off.

"I don't understand," she said, the pressure in her chest like an anvil was sitting on it.

"I know. That was the beauty of it." He gave her a tight smile. "See you around our stores, Cami."

She stared at him. "Is this goodbye...for good? Are you that afraid of Penny?"

"I know what she's capable of, and I know what she could do to you. Your business, your life, your reputation. Not worth the risk."

"Please," she scoffed. "I survived a husband who was

married to one woman and living with another. I can survive your nasty sister-in-law."

But he just closed his eyes. "You don't know what nasty is, darlin'. I can't let that happen to you."

"So...that's it? We're done? *C'est la fin?*"

He stabbed his chest with an invisible dagger. "Don't speak French. I can't take it."

"Then why are you doing this?" she asked.

"Because I really like you. Goodbye, Cami."

Once again, a wave of nausea threatened and her chest ached, so she just nodded and whispered, "'Night...Buck."

She climbed out and walked to her door, painfully aware that he cared enough to wait to make sure she got in, but not enough to walk her to the door. Not enough to give her that promised kiss.

Inside, she let the tears flow and finally did what she wanted to do all day...collapsed on her bed in bone-deep, inexplicable exhaustion.

Chapter Fourteen

Claire

Was that a phone vibrating at six in the morning?

Claire frowned as she headed down the hall, the sound so strange in a house that was usually quiet when she dressed and left for her morning walk with Eliza. Sometimes Noah was up, but that sound wasn't coming from his room.

She inched the door open to the dark bedroom where DJ slept while the phone next to him hummed and lit with an incoming call.

"DJ." She came closer and nudged him, peering at the name on the screen. "Your phone. It's Sophia. Should I answer for you?"

With a grunt, he pushed up, and she handed him the phone. He tapped the screen, and, whether on purpose or by accident, put it on speaker. "Hey. Hey, baby. You okay?"

Nothing, just a gasp and a sob.

Claire reached to turn on the light, spilling a soft golden glow in the room and making it bright enough to see the raw turmoil on DJ's face.

"Honey? Are you there? Soph? Talk to me."

"He cheated on me, Dad! Kyle totally cheated on me

with Bethany!" She wailed the last few words, gasping for air.

"Who's Bethany?" he muttered, sitting straight and trying to shake off sleep.

"My best friend!" she screamed, sounding indignant that he didn't know and making him inch the phone away. "What am I going to do?"

"You're going to calm down. Just..." He blinked the rest of his sleep away. "Calm down. Where are you?"

"I don't know. Driving around...somewhere. Half Moon Bay, I think."

He squinted at the screen. "Half Moon—it's three in the morning out there!"

"I don't care. He cheated on me, Dad. Do you understand what that means? It's over! My whole life, the rest of this year, everything. I hate him! I hate her!" Sophia finally gasped, her ragged high-pitched wail cutting through the peace of dawn. "I can never, ever set foot in that school again!"

"Whoa, whoa. Honey. Calm down. Why aren't you home? Why not talk to your mother?"

"Is that your answer for everything?" she shot back. "Talk to Mom? She's not home, Dad. She's shacked up with *her* boyfriend. At least she has one. I'm all *alone!*"

"Sophia, listen to me." He stabbed his thick hair with his hand, mussing it even more as he gave Claire a helpless look. "I really don't think you should drive when you're this upset."

"Well, what can I do? I have to figure this out, Dad! I can't walk in that school tomorrow! Every single person saw their picture on Instagram! I'm ruined!"

"You're not ru—"

"Yes, I am! My life is *over*. I didn't apply to college and it's too late to get into anything but a community college because he told me we were going to get married and be rich and happy and, oh my God, *Daddy*! Why don't you come home and *fix this*?"

The drama voice had reached peak decibel level now, matched by the raw discomfort on DJ's face.

"You always say live in the moment and do what feels good," she said.

"That's not exactly—"

"Well, why can't you live in *my* moment and make this feel better? Why are you three thousand miles away when I need you!"

He looked at Claire, sucker punched and silent. Instantly, she put a hand on his arm. "Tell her to come here," she mouthed.

He shook his head as if that would be a complete waste of time.

"Just ask," she urged silently, giving a squeeze. "We have room."

"Honey. Soph." He shifted and took a breath. "Why don't you come here? I know it's not ideal but—"

"I don't want to go to freaking Florida! What if he wants to make up?"

"Sophia, you are not going back with a guy who cheated on you." Now, his voice was stern and rich with fury. "That's not who you are."

"See? See how much I need you? Please come home, Dad. Quit running and hiding your head in a pizza oven. I need you here."

Claire cringed at the words and tone, while her heart broke at DJ's bereft expression.

"I do the best I can with what I have," DJ said, steady and strong. "And I love you very much, even though you are upset and can't see that right now."

She was silent for a moment, then said, "Please, I'm begging you, Daddy. Come back here. I'll go to Carmel with you and help you make pizza. I don't need to graduate and God knows I'm not going to prom now. Not with Bethany and Kyle reigning as king and—oh, crap! Seriously? Is he serious right now?"

"What's wrong?"

"He's pulling me over?"

"Sophia? What's going on? Why are you being pulled over? What were you doing?"

"Eighty-five," she said with a sniff and a soft curse. "Maybe eighty-eight. I better go, Dad."

"Listen, So—"

But the phone beeped with a disconnected call, and he fell back on the headboard with a thud.

Claire instantly curled next to him. "It's teenaged drama, DJ. She's using guilt because she's hurt and angry. You can't—"

"I can't ignore that plea, Claire." He closed his eyes, fighting tears. "Honestly, I've waited for it for so many years."

"To hear her crying in the middle of the night over a cheating boyfriend?"

"To hear her ask for my help instead of Rachel's. To need me. She never needed me."

As he spoke, he stared ahead, expressionless, which was almost harder to bear than if he exploded or cried.

Claire just studied him, thinking one simple thought. *We need you. Noah and me.*

But telling him that would tear him apart even more, so she held his hand, silent.

"I really have no choice, Claire." He finally looked at her, his dark, dark eyes intense with pain. "She's my daughter and she's in trouble and I have to go back."

She nodded, unable to argue with that no matter how much she hated it. "Maybe you can convince her to—"

"I'm staying there."

Oh. She swallowed, a little stunned by that, but not really.

"How can I do anything else? I can't rob her of her senior year, I can't let her drive eighty-five miles an hour around Half Moon Bay in the middle of the night. Someone has to help that kid get her head on straight and that someone is her father."

"I understand."

"I can work with her. Teach her things I haven't had a chance to because of the divorce. Maybe this is a blessing in disguise."

"Not for...us," she said softly, hating to add to his inner turmoil. "Not for Noah and me."

"Hey." Noah tapped on the door, which was ajar, so he nudged it open.

"Come in, man," DJ called.

"I was just getting up to go to Shellseeker and I heard you guys talking. Well, I heard someone female who wasn't Claire kind of screaming. Is everything okay?"

Claire didn't answer and DJ didn't have to. His face practically crumpled at the sight of Noah.

He was up and out of the bed in an instant, arms outstretched.

"C'mere, son."

Fighting tears, Claire just watched them embrace. Noah, a little surprised, not that his father's emotions shocked him anymore. And DJ, wearing sleep pants and his favorite Caputo Flour T-shirt, his strong arms squeezing the son he'd only recently discovered he had.

She didn't want life without these two men together. They belonged together, with her. It was right. It was family.

Except, so was Sophia.

"What's going on?" Noah asked as they separated.

"My daughter needs me," he said, pulling back. "She's in trouble and needs a father."

"Sure, sure." Noah nodded. "You gotta take care of stuff in California, man."

"It's more than..." He sighed sadly. "I'm going to stay for a while, Noah. Rent a place, get her through this semester and figure out how to get her on her feet."

Noah tried, really tried, not to look stricken by this

news but Claire knew him well enough to know it had rocked him to the core.

"Will you...be back?"

"Eventually," DJ said. "Would you consider coming with me? Getting to know your sister and life in California?"

Claire fisted her hands and held her breath. What would she do if they both went out there?

"No," Noah said simply. "We're here now. This is home."

"I get that, son, I really do, but just for a while? Maybe you both could come?" he added, turning to Claire. "Your firm has a Northern Cal office. We could make some pop-ups happen there and help Sophia..."

"I'm not leaving Katie, Dad. I've moved around for twenty-six years, and I'm not doing it again."

"And I'm not leaving Noah," Claire added. "If I did, it would have to be back to New York where I'm supposed to be. I'm so sorry, DJ. I hate to put you in the middle, but..."

He held up his hand and squeezed his eyes closed. "I know, I know. I can't blame you, but I can't abandon her. I did that once. Heck, I did it for her whole life when I put my job before my family. I can't do it again. You know what Paulo Coelho would say."

"'A mistake repeated more than once is a decision,'" Noah replied without a nanosecond of hesitation, getting a bittersweet look of satisfaction and sadness from his father.

"You've been reading that book I gave you."

"And listening to you." Noah put a hand on his father's back and suddenly looked so mature that Claire almost whimpered.

She didn't have to, though, because DJ did. He hugged his son and couldn't even say a word while he accepted Noah's comfort.

After a moment, emotions got the best of her and she pushed up from the bed to wrap her arms around both of them.

"We're a family," she whispered, as much to herself as to them. "And we can survive anything."

"We already have," Noah said. "And we're just getting started. Right, Dad?"

Dad. The word hung in the air, somehow both poetically perfect and sadly late.

Chapter Fifteen

Eliza

"What do you have for three very glum girls?" Eliza asked, only half-jokingly, as she dropped her elbows on Teddy's kitchen counter and pretended it was a bar. "Because that's who we're having over for tea and sympathy tonight."

Teddy made a face. "Lemon balm, of course. Maybe some chamomile with ashwagandha, which is very soothing. Some St. John's wort with a sprinkling of basil or mint. What do you think?"

"Hmm." Eliza thought about it. "For Liv, a woman who's about to say goodbye to the man she loves? And Claire, who just said goodbye to the man she's falling in love with? And Camille, who got kicked to the curb for no logical reason? I'd go with...wine. Or maybe straight-up vodka."

Laughing softly, Teddy opened the fridge and brought out a cold bottle of chardonnay. "You're right. This might be too much for my plain old tea." She sighed as she put it on the counter. "How did this happen in the space of a week? They were all so happy, then, wham! Maybe Mercury is in retrograde."

"All three of these situations are driven by men trying to do the right thing," Eliza mused. "But none of them *feel* right, you know?"

"Oh, I know. At least things are going well with you, and Miles isn't flying off for some noble cause."

Eliza smiled. "They are going well," she said. "But I'm keeping him at a relatively safe distance. I don't want to be Broken Heart Number Four around here."

"And is that okay with him?"

"Everything's okay with him, Teddy." Eliza tipped her head, remembering some of her more personal conversations with Miles. "He's so patient, and all he wants..."

"Is for you to be happy?" Teddy finished when Eliza's voice trailed off.

"If marrying him would make me happy, then yes."

Teddy's blue eyes widened and she sucked in a soft breath. "You've talked about marriage? You've barely kissed the man."

"He's talked about it. To Nick, when they were alone. I overheard him telling Nick that was his, well, endgame, although he didn't use that word. I asked him about it later."

"You did?" Teddy searched her face. "And how do you feel about that?"

"Like it's less than a year since my husband died."

"Oh, that pesky one-year mark," Teddy tsked.

"I know it seems silly and arbitrary, but I simply can't do anything more than have lovely dinners and dates and kiss him goodnight until I've passed that milestone, and that's a month from now."

"And then?" Teddy asked.

"Well, I am not going to marry him, not..." She swallowed. "Not ever. And not because he's not, I don't know, worthy. He's a catch and a half, a fine and bright and fantastic man, and I'm incredibly attracted to him."

"So why would you want to marry a schlump like that?" Teddy teased, just as they heard footsteps and women's voices on the steps outside.

"Because I can love again. I can be with a man and give him my heart and enjoy a wonderful relationship. But I married once, and will never say the vows to anyone else." She looked at Teddy and angled her head. "I'm sorry, that's just how I feel."

"I understand," Teddy said, getting up to greet their guests. "Let's take care of the Broken Hearts Club now."

Camille came in first, looking flushed but still beautiful in an eggshell maxi dress and...flat shoes? That was a change.

"Camille, darling." Teddy put her arms around the other woman, who accepted the hug, then inched back.

"I don't need sympathy. These two?" She shot her thumb over her shoulder. "They need all you have."

Eliza's heart cracked when Olivia walked in, so dejected she couldn't even smile.

"Livvie Bug." She went to her daughter to hold her, but Olivia held up both hands.

"I'm fine, Mom."

"Did they leave yet?"

"Tomorrow morning. All packed and ready to go at the break of dawn."

"Are you sure you don't want to be home tonight?" Eliza asked.

"I'll leave early, but he's down at the cabana with Noah, giving him a crash course on the business." She finally hugged Eliza. "Thanks for letting him slide over from the tea hut to the rental business. If he rents stuff the way Deeley does, that kid'll have a lot of money soon."

"It's fine. If they aren't going to run a pizza business, the tea hut can go back to the honor system," Teddy said as she came closer with Camille. "I told Deeley that today when he took me to lunch to say goodbye, which was very sweet of him. Where's Bash if Deeley's at the cabana?"

"Bash?" Livvie looked skyward. "You mean the kid who suddenly decided his favorite expressions are, 'Okay, Wibbie,' and, 'Am I good boy, Wibbie?' and just to make things absolutely impossible, 'I wuv you, Wibbie.'"

They all cooed with the sadness and sweetness that news deserved.

"He's so good when he's with Deeley and Noah, just playing in the cabana with his toys." She gave a sad smile. "It's like when your hair is perfect the morning of the salon appointment you made to cut it off."

"Livvie." Eliza hugged her again. "Are you doing okay, though?"

"I guess. Very moody, but then, I'm probably about to

slide into epic PMS that I will treat appropriately with mountains of chocolate, bags of chips, miserably sad movies, and way too much wine. Speaking of..." She snapped her fingers playfully.

"Open and ready to pour," Teddy assured her, breezing back into the kitchen. "Where's Claire?"

"She came with Noah, but we saw her down in the garden on the phone," Camille said.

"I think DJ's plane just landed in San Francisco," Olivia said. "Have you talked to her, Mom? Is she doing okay?"

"Yes, we spent a lot of time together today. My sister is a strong woman, and the fact that Noah wouldn't leave meant the world to her. And, if you want my opinion? DJ will be back. He'll straighten things out with Sophia, but I think his connections here are strong. He obviously adores Claire and hasn't wiped the smile off his face since the day he arrived and met Noah."

As Teddy poured wine, they commiserated about the changes that seemed to be sweeping over Shellseeker Beach. When Claire came up and confirmed that DJ had made it to San Francisco and already missed her more than he wanted to admit, they settled in the living room with drinks and snacks.

"Okay," Teddy said as if she were calling the meeting to order. "Camille first. We've heard bits and pieces about what happened, but we need the entire story in living color. Do not leave out one detail, especially the juicy parts about Penny."

"Every drop of juice," Olivia said as she made a show of taking a sip.

"She was horrible," Claire agreed. "Tell them, *Maman*."

Camille kept them mesmerized with a blow-by-blow description of a shocking scene in a restaurant bathroom, leaving the entire group with nothing but disbelief and questions.

"Why would she do that?" Claire demanded.

"What's the big secret?" Eliza chimed in.

"And how could Buck think letting you go is the answer?" Teddy's question was the hardest of all.

"Maybe he's genuinely afraid of his former sister-in-law," Olivia suggested. "She's kinda terrifying."

Camille just shook her head and took a deep drink of her wine. "I truly think he thinks he's protecting me."

Olivia groaned. "Enough with these men who are killing us by protecting us. We can handle a little stress, am I right?"

"I don't know," Camille said. "The whole thing has left me sick and tired. Literally."

More sympathy poured her way, but Eliza was stuck on some of the things Penny had said. And the response.

"So, this big secret," Eliza said. "She thought you knew something about him that you don't? What could it be?"

"I have no idea, and he said he knew I didn't know and that's why I was special, or some such thing. I knew he was breaking things off and I was fighting..." She pressed her hand on her chest.

"What?" a few of them asked.

"Nothing. A broken heart, I guess. It hurts."

"*Maman*, is something wrong?" Claire inched closer. "Does your chest hurt?"

"No, please, nothing is hurt but my ego. And my..." She sighed. "Expectations. The man made me feel so good, I didn't want to pass judgment or make snide remarks. Whoa, did I say that? Maybe I am sick," she added on a laugh. "Or don't want to be like Penny."

"You're happy," Claire said. "You've got your life in a nice place—literally and figuratively. A successful business, a beautiful new home, and a grandson." She smiled. "You lost your edge because life got so good."

Camille lifted a dubious brow.

"But what is the secret?" Eliza insisted, still hung up on it. "What exactly did Penny say? Word for word. Can you remember?"

"You don't forget when someone says, 'You know and I know that you know and you know that I know'—not with that godawful hair that looks like it was cut with pinking shears."

"And she's back," Olivia joked, raising a glass.

"That's all?" Eliza asked.

"And a minute later, she peered through her Ben Franklin bifocals and said, 'You really don't know?'"

"What could it be?" Eliza asked again, looking at Teddy. "Do you know any of this family's secrets?"

"They're very...insular," Teddy said. "For all the power they have, they don't let just anyone in their inner circle. And remember Penny's grandson said that Buck had health problems. Maybe that's the secret."

"That wouldn't make her threaten me, would it?" Camille asked.

"Who knows?" Olivia shrugged. "I mean, they think you and your sexy French accent are going to...put him over the edge."

Camille snorted. "I didn't even get a chance to try."

"Are you sad, *Maman?*" Claire asked.

They all expected her to flick her wrist and pop off some French phrase that was the equivalent of "couldn't care less," but she surprised them with a nod.

"I am. He made me feel young," she said on a whisper. "No, he wasn't my type, not that I even have one anymore, but he made me laugh and flirt and forget about aches and pains and insomnia and that very real sensation that life is...slowing down."

"Maman!"

"Please, Claire. I'm going to be seventy-two years old on my next birthday."

They all just stared at her, and for the same reason. Camille never, ever admitted her age. Or wore flats. Or was quite this honest.

Maybe she *was* sick, Eliza mused.

"I just enjoyed everything he made me feel," Camille continued. "I'm going to miss it, that's all."

Eliza pressed her hands to her lips, thinking. "If you knew what this deep, dark family secret was, maybe you could get him back. I mean, if you want him."

"*Do* you want him?" Claire asked.

She lifted her shoulder, halfway through her *laissez-faire* French shrug when she froze, let the shoulder fall, and sighed. "Yes," she said on a breath. "I like him. A lot. And I miss him already."

"So call him," Olivia said. "It's the twenty-first century, Camille. Women can pursue men."

Camille shot her a look. "Not *this* woman."

"Maybe Miles can find out," Eliza said, letting the words pop out the minute they occurred to her. "I know he's the people-finding expert, but you would be shocked at the dirty laundry this man knows. Maybe Buck had an affair and they're holding it over him."

"Maybe Polly did," Teddy said. "There wasn't a man in this county who didn't want to be near her."

Camille groaned. "Just what I love. Competition."

"She's dead," Olivia reminded her.

"Dead competition." Camille looked skyward. "The worst kind. No one can compete with a memory. And I'm officially done with this subject." She reached a hand to Claire. "You're not happy, *cherie*, and that hurts me even more."

"Oh, I feel like you do, *Maman*. I'd rather not talk about it. It was a bittersweet goodbye, but the call from Deeley asking Noah to take over his business? That made my son very happy." She turned to Olivia. "Thank you for suggesting that. I know that helped speed up his decision, so you were very selfless to offer it to Noah."

"That and other things," Olivia sighed noisily. "It's fine. He needs to go. It's the right thing, I guess. But..."

She made a face. "I'll happily talk about it for hours, but expect me to cry, because it seems that's all I do lately."

Eliza instantly forgot about Camille and Claire, and focused on the young woman she loved the most in the world.

"What can we do for you, Liv?" she asked.

"Nothing. But don't judge me tonight when he texts and says he's done training Noah and wants to go home. Because I will run to spend my last night with that man."

"No judging," Eliza promised.

"And if you want more wine, I'll drive you," Claire offered.

Camille put a loving hand on Olivia's arm and Teddy slid a big blue crystal across the table. Olivia dropped her head back and half-laughed, half-sobbed in response.

"Livvie!" Eliza crooned, her whole body physically hurting for her girl.

"It's okay, Mom," Olivia said, much more in tune with her than any of the other women surrounding her. "Don't be upset."

"I'm sorry," Eliza said. "But a wise woman once told me a mother is only as happy as her kids are."

"Who was that?" Olivia asked.

Eliza pointed at Teddy. "This wise woman. The wisest."

"And I don't even have kids," Teddy joked.

They all laughed at that, but Eliza's smile wavered. "And if she's right? Then I'm in trouble. Olivia's a crying mess and I got a text from Dane the other day, and I'm not sure he's in such a great place, either."

"You, too?" Olivia asked, wide-eyed. "He texted me in the middle of the night and made some weird comment about hating Silicon Valley. Wait, I'll read it to you." She reached in her bag and pulled out her phone. "Oh, I just missed Deeley's call. He must be done at the cabana. I'm going to..." She gave a tight smile. "Have our last night together. We've argued so much lately, I just want tonight to be calm and peaceful.

A chorus of, "Oh, Livvie!" echoed through the room as they hugged and squeezed and wished her the best.

When she left, the four of them sat in a moment of silence, sharing sad expressions and sipping their wine.

"We need a happy subject," Teddy announced.

"Yes," Claire agreed. "Any news on *The Last Resort*?"

Camille snorted. "You mean the opportunity that Penny the Horrible tried to squash?"

"But failed," Eliza reminded her. "Just like she might fail to wreck your relationship with Buck."

"Abner. I never call him Buck, which is just a stupid nickname."

"How did he get it?" Claire asked.

She rolled her eyes. "Evidently, Polly called him that and it was 'personal' so...use your imagination."

"Ew." Claire curled her lip. "Not sure I want to."

"Seriously!" Eliza agreed as they all laughed. "I wonder if—" She frowned, cocking her head at the sound of footsteps. "Is Livvie coming back?"

"Maybe she decided we're better company than her last night with the boys."

"I doubt that," Eliza said, pushing up as Teddy did.

"You stay, Teddy. I'll go talk to her and find out what's going on."

She headed out to the deck and glanced at the stairs, stopping at the sight of a teenaged girl she'd never seen before. Maybe one of the guests? Doubtful. She wouldn't forget someone this beautiful, with a mane of ebony curls and eyes to match.

"Hello," Eliza said. "Welcome to Shellseeker Cottages. Can I help you?"

"I don't know. I guess. I'm looking for a guy who lives here, or did. I don't know his address but this was the only place he ever mentioned."

"Of course. Who is it?"

"Dante Fortunato," she said. "He goes by DJ."

"Yes, we know DJ. As a matter of fact, he took a flight to California this morn—"

"What?" she exclaimed. "He went *there*?"

"He did, but we can...what's your name?" Eliza blinked just as Claire stepped out onto the deck.

"He went to California and didn't tell me? I came to him."

"Sophia!" Claire exclaimed, coming forward. "You're Sophia, right? I recognize you from the picture DJ carries. I'm Claire."

The girl took in a soft breath, staring at her, silent for a long moment. "You're really not what I expected."

"Well, I certainly didn't expect you," she said. "I think your planes must have passed in the air. Why didn't you tell him you were coming?"

Narrow shoulders sank with a very noisy and theatrical sigh. "Because I'm the worst human alive."

"Not true," Claire insisted.

"It is true. I was awful to him. I was mean and hateful and nasty and..." Her face collapsed into a sob as her voice rose with each word. "I'm so sorry and I came to tell him I'm sorry. Will he come back? Will he forgive me?"

"Of course." Claire reached out and put her arms around the girl, who was sliding right into a full-fledged meltdown. "He will be over the moon when he hears that you've come. He'll turn around, fly back, and be here tomorrow."

She shuddered with another sob. *Oscar-worthy*, Eliza thought, or truly repentant.

She left them to talk privately, slipping back into the house to tell the others this news.

"That means DJ will come back," Teddy said in a happy whisper.

"But will he stay?" Camille asked.

Eliza shrugged. "No clue. But all I know is Claire will be getting her man back. That's one glum girl who'll be happy. Not much we can do for Olivia right now. But you?" She looked at Camille. "What are we going to do for you?"

Camille's eyes narrowed to dark pinpoints. "Call Miles. See if he can get me some answers, Eliza. I refuse to be beaten by that witch."

"That's my girl," Teddy whispered, putting an arm around her. "You're a fighter, Camille, and that what I love about you."

As they hugged, Eliza inched back and watched the exchange of genuine affection between two woman who both once loved the same man and vied for this property. Now they were like sisters, which was nothing short of a miracle.

Men might come and go in their lives, but friendship like they had? Lasting, and priceless.

Chapter Sixteen

Olivia

The all new and improved version of Bash held all the way home, through bath time, and right into bed, where he curled up with Olivia to read.

Why did he have to be so perfect? It was just going to make this night harder.

"Baby, all of your books are packed to go see your Aunt Christine in North Carolina."

They hadn't actually told him the trip was *forever*. Mostly because they figured he didn't quite get that concept, and also because...neither one of them wanted to say the word.

And the closer the clock ticked to that forever, the harder it became.

"Tell me a story, Wibbie."

"Oh? A story, huh?" She climbed onto the bed next to him, nestling his freshly washed body so close she could still smell the baby shampoo in his hair. "About what?"

"Water." He looked up and gave that baby-toothed smile that melted her heart. "I wuv water."

"I know you do. Bath water. The Gulf of Mexico. You even like rain, you silly goose."

He giggled when she pretend-tickled him, but the

door to the garage slammed and his eyes got wide. "Where Deeley?"

"He's packing up the truck for your trip."

He frowned, like something in that sentence didn't make sense. "Mine?"

"You and Deeley," she corrected. "I'm staying here."

The slightest look of...was that panic? Something flashed in his eyes. "Where Mommy?"

Her heart folded in half at the question. He'd stopped asking for his mother after about a month or so, and Livvie figured he was slowly forgetting about Marcie Royce.

It wasn't like she was the world's most attentive mother. But she was gone from this Earth, and Olivia and Deeley had agreed they would paint a rosy picture of his mother for little Bash, who had no reason to go through life knowing he was literally abandoned.

Let him think she died on an out-of-town trip, not a joyride with a loser to get married in Vegas.

"She's in heaven, buttercup. With all the angels and Jesus and...and all the people who belong there." Probably not Marcie, but, again, TMI for a not-quite three-year-old. "Oh!" She sat up with a realization. "Your birthday's coming up." And she was going to miss it! Teddy would have had a party and everyone would be there and...she squeezed her eyes closed.

Don't go there, Liv.

He grinned and held up three fingers. "Free!"

"Yes, you'll be free," she said, hearing the sadness in her voice. Free to run around a vineyard and get spoiled by his Aunt Christine. What would he call her? *Cwissieeeeeee.*

She bit her lip to keep from letting out a whimper of sadness. "Okay, a story about water?"

He nodded. "And trucks."

"Ah. That's a challenge, but I'm up for it." She scooted a little higher on the pillows, easing him closer. "How about a story about a boy who could drive a truck through deep rain puddles that splashed mud everywhere?"

"Allllllll over!" He swept both hands. "So much mud."

She laughed. "Once upon a time, there was Sebastian the Truck Driver."

"My name," he said proudly.

"Yes, it is. And a great truck driver name, for sure. He was on his way to make a delivery of..."

"Porcupines!"

She laughed, mostly at his enthusiasm and sweet, sweet face. "A delivery of porcupines it is. They were going to the porcupine farm, which was on the other side of a big river and it had been raining for days and days. But Sebastian had to get there because the porcupines were..."

"Hungry," he helped.

"Oh, yes, very hungry porcupines and the only food they could eat was at the farm. So, Sebastian fired up his truckload of porcupines and rumbled fearlessly toward the river. Nothing scared him. Not a little water! Not for Sebastian. He was..."

She purposely hesitated and let him finish.

"Just like Deeley," he whispered.

"Aww, yes. Brave and strong like your...like Deeley." Who *would* be his daddy someday, she had no doubt. After a year or two, Deeley would officially end the guardianship and adopt this child.

And Olivia wouldn't be there to see that day, to celebrate. His Aunt Christine would.

She shifted on the bed, trying really hard not to hate that woman, who was kind and good and loving and... getting everything Olivia wanted.

"And just when he got to the river," she continued, closing her eyes to try and see some dump truck on a muddy riverbank...but all she could see was Deeley and Bash and birthday parties and adoption days and first day of school and Little League and—

"What happened?" Bash prodded her, patting her thigh.

What happened? She fell in love, that's what. With this kid and his soon-to-be father and this life and it was all being taken away.

She opened her mouth to make something up but her throat was so tight with a sob she wasn't sure she could speak.

"He drownded?" Bash asked groggily.

"No." She choked the word, and swallowed the lump in her throat. "He made it across, splashing mud every-where. It was so messy but his big wheels rumbled and splashed and finally they made it across the river. Just when he got there, the porcupines cheered and then...he..."

She looked down, hoping he had an idea, but his eyelids were closed and his tiny chest rose and fell with the first few deep breaths of sleep. She smiled, because when he crashed, he crashed so hard and so fast, it always amazed her.

And she knew she could practically toss him over her shoulder—or Deeley could—and put him in his crib and he wouldn't wake up.

Slipping off the bed, she scooped him up in her arms, a sack of boneless child draped over her. She took him to his room and didn't bother with the light, already knowing the way to his crib and also knowing the path was clear of small toys because...they were all packed.

"Here you go, little angel," she whispered as she brought him to the side of the crib and eased him onto the mattress. She'd convinced Deeley to leave it, telling him that Bash was ready for a toddler bed. Of course, he'd have one in his perfect room at his perfect house with a perfect lady who wasn't his mother any more than Olivia was, but that didn't matter.

A tear slipped out as she pulled his blanket up and watched that thumb go right into its happy place, even though he was sound asleep.

Maybe Aunt Christine wouldn't let him suck his thumb, but Not-Your-Real-Mom Livvie would. Tonight, at least.

He could have anything he wanted.

Before she pulled up the side rail, she leaned over

and got close, taking one more whiff of baby shampoo and clean pajamas and darling boy. God, she loved him.

She gave in to the sob and cried softly, a tear falling right onto his shoulder.

"Oh, Bash," she choked. "I am going to miss you. I'm going to miss your exuberance and your dear heart and your wild soul and precious little fingers and curly hair and...all that energy you put into life. I'm going to miss mashing your bananas and your kisses goodbye at daycare and spending ten minutes every day looking for that toy... thing you call Greenie because it makes you so happy."

"It's a rabbit."

She straightened and turned to see Deeley's silhouette in the doorway.

"It was in the Easter basket I gave him last spring."

How much of that soliloquy had he heard? "Oh, I guess I knew that. Did you pack it? He loves Greenie."

He crossed his arms and leaned on the door jamb. "I packed everything, Liv. Or you did. Every single thing but that crib, and if you want me to get rid of it or take it to Goodwill before we leave, I can—"

"No." She closed her fingers over the railing as she raised it slowly and latched it into place, remembering how she couldn't even figure out how to work the sides when Deeley brought the crib over the Friday after Thanksgiving.

"No, don't take it. I..." Well, she couldn't admit she wanted it, could she? This piece of furniture that had zero function in her life and home? "I'll donate it to Jadyn's daycare. I bet she'd love to have it."

She waited for him to respond, to say, "Good idea," or something, but he was stone cold still and silent.

Sighing, she fixed the blanket again, trying to compose herself before she had to face Deeley in the light.

But when she turned, he was gone and the only thing she heard was a sniff. Was he crying, too?

She didn't want to know, so she stood over the crib with one hand on Bash's back and hummed a lullaby until her tears dried.

OLIVIA WOKE up with a sick feeling in her stomach, that dark sensation when she couldn't make the world do what she wanted it to do. Coffee usually washed that feeling away, along with a nice to-do list, maybe a spreadsheet, a check of her calendar, and a mental plan for the day ahead.

Failing all that, she would call or visit her mother for a good old-fashioned Eliza Whitney pep talk. That was definitely on the agenda for later this morning.

First, she had to say goodbye to Deeley and Bash. No. First, coffee.

While it brewed, she stared out the kitchen window at her little patio and backyard, already aching for all the things that wouldn't happen there. No games of tag with Bash, no blow-up kiddie pool like they'd talked about getting, no swing-set that Deeley said he could build.

And then there were the adult memories she

wouldn't be making. No cocktails after work with Deeley, no shopping for that new glider they'd liked the last time they were in Lowe's, no midnight kisses under the stars.

"You okay?"

She turned at the sound of Deeley's question, asked in that hushed whisper they'd learned to use when Bash was still sleeping.

"Yeah, sure. I'm fine."

He frowned and came closer, running his finger over her cheek with a feather-light touch, concern in his whiskey-colored eyes.

"I'm just sad."

"I know." He heaved a sigh. "I hope I'm doing the right thing."

"For Bash? For you? For your dad and sister and... yeah. It's the right thing, Deeley."

"What about you?" He inched closer. "I thought this was for you, to free you up to have the life you wanted and not raise some other woman's kid, but—"

"But he's not some other woman's kid anymore."

He nodded. "I saw that last night."

She held his gaze for a moment, a little lost like she always was with him. Before her stood a man who was having second thoughts, a man who cared deeply for her, and wanted always to do what was best for the people who depended on him.

It would be so easy to change his mind. One touch, one kiss, one whisper of, "Please don't go," and he might stay.

Then the echo of his sister's voice played in her head,

and she knew that his father needed him and Bash needed all that love, attention, and time that would make him a better little boy.

It was selfish to keep him here, and she knew that. If she really loved Bash, like she realized last night, she'd let him go. And if she really loved Deeley—

"I know what you want out of life, Liv."

"You better tell me, then, because I can't even remember what I want."

"What does that mean?"

She searched his face, memorizing every crease, color, and shape of what she saw, knowing she'd want to fall asleep every night remembering him.

"You know how I feel about you," she finally said. "And getting over you and Bash isn't going to be easy."

"Maybe I could..."

She put her finger on his lips. "Decision is made."

"I was going to say maybe I could come back. Maybe Bash won't be so happy..." At her look of sheer disbelief, he shook his head. "You're right. I can't do that to him. But we don't have to stay forever."

She let out a little whimper. "Don't give me hope, Deeley. It will paralyze me waiting for you. You're going or you're not. I can't live in limbo wondering if you two will—"

"Wibbie?" A squeaky voice echoed through a house that was small enough that a monitor was overkill. "Where you, Wibbie?"

It was Deeley's turn to look a little sick. "He calls you first now."

She just closed her eyes, not wanting to have this conversation now. It was too late. They were leaving, Christine had Bash's room ready, and his father had had an infusion of new life and energy when he heard they were moving there.

"He'll call his Aunt Christine first in a few weeks," she said, working to keep any bitterness out of her voice.

"Yeah, maybe," he said gruffly, inching back. "But I won't."

"You'll be fine," she said, waiting for the wail when she didn't show up five seconds after Bash demanded it. "I better go get him." She slipped away, stepping toward the door, but Deeley snagged her arm and turned her to face him.

"I will not be fine," he ground out. "I was fine before...Livvie. Months ago, when I had some problems and responsibilities I didn't want, some guilt I shouldn't have had to lug around, and a business that had potential I couldn't quite reach. That was *fine*. But now, I know that life can be so much more and I know that because you, Olivia Whitney, showed me exactly how to...love."

She stared at him, stunned by the speech, which was a lot of words and emotion for this man.

"So, yeah, now I know. And I'm loving Bash by doing this for him, and I'm loving you by freeing you to have the life you want, but just for the record, I am not happy about it. I am not...I don't want to leave you."

She almost said the two words that were screaming in her head. Two words, that was all it would take, two little words:

Then don't.

"Wibbie! Go potty?"

She closed her eyes and fought a smile. "I better get him." With that, she stepped out of the kitchen and changed her last diaper, then said her goodbyes in the driveway.

After the truck pulled out, she cried in the shower for fifteen minutes.

Then she made a to-do list, checked her calendar, reviewed her schedule, and texted her mother to say she'd be over soon.

Life had to go on, whether she liked it or not.

"For the record," she whispered to herself, echoing Deeley's tone. "I'm not happy about it, either."

Chapter Seventeen

Claire

"I'm leaving Orlando in a rental car," DJ said, the exhaustion after a cross-country—and back—trek clear in his voice. "I'll be on Sanibel in under four hours. How is Sophia? How was last night?"

Claire pressed the phone to her ear, thinking of how to answer that question as she sat on the edge of her bed, dressed for the day. "She's dramatic. Over the top. As big in personality as her father."

He chuckled softly. "Welcome to the Sophia Show. Was she nice, though? Did you guys do okay? God, Claire, I still can't believe she used that credit card that was supposed to be for emergencies only to buy a ticket and didn't tell a soul. It's a little terrifying just to think about it."

"Have you talked to Rachel?"

"Oh, yeah. She blamed it on Sophia's overly dramatic personality."

"It is that," Claire agreed. "But all that matters is she made it, and is currently sound asleep in your room. I changed the sheets and Noah warmed up some pizza from the fridge and we talked for a while. I actually think the two of them were up until well after midnight."

"Really?" His voice rose with hope. "I can't believe I missed my son meeting my daughter. Did they click?"

"Who doesn't Noah click with?" she asked with a laugh. "He made everything smooth last night, asking her questions without prying, but managing to bring her out of her shell and make her comfortable." She couldn't help but smile; she was so proud of that boy.

"Good, good," he said. "Did she talk endlessly about this idiot, Kyle?"

"A bit, but she talked a lot about her mother, too."

"Really?"

"Enough for me to know Sophia really doesn't like... Mike? That's his name, right? Rachel's boyfriend. Have you met him?"

"Once, in passing."

"Apparently he wants Rachel to move in with him, and help him with his kids, who are younger."

DJ was quiet for a beat. "I wasn't aware of that. What would happen to Sophia?"

"Well, they thought she was going to college, then found out she was getting married—"

"Thank God that stupid idea is DOA."

"But the point is, they don't have a plan for her," Claire explained. "I think that she's lost, and on top of that, feeling betrayed by everyone. Her mother. Her boyfriend..."

"Her father," he finished when she didn't.

"She's just a wounded little girl trying to be tough and strong, Deej."

Once again, he was quiet, but for a lot longer this

time. "We'll talk about it when I get there," he finally said. "I'll have to figure...everything out."

"You should talk to Noah, since I suspect she was more open with him last night after I went to bed."

"I will. I'll be home soon. Will you all be there?"

"I'm not sure. I thought I'd take her to Shellseeker Beach so I can show her around. She met Teddy and Eliza and my mother last night, but it was very brief. The beach seems like a good place to hang out until you get back. Just stay in touch and I'll tell you how to find us."

"Claire." His voice dropped to not much more than a whisper. "How can I thank you?"

"That's not necessary."

"But you were ready to let me go, and now..."

"Define 'ready,'" she joked. "I understand how important family is. I'm here with Noah, much to the dismay of my firm."

"Still no response to your suggestion they open an office there?"

"No. My boss has presented the idea to the other senior partners, but I haven't heard anything. Oh." She sat up. "I just heard a door close in the hall. Noah's gone to Shellseeker to work, so I'm going to see if Sophia needs anything. Stay in touch, Deej."

"You bet."

After she hung up, she took a deep breath in preparation for a conversation with Sophia. Noah had done the heavy lifting in the chatting department last night, and Claire had observed, as she preferred.

And from what she observed? The cheating

boyfriend was the excuse Sophia needed to wake her parents up and get some attention. She might be on the cusp of eighteen, but she was a girl, and right now? That girl's parents were deeply involved with families that didn't include her.

As Claire stepped into the hall, she heard the sliding door to the back patio open, so she headed there to join Sophia.

"Hey there," she said, leaning through the opening to see Sophia settling at the side of the pool. "Good morning. How'd you sleep?"

She shaded her eyes from the sun and looked at Claire. "Is that my dad's room I was in? Don't you two sleep in the same room?"

The question threw her a little, but she'd learned last night that Sophia was blunt. "Not...always," she replied. "I'm going to get some coffee. Would you like some?"

"Iced, with tons of milk and sugar."

"You got it." Claire stepped back inside and prepared the coffee as requested, and got one with no ice and no tons of sugar for herself, taking them both out to the back.

Sophia sat on the pavers with her feet in the water, leaning on her hands, face toward the sky, eyes closed. Her thick dark curls cascaded down her back, darn near touching the ground.

"Here you go," Claire said, offering her the iced coffee. "Can I join you or do you want some alone time?"

She heaved a sigh, her punctuation and response of choice. "You can stay. We didn't talk much last night."

"Noah's much more talkative than I am," Claire said,

lowering herself to sit next to her and drop her feet in the water, too. "And your father loves to talk. I'm the quiet one of the..." She stopped and caught herself, sensing that "family" wasn't the right word to use. "Group," she finished.

"So how'd you meet?" She took a drink and gave a questioning look over the rim of the metal tumbler full of coffee.

"Your father and Noah? Didn't Noah tell you that I hired an investigator to—"

"No. My dad. When you were together and you got pregnant. You were my age."

"I was nineteen and we were at Fordham together. I was a freshman and he was a senior."

"First guy?" she asked. "For, you know..." She fluttered her fingers.

"Yes."

"And you got knocked up." She blew out a breath, putting her coffee down next to her phone. "Bad luck."

"Not when I look at Noah," Claire said with unabashed love in her voice. "Nothing's bad about him."

"But how'd you manage? What did your parents say?"

"I never told them," she admitted. "My mother was a flight attendant and traveled constantly. I didn't really show that summer I was home, and then I went back to school and the university helped me arrange the adoption. That didn't actually work out as planned, though."

She nodded. "Noah told me about his parents being

killed in 9/11. Really sad." She turned toward Claire, her dark eyes shockingly intense. "But my dad just...blew you off?"

"No! I didn't tell him, either."

"Why not? He deserved to know!"

She took a sip of coffee, using it as an excuse to formulate her answer. "I believed, in my heart, that he didn't want a baby at that age," she said carefully. "He was focused on getting his advanced degree and had...big dreams."

"Big dreams that he achieved at the cost of his family," she said bitterly. "First family," she corrected. "Or is it his second? I guess technically you beat us to him."

Claire let out a soft sigh. "It's a complicated situation, Sophia, but you need to know that your father loves you so much. He left yesterday with every intention of staying in California, letting you move in with him, and...and..."

"Leaving you," she finished.

"You are his priority."

She closed her eyes for a second, then turned to stare straight ahead. "*Right.*"

"You are."

"I'm no one's priority, Claire. Not Kyle, who was my first, too, but thank God I didn't get pregnant. Not my mother, who is in a love bubble where I'm not welcome. Not my father, who has discovered he has an instant new family. Not my sister, who is so busy being the queen bee at Stanford she doesn't even text back, just buys me a ticket and says I should go. And I'm sure not a priority to my best friend, Bethany, who decided to bang my boyfriend." She threw a spray of water in the air with her feet as if to punctuate that. "I am no one's priority and that is the worst feeling in the world."

Before Claire could answer, Sophia jumped into the water, cannonball-style, soaking Claire with the splash and disappearing underneath for...too long.

Claire stared at the fully clothed girl, holding herself in a ball, staying underwater like she...like she...

She wouldn't try to drown herself, would she?

"Sophia!"

It had to be twenty seconds now. How long could she hold her breath?

"Sophia, please!"

Claire stood slowly, absently taking her phone from her pocket and placing it on a glass table behind her, never taking her eyes off Sophia.

Could she dive down there and bring her up? Would Sophia fight her? Was this all for dramatic impact? Of course, and it was working.

Well over thirty seconds now.

"Sophia!"

Nothing. She actually wasn't moving at all, just rolling around like a ball in the fetal position.

Swearing softly, Claire jumped in, throwing herself knifelike into the deep end, her body shooting to the bottom so fast she felt her feet touch it. She kicked closer to Sophia and grabbed her. For a moment, she didn't move. Didn't react. And Claire's whole body went limp at the idea of—

Suddenly, her eyes popped open and she grabbed Claire's arms, both of them kicking to the surface in one brief second. They popped up for air, with Sophia gasping much harder than Claire, but still staring at her.

"What were you doing?" Claire demanded.

"Testing you," she fought for a breath.

What the—

"You passed," Sophia said on one last ragged breath, kicking to the side and holding on as her chest heaved.

Claire followed, only a little weighed down by her shorts and top. "Why?" she managed to ask. "Why would you do that?"

Sophia wiped water from her eyes, blinking at Claire as more poured down her cheeks from her wet hair.

"Because I need to know what you're made of."

"I'm a human being made of flesh and blood who wasn't about to let you drown." She couldn't keep the anger out of her voice.

Sophia stared at her for a long time, both of them still panting from the experience and the emotion.

"Can I stay?" Sophia asked softly. "Here? In this house? With this family? Can I stay?"

"Of course," Claire said without even a second's hesitation. "Just don't pull another stunt like that."

Sophia studied her for a long time, then pushed herself up and out of the pool. "You should have told him," she muttered. "He'd have married you and you'd have been a heck of a lot better for him than my mom was."

"You don't know that," Claire said, scooting to the ladder to climb out. "You can't change history."

Sophia shrugged and walked around the pool, dripping. "But you can change the future."

Claire couldn't argue with that. She had a feeling that Sophia Fortunato was about to do just that.

Chapter Eighteen

Camille

When Camille opened up Sanibel Sisters in the morning, she always stopped to take a deep inhale of the perfumed air. She didn't know anything about perfumed air, having spent her working years on airplanes, but Livvie sure understood the power of a good diffuser. Apparently, women stay longer and spend more in a boutique that smells like wild mint and bergamot.

But today, something smelled...different. Something was heavier than the clean and beachy fragrance that had become so calming and welcoming to her. Today, she smelled...a man.

Not just any man, but the one who'd been haunting her dreams and making her heart ache more than it did all by itself.

Had Abner been in the store?

By unspoken agreement, they kept the secret door that connected the back offices of Sanibel Sisters and Angler's Paradise unlocked from both sides. Although the door opening had been built for the former owner's husband to hop back and forth between the two stores, Abner liked that she and Olivia had opted to keep the door functioning. He believed it was a safety issue, and that women alone in a place of business should have an escape route. Since there was no back door to this establishment, it did make sense.

But it also gave Abner access to her store and...she inhaled deeply. It sure smelled like he'd been here.

Why?

It had been a few days since that fateful date, and she hadn't seen anyone from next door yesterday. Not Abner, not his nephew, and certainly not his mean sister-in-law.

Glancing around, everything looked to be in order, so she headed to the back office, half expecting the secret door to be wide open, explaining why she could smell that manly fragrance of Old Spice and...live bait.

Stepping into the undersized work area, she froze. She hadn't been expecting *that*.

A single red rose lay across the desk, a matching crimson ribbon around the stem.

"Oh, Abner," she whispered, staring at the flower and knowing exactly who'd put it there. She took a few steps closer and reached for it, taking a whiff before she realized that someone had carefully removed the thorns.

Her whole chest squeezed and her eyelids stung, surprising her. She wasn't a woman who cried at much of anything, but...*mon Dieu*, she liked this man. And it seemed like he must like—

A soft tap on the other side of the secret door shelf grabbed her attention. Before she could respond, the shelving unit moved, slowly swinging in.

Abner stood on the other side, a slow smile breaking

across his face. "A rose by any other name would be... Cami," he said softly.

She exhaled and pressed the gift to her chest. "Peace offering?"

"We didn't argue."

"And yet, you left me high and dry and without that kiss."

A pained expression passed over his face. "Can I come in?"

"Unless you're afraid Penny planted a camera back here in her effort to ruin my good name."

He puffed out a breath and looked skyward as he stepped through the door and filled up the tiny office. "I didn't get to be the man I am today by being afraid."

"And what kind of man is that?" she asked.

He opened his mouth to answer, then shut it, slowly shaking his head. "I'd love to give you a flowery apology, Cami, but..."

"You gave me a flower instead." She lifted it an inch and let him off the hook. He wasn't the kind of man to grovel, and she wasn't a fan of groveling men. "Thank you."

"I'm forgiven?"

She lifted a brow. "I wasn't mad at you, Abner, just disappointed and confused. You don't owe me an apology, but an explanation would be nice."

He tucked his hand in the pockets of his faded jeans and regarded her with a steady gaze. "Nothing to explain. I don't want you to—"

"What was she talking about in that restaurant?"

Camille demanded, not wanting to dance around it any longer. "What do I not know that she thought I did? What secret are you keeping from me, Abner?"

"Nothin' that matters, Cami. But I—"

"But there is something, right? There's some story or mystery that you don't want me to know..." She frowned. "Is she blackmailing you?"

He barked a laugh. "Good one." Then his smile faded. "And not that far from the truth, but no, nothing like that." He took another step closer but she held up her hand, stopping him.

"No. Complete honesty. Complete candor. You have to tell me what this...this mystery is. Why is Penny so adamantly opposed to you seeing someone? Please remember that my husband was a bigamist and I've been through enough with men. I don't need another stinking secret to discover some dark day in the future."

He flinched at her tone. "You sure you want to hear this?"

"Why wouldn't I?"

"Because it involves my late wife."

She shrugged. "I'm not jealous of your memories, Abner. I know she was beautiful, and I know you loved her very much. I also know that she, sadly, is no longer here and you remember her with nothing but fondness. None of that upsets me. Should it?"

"I did love her," he said. "Enough that I, uh, made a promise that I would never be with another woman again."

She blinked at him.

"And Penny was in the room," he added.

Slowly, she dropped into a chair, an extra from the dressing area. "And she's going to hold you to a deathbed promise?"

"I made the promise...to both of them. To the whole family, in fact."

She took a moment to process that, and to imagine what it meant. "Why would you do that?"

"Because she asked and never in my life, not once since the day I met her, did I say no to Polly McPherson."

"Okay," she said, holding out her hands as a low grade of frustration crawled through her. "Why would she ask that of you? I mean, you were in your sixties, with plenty of life ahead. Why would she be so selfish?"

He grimaced and she regretted the word. Of course he'd be protective of his late wife. She shouldn't have used that word, but was there another one for a woman who would elicit a promise like that from a man?

"It doesn't matter," he said. "She did."

She searched his face and eyes and saw nothing but... okay, maybe not love, but certainly attraction and attention. And he was standing here, giving her a rose. What did he want?

"So now what?" she asked. "Secret trysts through our magic door? An affair, like I'm some kind of mistress that you don't want Penny to discover or Polly to see from her cloud in heaven?"

He just looked at her, silent.

What did it matter if they kept this secret? She didn't want to marry the man, and God knows she'd done dumber things in her life. She'd married Dutch and their relationship was Unorthodox with a capital U. What difference did it make?

Very slowly, she stood, only half aware that she was shaking her head.

It made every difference. She'd made enough mistakes giving men the benefit of the doubt in this life, and she didn't need to do that ever again.

"No, thank you, Abner. Not interested in that."

"I would never ask you to be a secret mistress, Cami. I care too much for you. That, in fact, is the problem."

She gave him a questioning look, waiting for an explanation.

"I've never met a woman like you," he said softly. "And that includes Polly. You intrigue me and enchant me and make me want to..." He took a very deep breath. "Break promises."

The words nearly folded her heart in half. "Well, will you?"

"It could get very, very complicated."

She lifted a shoulder. "Complicated doesn't scare me. Does it scare you?"

He reached out and took her hand in his. "Not being able to look into those bottomless brown eyes scares me. Not getting close to you and sharing what's left of my life with you scares me. Penny..."

"Also scares you," she finished with a laugh.

"Penny is going to do whatever she can to make you leave me."

She still didn't understand a woman being that small

about her sister's husband, but Camille gave her best shrug. "Bring it, Pen. And while you're at it, get a better dye job and attitude."

He brought her hand to his lips and kissed her knuckles. "I hope you know what you're in for."

"I hope *you* do."

Throwing his head back, he gave a hearty laugh.

"Hey, Uncle Buck? You back there?" His great-nephew Davis appeared in the doorway, scowling. "What's going on?"

Abner lifted their joined hands, a challenge in his eyes when he looked at Davis. "I'm just having a little morning chat with my girl, Cami, son."

Davis looked...sick.

He nodded and backed away, without even acknowledging Camille.

"Told ya," Abner muttered, tugging her closer. "Dinner tonight? On my boat? I'll cook."

She took a deep breath, once again smelling his cologne and manly fragrance. "Yes."

Chapter Nineteen

Eliza

S he didn't want to rush a call with her son, so Eliza almost didn't answer when she saw Dane's name on her phone. Miles was on his way over to pick her up for lunch and he said he had some news.

But...Dane.

She hadn't talked to him in nearly a week, and he didn't call that often. Mostly they texted. Dropping down on the sofa, she tapped the screen and put him on speaker, gazing out at the Gulf, but seeing her handsome, if somewhat nerdy, son in her head.

"To what do I owe this honor, my darling boy?" she asked. "And so early in California."

"Hey, Mom. Not that early. Eight-thirty. Even slacker engineers are at their desk by that time."

"And no one ever called you a slacker. How are you doing, Dane?"

"Eh, you know."

What she knew was that note in his voice, one she'd heard every time they'd talked in the months after Ben died. She and Livvie had mourned—deeply—but sometimes she worried that her husband's death had actually broken her son. He took it so hard.

"Having a blue day?" she guessed, not sure how much he wanted to share. But he did call, so he obviously wanted to lean on her shoulder.

Last night, that shoulder had been soaked in Livvie's tears. Today, it would be Dane's, figuratively. If that old adage that a mother is only as happy as her kids was true? Then poor Eliza was not destined for happiness today.

"Having a blue quarter," he replied. "And it's only January. By the fiscal year-end, I'll be purple."

She wasn't sure when the fiscal year ended for his artificial intelligence engineering firm, but she got the idea. "Is the piano helping?'"

She'd been happy to give him the baby grand from their family home in Los Angeles, knowing that a hobbyist composer like Dane would truly get the most use out of it. Plus, she loved the idea of keeping the beautiful instrument in the family.

"The piano...is killing me."

"Dane!" She frowned, confused. "You always get such pleasure from playing. Like I do from singing." And she couldn't do that for months after Ben died, she recalled. "Are you having trouble composing? Hitting a block?"

"I'm having trouble living, Mom. Hitting a block every time I walk into this stupid, soulless, painfully corporate place and sit in a meeting with pompous geniuses who think they are going to change the world."

She drew back, her eyes wide. "Maybe it's time you, uh, looked around for a company with more soul and less...pompous geniuses."

"In Silicon Valley? That's all there is."

She wasn't sure how to answer, not sure if this was a serious career glitch—which would be tough for a job that paid like his—or remnants of grief. Work issues usually sent him to Ben for a chat, and she suddenly felt woefully inadequate for the job.

"So, what's the problem with the piano?" Although even as she asked the question, she suspected the problem was with Dane, not the instrument.

"All I want to do is write and play," he said. "Every minute that I'm doing something else is, like, physically painful."

"Wow. That's a passion. I mean, you've always loved music but..."

"But I had to work. I had to achieve. I had to excel. I had to use my left brain because, well, I had it."

"You sure do," she said on a laugh, remembering what a remarkably gifted student he'd been.

"But I also have a right brain, Mom. I need to use that. I love to use that. It's my spirit. But take it from a guy who programs robots on one thing: this world is headed straight in the direction of humans—or some reasonable facsimile—that don't have or need a right brain."

She didn't quite get that, but she knew he worked on very advanced technology and artificial intelligence. Too much time on that subject could actually be a little depressing, she imagined.

"What are you saying, Dane?"

"I want to pursue music."

She pulled the phone away, not sure she'd heard that right. "Like, as your job? For a living?"

"Yes. I want to throw myself into music and compose and produce an album. And then sell it. And while I'm doing that, I want to sell some songs. I've been writing a lot lately, and some of it is really good."

"I'm sure it is." He was extremely talented and had written some beautiful ballads and even orchestral music. "But...can you do that? Don't you need a band? A manager? A...plan?"

"Music isn't what it used to be, Mom. Everything is done electronically and virtually now. I can compose a symphony with software and play nothing but keyboard. In fact, I have."

"Wow! That's amazing. But..." Gosh, she hated to be a killjoy mother, but twenty-seven-year-olds shouldn't walk away from jobs like his. Not only did he make an extraordinary salary with fat bonuses, he'd worked so hard to get there. He'd earned an impressive degree from Caltech and a string of jaw-dropping internships. "Can't music be a hobby? Something you do at night?"

"This place is killing me!"

"Maybe another company?"

"They're all the same, Mom. They're all hell."

She cringed, unused to him being that passionate about anything. Dane was rock solid and steady, the quintessential engineer who carefully examined all aspects of a problem before calmly solving it. What had happened?

"Dad would totally support this, you know."

Oh. *That* happened.

"Dad...had a keen business mind," she said, not sure if that's what he wanted to hear.

"His business was the arts," he said sharply. "Making movies, remember?"

"And so was mine," she reminded him. "Managing actors. But at the core of what Dad and I did—especially Dad—was run a business. And we know that it's not always fun. Your father frequently said, 'That's why they call it work.'"

"He also said, 'No guts, no glory.'"

"Yes, he did," she agreed. "So, did you call because you need me to give you permission to quit your amazing job and pursue music? Because you're a grown man, Dane, and you don't need my approval."

"No, but I need your support and enthusiasm."

She sighed, torn. "Of course I'm going to support anything you want to do and I never want to think of you being unhappy at your job. But—"

She heard a tap on the sliding glass door and turned to see Miles waiting for her. Beckoning him in, she mouthed, "One second" and he nodded, coming to sit in the living room.

Now, she was truly torn because this wasn't a conversation to rush, but she didn't want to make Miles wait.

"But what, Mom?" Dane pressed. "I should go through the rest of my life miserable?"

"Dane, are you really that unhappy?"

He didn't answer and she held Miles's gaze, but he just nodded and gestured toward the outdoor deck. "I'll wait," he whispered, giving her hand a squeeze.

She smiled at him, a wave of affection rolling over her for his patience and class.

"Yes," her son said. "I'm that unhappy."

"Are you sure this isn't grief?"

"It's part grief. I mean, my dad died. I feel...mortal, you know? Like life is short. He died in his fifties, Mom. What if I—"

"Stop," she said, almost unable to have the conversation. In fact, she *was* unable to have one this deep right now. "Honey, can I call you tonight? Someone's waiting for me and—"

"Is it that Miles guy?"

She inched back in surprise. "You've been talking to Livvie."

"Yeah. She told me you have a boyfriend."

She couldn't resist looking over her shoulder, grateful he'd stepped outside and couldn't hear her half of this conversation. "I do not have a—"

"I hope not, because it's really too soon."

"I know," she said, emphasizing the words. "But it's not too soon for me to have friends, Dane."

"How serious is it?"

"Serious enough that he's outside in the blazing sun waiting for me because I told him I'd be ready to go ten minutes ago."

"Livvie said it's really serious."

Exasperation made her suck in a deep breath. "Then maybe you should ask these questions of Livvie. If you want my side, I'm happy to tell you that it's not serious, Dane. We're friends and we like each other and I'm painfully—and I mean *painfully*—aware of how long, or short, it's been since Dad died. I think about him every hour. Every...minute, even."

He answered with a long, dead silence. Then, she heard him try to speak, but a sob got the better of him.

"Oh, honey. Dane. Don't."

"I miss him, Mom. There will never be another man like Dad. And he'd want me to follow my dreams, I just know he would."

She just closed her eyes, fighting the old grief that mixed with pain because her children hurt. Sometimes she hurt more for their loss than for her own. She hadn't felt it for so long, but here it was, familiar and sharp.

"He was a great man," she managed.

"So, I guess I won't go into HR and give my notice," he said with a dry laugh. "Mom thinks it's a bad idea."

She smiled. "I think you should consider every angle and solve the problem, because that's what you do."

"Or I could call Liv."

"Or that." She smiled. "She's big on starting over. And I did it, so..."

"So why not me?" he asked. "Why should only the female Whitneys get a second chance?"

She thought about that, suddenly seeing his dilemma in a different light. "I don't know, Dane. Maybe you should."

"It's okay, Mom. Go out on your date now. Have fun, but not too much."

She laughed softly. "Thanks, honey. I love you so much."

"Love you, too."

She sat for a moment, replaying the conversation in her mind before she got up and gave Miles the proper hello hug that he deserved. She did her best to leave Dane's problems behind and simply enjoy her time with Miles. That wasn't ever difficult to do.

THEY WERE ALMOST DONE with lunch at Doc Fords when Miles leaned forward and said, "What I'm about to tell you, Eliza, is confidential."

She lowered her glass of iced tea and inched forward. "Oh, I'm intrigued. Is it Buck Underwood gossip?"

"It's not gossip. It's some serious factual info that is going to blow your socks off."

"Really?" Her brows shot up. "Please tell me there are no bodies in his basement, because Camille told Claire they're back on."

"They are? What does that mean?" Miles asked.

"Well, I guess they're going to continue seeing each other, despite his family's disapproval, which makes sense."

"So when they decided this, did he share anything personal with Camille?" he asked.

"Just that he'd made a deathbed promise to his late wife to never...get involved or date or marry—I don't know the details—and that her sister, Penny, was in the room. I guess she wants to hold him to that, but honestly, he doesn't owe anyone anything."

"You can say that again," Miles muttered.

She frowned, not sure what he meant.

"He doesn't owe anyone anything, and his family wants to keep it that way."

"Why?"

"Oh, they have their reasons." He swallowed and inched closer to whisper, "About a hundred million of them."

"A hundred million..." She gasped and he held up a hand to keep her voice at that intimate whisper. "*Dollars?*" she managed, breathing the word in disbelief.

He nodded very slowly. "And apparently *that's* how Abner got the nickname Buck. He evidently knew how to make one. Many of them, in fact."

"He's a multimillionaire? How?"

"Real estate. That strip center where his bait store is, and Sanibel Sisters? He sold it and a lot of others like it all over these islands and all of Florida. He's a quiet mogul, just loping around in his jeans—"

"And living on a boat!" she added in a hushed whisper. "I actually thought he might be too poor for Camille's Chanel and champagne tastes."

"Classic example of one of those people who you never know is loaded. Lives under the radar, not one ounce of ostentatious in the guy. And he doesn't *want* anyone to know. The only thing he spends money on is charity and his church."

She dropped back against the leather banquette of the booth and stared at Miles, processing this news. "And they think that if he gets serious with Camille, she'll marry him and inherit it all."

"Bingo. They have quietly ruined any chance the man has ever had at finding love again since Polly died ten years ago."

"How have they ruined it?"

"Just made life miserable for any woman he dated, although I don't think there've been many. There was a lady he liked at church, but they wrecked that by spreading rumors that she'd been a little too cozy with a guy in the choir."

"No!"

"They're ruthless. And there was a snowbird who kept a boat near his in the marina."

"What did they do to her?"

"Penny made sure that boat couldn't pass city inspections and had to move to another marina. Then the poor lady quietly disappeared, but not before she was accused of shoplifting at Bailey's."

"How did you get all these juicy details, Miles? This isn't the kind of stuff you get off the internet."

"I called in some favors," he said, always so vague about his investigative techniques. "Enough to know that Penny and Frank are deeply disliked, and feared. There are others on this island and Captiva who'd very much like to unlock the stranglehold those two, and their family, have on local politics and governing. But...they have the money."

"*Buck* has the money."

"He gives them plenty, because he doesn't have

family of his own, and he and Polly never had a child. Evidently, he raised himself from the time he was fourteen, like a regular little Huck Finn."

"Buck Finn," she joked. "A very, very rich Huck Finn."

Miles chuckled at that.

"A hundred million?" She let out a whistle. "Camille is going to—"

"No." He reached over and put a hand on hers. "You can't tell her. She cannot know."

"Why not?"

"That was the stipulation from my connection. No one can know."

"But you told me," Eliza said.

"You're...different. First of all, you made the specific request for information."

"So I could tell Camille," she clarified.

"You cannot. If he tells her, fine, then it's out of our hands. But this is not commonly known information. He has his money so spread out that no one at any bank or financial institution knows."

"What was the second of all?" At his confused look, she added, "You said, 'First of all, you made the specific request.' Was there a second of all?"

He studied her for a long time, holding her gaze, his lips lifting in that half-smile that sent the old butterflies aflutterin'.

"Second of all," he said softly, reaching over to take her hand in his. He made her wait for a few heartbeats, rubbing the pad of his thumb over her knuckles. "I can't keep a secret from you. I trust you completely. I don't even have to think about it."

The compliment warmed her along with his touch. "Thank you." Then she made a face. "But that means I really can't tell Camille. Or Claire. Or Teddy. Or Olivia." Her eyes flashed. "Who can I talk to about it?" She was only half teasing.

"Me. You can talk to me about anything."

She sighed. "That's a lot of seriously important information I need to share."

"You can help her, guide her, advise her, but you can't tell her she's dating the richest guy on Sanibel Island."

"Dang," she muttered. "And I'm dating the most resourceful."

He laughed. "Oh, we're dating, huh?"

"What would you call it?"

"Really nice," he answered without missing a beat.

She smiled at him, lost in his green eyes. "You know, that's exactly what I told my son on the phone."

As he gave his credit card to the server, he lifted an interested brow. "And how did that go?"

She lifted a shoulder. "Like you might guess. He's still mourning his father—I mean, we all are. But sometimes I think he's taken Ben's death the hardest. He's actually talking about walking away from his incredible job in AI engineering to...be a musician." She wrinkled her nose. "I see starvation in his future."

Miles considered that, not laughing at the joke. "You

know, Eliza, when a man's father dies, he's faced with his own mortality."

"That's exactly what he said."

He nodded. "I remember the feeling all too well when I lost my dad. There's a feeling of...'Is that all there is?' It can be extremely debilitating. He's second-guessing everything, even his job."

"That makes sense," she said. "But did you quit your job and follow your dream when your father died?"

"Yes."

She blinked at him. "That was when you left the Navy and JAG?"

"Exactly. And it was considered a really dumb move by a lot of my peers," he added.

"I thought you saw the potential in the PI business and you'd honed your skills."

He smiled. "Just as your son—a gifted musician, if I recall correctly—has honed his."

"But being a PI isn't being a...piano player." Even as she said those words, Eliza knew that Dane was so much more than that. He was a composer, an artist, and a true talent.

"All I'm saying is, don't fight him too hard," Miles said. "And maybe take the time to see life from his perspective. Losing a father rocks a man's world in a way that's hard to describe. If his way of coping is leaving engineering to pour his feelings into music, then..."

She nodded a few times, getting all that. But still...

"I hate to be the voice of practicality, Miles, but Dane makes a lot of money. He has stock options, too, and...

and..." Her voice trailed off at the look in his eyes, like she was trying to fight the tide. She laughed softly. "I guess I should tell him you like the idea."

"Please do. Then maybe he'll forgive me for falling for his mother."

"Maybe," she teased. "I guess it depends on how hard you fall."

He lifted her hand and gave it a kiss. "Very hard. Very far. Very fast. Can't wait until you join me."

She didn't have to answer. She was halfway there.

Chapter Twenty

Olivia

Nothing. Still nothing. Not a call, text, email, or smoke signal from Deeley and it had been...how many days? Too darn many. Enough that he should be settled at his sister's and...missing her.

Olivia locked the register and considered sitting in the back office for an hour running a P&L, to get solace from a good spreadsheet and the thrill of crossing something off her to-do list.

Except that list was woefully short.

Workwise, she had just about everything covered, from accounts receivable to inventory management. Her marketing strategy was set and rolling out through her ever-growing customer email list and some social media ads. They were making money at a decent clip, had paid the monthly mortgage ahead of time, and were on excellent terms with every vendor.

On the home front, all her furniture had arrived from Seattle, her house was decorated, cleaned, and looked like a showplace. She'd even had Noah pick up the crib and take it to Jadyn's daycare center.

She had no outstanding debt, nothing she needed to

buy, a full fridge and pantry, and she'd already worked out that morning, so she didn't need to hit the gym. Her teeth were cleaned, her hair freshly trimmed, her emails read, saved, or deleted, and her car was serviced and full of gas.

Olivia Whitney was living in a state of complete and total control over every aspect of her life and she'd never been more...

"Miserable," she muttered as she took the cash drawer to the safe in the back.

What she needed was a good mashed banana and peanut butter mess to clean up. Or maybe that sickening feeling when she'd taken the last Pull-Up from the package and didn't have a backup. How about a decent traffic jam when she was late, a meeting she couldn't reschedule, a missed workout, a burned dinner, a screaming toddler in the next room, and a man in her arms who wanted her to forget it all and just kiss him.

She missed the chaos of her life with Deeley and Bash. She missed it so much there were tears in her eyes as she locked up the cash drawer. The last thing she wanted to do in the entire world was go home to that picture-perfect life and open up her to-do list to find it...finished.

So, when she got in the car, it was only a little surprising that she gave up control and let the wind and wheel take her where she wanted to go...Shellseeker Beach.

This late on a weekday, the beach would be nearly

empty. And that was what she needed—some solitude at the beach. Maybe a stroll down to Deeley's—Noah's—cabana so she could really wallow in self-pity and loneliness.

She parked in the lot and walked toward the beach. Something in the sky over the sand caught her eye. Something red fluttering up and down and all around. Was that a kite?

Oh, Bash would have loved a kite, she thought with a punch to the gut. Why hadn't she ever gotten him a kite? What were they thinking?

Guilt and regret felt like it could swallow her whole, slowing her step and forcing her to take a deep, deep breath.

Stop it, Livvie!

She listened to the harsh whisper in her head, her own voice making the demand. But she had to listen. She had to snap out of this. But how?

Pausing at the rise in the garden that looked out over the beach, she momentarily forgot her blues as she scanned the people gathered on the sand and in front of the tea hut and garden.

On the beach, Harper ran back and forth, her falsetto screams barely audible as she worked to keep her kite in the air. Noah jogged beside her, giving instructions like the loving father she sensed he would most certainly be to that child.

Katie and her sister, Jadyn, watched from nearby, lounging on canvas chairs and sipping drinks. They looked like a travel ad promoting sisters at the beach, chatting with their heads close, occasional bursts of laughter between them.

Teddy stood at one of her garden tables, carefully cutting the stems of herbs and flowers that she must have just picked, readying her collection for tea brewing that Noah would sell the next day.

Not far from her, Camille lounged on a chaise, a book in her hand, but she seemed to be looking over it, gazing out to the water, deep in thought. Roz and George sat with Asia at a round table, a baby carrier with the shade cover between them. Roz had a collection of shells in front of her and a canvas, giving Asia a lesson on how to make shell art, whether the young woman wanted it or not. Olivia suspected she did not.

At the tea hut, three people sat like customers at a bar and Olivia recognized Claire and DJ and the still unfamiliar curly dark hair of DJ's daughter, Sophia. They'd been scarce since she arrived, so this was a rare treat.

And there was Mom, sharing a table with Miles, playing chess.

Wait...*what*?

Never once in her whole life had Olivia seen her mother play chess. Checkers when they were kids, sure, and she played a mean game of poker. But chess? When did she learn that?

But there she was, studying the board intently, sipping a glass of wine and talking to the man who just might be Olivia's stepfather someday. Imagine that.

Taking one step closer, the phone in the pocket of her sundress vibrated, making her gasp softly. Was it Deeley?

Before she grabbed the phone like a drowning woman being thrown a life preserver, Teddy looked up and called a greeting, and all those other faces turned and responded with the smiles and expressions that welcomed her.

This was her life now—these people—not Deeley.

She knew what she should do—ignore the call. If Deeley were down there on that beach, she wouldn't even give answering a phone call a second thought. Whoever wanted her would leave a message.

But what if it *was* him calling? Finally, after all these hours and days?

Well, so what? This beach was filled with the people who really did love her, were obviously thrilled to see her, and ready to cheer her up because they all knew—every last one of them—that her heart had been shattered.

Who mattered more? The man who left her who *might* be calling...or the people who were right here?

"Livvie!" Her mom stood and beckoned her down. "Come and join our impromptu party."

The phone hummed again and Olivia, queen of control, ignored it. And, for some reason, that made her really proud of herself.

*

"I DON'T KNOW what's more stunning," Olivia said as she sipped some wine from a plastic cup and settled in at the table with Roz and Asia. She'd positioned herself so she could keep an eye on the chess game and the kite flying but still admire baby Zane. "That we've got booze at the tea hut or my mother is playing chess."

"And winning," Miles muttered, making her mother laugh.

"He's just teaching me," Mom said. "I've always wanted to learn. Oh..." She slid a chess piece and picked up one of his. "Look at that. I got your...castle thing."

Miles rolled his eyes. "I've created a monster."

"The wine is illegal," Roz told her. "If one member of the city council or a friend of the mayor's cruises by and thinks we're selling it—"

"We're not," Teddy called from her cutting table.

"—then we're doomed," Roz finished.

"What could they do?" Olivia asked. "Other than slap a fine on the place, obviously."

Camille slammed her book closed. "Well, I for one am not scared of the mayor or his wife. Abner says they're just full of hot air and imagined power. Drink the wine, I say, legal or not."

Her mother and Miles exchanged a look that was... kind of meaningful. But before Olivia could give it much thought, Zane shuddered with a sweet baby sigh in his sleep, and Asia instantly stood to scoop him up.

"Never wake a sleeping baby, Asia," Roz insisted, a frown furrowing her dark brows. "Even if he opens his eyes, he might go right back to sleep."

"And the sky might fall," Asia shot back as she unlatched the safety belt in the little carrier. "My baby, my rules. I need to love him, awake or asleep."

Roz rolled her big brown eyes and opened her mouth

to argue, but her husband put a hand on her arm. "Rosalind Turner, we discussed this," George said.

And that shut her up and made more than a few of them smile.

"How are you doing, Livvie?" Asia asked softly as she cradled her son, but looked at Olivia. "Been a few days, huh?"

She resisted the urge to announce days, hours, and minutes since the bottom fell out of her world.

Instead, she shrugged. "I'm fine." She leaned forward when Zane's eyes opened and focused on her. "Not as fine as this little man," she said in baby talk.

"Why don't you hold him?" Asia suggested. "I know you love that."

"I do." Olivia reached out her arms to the baby. "Gosh, I miss our playdates at the park, Asia. I don't get to see this guy as much." She gave a soft moan of happiness when Asia delivered him right to her arms, always surprised at how light the baby was after carting Bash around. "I probably am doing this wrong, eh, Grammy?"

"Not at all," Roz assured her, standing up. "You're a natural. So good I'm going to get more wine."

"And I'm getting tea." George rose, too, and put his arm around his wife. "So proud of you, learning to let go of control, Roz."

"Don't get used to it," she quipped as they stepped away and left Asia and Olivia at the table, smiling after them.

"She is chilling out a bit," Olivia noted. "I like that you two are laughing about your differences now."

"She has her moments, but most of the time, she tries to call all the shots." Asia leaned over and smiled at him. "And we all know who's really calling the shots, right, Zee? My sweet angel baby."

An unwanted wave of envy rolled up and Olivia gave the baby the lightest squeeze. She tried to respond to that, but her throat felt tight and the last thing she wanted to do was burst into tears.

"Hello there, my precious," Olivia cooed instead, tapping his button nose with her finger, his delicious brown skin so soft and irresistible. "You are just what the doctor ordered for my heart."

Asia beamed at them. "Yep, that's little Zee's super-power, bringing peace and joy. And spitup."

Olivia chuckled and stroked his cheek and the curly cap of black hair that would no doubt be as wild and beautiful as his mother's. She didn't speak, but just drank him in, loving the feel of him in her arms and that sweet baby smell.

"Have you heard from him?" Asia whispered.

Olivia shook her head, thinking of the phone in her pocket...that hadn't vibrated again.

"It's okay, Liv," she said, putting a hand on Olivia's arm. "You'll recover. I know this from experience."

She searched Asia's face, so tempted to ask her what had happened in her past, but there were too many people around. Instead, she nodded, and accepted the comfort.

"You can come and hold him anytime," her friend

replied. "And if you want one of your own, Livvie, you know you don't need a man."

She blinked and cursed the sting in her eyes.

"I know, I know," Asia whispered. "Wanting isn't needing, and you wanted the man you had."

"I did, but—"

"I need air!" Sophia announced, marching away from the tea hut to the boardwalk and onto the beach, somehow getting every eye to watch her, but no one to follow.

After a minute, Claire and DJ came over.

"I'll go talk to her," DJ said as he pulled a chair out for Claire.

As he took off after his daughter, Olivia leaned in. "So, how's it going? Or shouldn't I ask?"

"It's life with Sophia," Claire answered. "Every moment more exciting than the last."

"She's a bit of a drama queen," Asia noted. "Not to, uh, state the obvious or anything."

"She can be over the top," Claire agreed. "But she's really confused now. She needs to finish school and doesn't want to, at least not in California. DJ isn't sure what the right thing to do really is, because it might be too late for her to graduate from a high school here, since the requirements are different. He offered to go back with her, but she..." She gestured toward the two figures walking past them on the sand. "Didn't love that idea."

"Could she—"

"Oh! Oh!" The exclamation from Olivia's mother cut into Asia's question, making everyone turn.

"Checkmate?" Olivia guessed.

But her mother was looking at her phone. "It's Mia from *The Last Resort!*" she announced, getting a noisy reaction from everyone. "This is the call, I think. To tell us if we made the next cut for Hidden Gems of Florida."

She stood, abandoning the chess board and the noise of their little group. "Wish me luck!" She hustled toward Teddy and put an arm around her, ushering her away to a quiet section of the garden and leaving them all exchanging looks of anticipation.

They kept up some small talk and cooed over the baby and laughed at how many times Noah had to pick up the fallen kite, but mostly everyone kept one eye on the two women at the other end of the garden, talking into a cell phone on speaker.

Noah and all the girls came up from the beach and they filled them in on the call. After a bit, everyone gave up talking and just watched Eliza and Teddy. There was no way to hear them or the person on the speaker phone from this far away, but they couldn't help but make a few guesses based on body language.

"Long conversation," George mused.

"And no celebratory fists in the air," Roz added.

Olivia chewed on her lip and watched how her mother leaned in and listened, then reached over to put a hand on Teddy's shoulder while she talked.

"There's a complication," she guessed. "My mother is trying to compromise. That's her, 'Okay, this didn't go as planned but let's figure it out' position."

Miles threw a look over his shoulder. "You're right, Liv. If she were happy, Eliza would be tapdancing."

Olivia laughed, warmed by how well he knew her mother already.

"And Teddy would surely be waving her hands up to thank the universe," George added.

"Maybe they didn't get it," Camille said, sounding a little darker than the rest of them. "Maybe that witch Penny put a curse on the whole thing." When they all turned and looked at her, she threw both hands in the air. "What? I'm just saying what you're all thinking."

Finally, the call was over and Mom and Teddy talked for a minute, then came back arm-in-arm as they were peppered with ten different variations of, "What happened?"

Teddy finally subdued them all. "It's down to three properties in southwest Florida," she announced.

"And we're one of them?" Claire asked.

"Yes," her mother and Teddy said together, eliciting a cheer. "Along with Tarpon Villas—"

"Save me from ghosts," George muttered, then shook his head with indignation. "I have an *actual* message in a bottle written by Teddy Roosevelt, they have some bogus pirate story and no proof it ever happened."

"Who else?" a few of them asked in unison.

"Sunset Palms Inn on Captiva," Teddy said, looking at Roz as if she'd truly understand why that mattered.

And Roz reacted with a heartfelt grunt. "Oof. That place is...whoa, geez, yeah."

"What?" Claire demanded with a laugh. "What about it?"

"It's the real competition, hands down," Roz said. "Tarpon Villas is on par with us, plus the ghosts, but Sunset Palms is swanky and top-notch, but super low-key with an amazing staff. And gourmet food. And an award-winning spa. And parasailing—"

"Stop," Olivia whispered as she watched her mother's face fall with each amenity.

"So what happens next?" Miles asked as he reached for Mom's hand and guided her to the seat next to him, just as in tune with her emotions as Olivia was. "How can we help?"

"There's a committee that will visit each location once more for a half-day, and then they vote on the properties," her mother said. "It sounds like Mia has the final say but she's deciding based on their collective input. She loves Shellseeker Cottages and has great memories of her time here, but between the lines I could hear that she thinks we might not be quite as special as the others."

That was greeted with a chorus of incredulity.

"We are special, of course," Teddy said, calming them. "But they're looking for a...what did she call it, Eliza?"

"A wow factor," she replied. "Something that makes the property not just special but...well, she called it a place where people emotionally connect in addition to having fun."

"Connect with each other or the place?" Claire asked, looking a little confused.

"Both," Mom said on a sigh. "She was a little vague on...how to wow."

"You'll wow them," Noah said confidently. "Our cottages are so nice."

Next to him, Katie grimaced. "They are, but you haven't seen Sunset Palms' rooms. They had an open house once and I went out of curiosity. Marble floors, four-poster antique beds, and bathrooms that could make you cry."

"Honestly, those things are like the ghosts to me," Olivia said. "Who comes to a beach to walk on marble and cry over the bathroom?"

"Lots of people," Jadyn said. "That's exactly where my mother would stay if she visited here."

For a moment, they were all quiet, thinking, commiserating, and just being the group of like-minded souls Olivia loved so much. And with that thought, another tidal wave of emotion rolled over her, but this time it felt different.

This wasn't angst or loneliness or self-pity. This time it felt like a problem to be solved, and deep inside, somewhere, she sensed she had the answer. She just hadn't found it yet.

"What do we have to offer to compete with that?" Teddy sort of groaned the question. "Gardens and tea?"

"Pop-up pizza," Noah suggested, refreshingly optimistic. "Best in the state."

"And the gazebo!" Katie added. "The only 'honesty house' built on sacred Calusa ground."

"And unparalleled shellseeking," Jadyn chimed in.

"We're called Shellseeker Beach." Harper's little voice, and her oh-so-serious tone, broke the tension, making them laugh.

"I love the input," Teddy said, looking from one to the other with genuine affection in her eyes. "But I'm afraid those quirks of our homey resort aren't going to win us the Hidden Gem status. We need something spectacular and memorable."

As they thought and threw out some ideas, Olivia leaned back, still holding the warm, sleeping baby. Silently, she let her gaze move from person to person, inhaling the energy and concern that vibrated through the group, the love and support and sense of family so strong she thought a stranger could sense it just walking by.

"We just don't have anything—"

"Oh, yes we do." Olivia sat straight up as the answer hit her with a jolt, the move sudden enough to make Zane whimper. "And he agrees."

Smiling, Asia automatically took the baby from Olivia's arms, which freed her to stand and make her point. And by the way all these people were looking at her, it better be good.

"We have what *everyone* goes on vacation to find," she said.

"Sun, sand, and surf?" Miles guessed.

"Rest and relaxation?" Noah chimed in.

"Local color and morning tides that leave a million shells?" Claire added.

But the rest were quiet, watching and waiting for Olivia to continue.

"We have the essence of what makes a family," she said. "And it's right here on this sand, in those villas, along that boardwalk, in that tea hut, and all through the shell shop."

A few of them look confused, but her mother's eyes widened as if she was following Olivia's thoughts exactly.

"When a family goes on vacation, what are they trying to find?" Olivia asked them. "A break from work and the mundane stuff of life? Of course. An adventure like parasailing or a run-in with Casper? Maybe."

That drew soft laughter.

"They want that moment, that rush of dopamine when everyone is connected and cares. They want inside jokes and sandcastles made by two siblings who aren't fighting. They want game night on the deck and new memories every morning. They want the best of each other. A family, united and supportive and appreciative and loving and...and..." Son of a gun, the tears started again.

And so did Teddy's. "Oh, Livvie! What you just described is what guests always tell me is why they come back again and again, and bring their grandchildren when their own kids are adults."

"That's the *real* history of Shellseeker," Claire said. "The families who come here and change."

"Finding family really is what Shellseeker Beach is all about," Noah added excitedly. "It's exactly what happened to me when I got here. And..." He turned and gazed at DJ and Sophia, who were slowly making their way back to the group, still deep in conversation. "I think it's happening to Sophia. She honestly doesn't want to leave."

"Same here!" Jadyn interjected, slipping her arm around Katie. "I got here hoping to take you away, and ended up staying for good. Because...family." She pointed to Olivia. "I think you're on to something, Liv."

"Oh, yes, you are," Mom said, beaming at her. "This was the reason I wanted you in on our pitch from the beginning. This was the marketing magic I knew you would be able to create."

"It's not marketing, Mom," Olivia said quietly. "It's the truth. I didn't even want to come to *Shellshocker* Beach, remember?"

While they all laughed at the nickname, Mom and Olivia held each other's gazes, mentally sharing the memory of how neither one of them had high hopes for the place. And now they lived here and loved it.

"But how do we create that?" Teddy asked. "It happens organically and over time, not in a week."

"Share the stories," Olivia said. "I suggest we carve out opportunities with this visiting council for each one of us to tell them how this happened to us. Maybe find a long-term guest who's been coming back for years to talk to them and tell them what this place has meant to their family?"

Mom looked immediately at Teddy, who responded with a nod, so whoever they had in mind, they agreed.

"I'll share my story," Camille said. "And I don't really

care if it has some dirt and scandal. That's what got me here."

"And I'll share mine," Jadyn said, squeezing her sister.

"I have a good one myself." Eliza smiled at Teddy. "I literally came for one night and still haven't left."

Noah put a hand on Claire's shoulder. "My mother and I sure could tell a great story about what Shellseeker did for us."

Claire looked up at him, her own eyes filled with tears. "I would be proud to share that, Noah."

Just then, DJ and Sophia joined them, looking far calmer than they had when Sophia had marched off.

"Well, since I have you all gathered," DJ said. "Let me announce that my daughter has won. She's finishing her last semester of high school next fall, but it means she'll have to take classes at the local high school this spring and at least one class this summer in order to graduate."

Instantly, as the others reacted to the news, Claire rose and came around the table, reaching her arms out to Sophia. "I'm so happy to hear this," she said, giving and getting a genuine hug.

Noah hugged her, too, which was touching.

As everyone chatted, laughed, and slipped back into the very family unit she'd been describing, Olivia quietly pushed up and walked toward the boardwalk, drawn to the beach. Still vibrating with emotions she didn't understand, she inhaled the salty air, trying to clear her head.

Her gaze moved left, over the sand, landing on the

thatch-roofed cabana that had become such a familiar stomping ground to her.

Deeley.

He'd have the best story of all, saved by Teddy in the darkest days, then building a life right on this beach. Then he'd gone and saved another family, passing on the love.

No longer able to resist the temptation, she slipped her hand in her pocket and pulled out the phone, squeezing her eyes shut before she looked at the screen to see who'd called earlier.

Please be him. Please be him. Please be—

Air whooshed out of her lungs at the screen bearing the words *Dane-not-Dave* that she loved to call her brother.

Okay, not Deeley. Not him. Not him at all. Without giving it a second's thought, she tapped the button to call Dane back, remembering that her mother said he'd been struggling.

"Hey, Liv."

"Sorry I missed your call," she said, pressing the phone to her ear and pushing away the tendril of disappointment she felt at not hearing the wrong male voice. "Everything okay in your life, dimwit?" she teased, as she always did with this uber-serious genius who'd gone from pesky little bro to impressive and successful tech guru.

"Couldn't be better."

"Really? I'm so happy to hear that. Mom told me that last time she talked to you—"

"I quit my job."

She inched back and blinked in shock. "What?"

"Handed in my resignation. I am no longer an artificial-intelligence engineer, Liv. I'm...a musician."

"Excuse me? Do you even *look* at your paycheck, you idiot?"

"Says the woman who waltzed away from corporate to go live on an island."

"But, Dane, I wasn't in your league. And I started a business, not..."

"Decided to become a starving artist," he said with a dry laugh. "Yeah, yeah. Let me tell you something, Liv. I have never felt better. Never, not once. Dad would be so proud of me. You know he'd say—"

"No guts, no glory," she finished for him.

"Exactly!" He laughed, sounding so much like that very man they were quoting.

"Yeah, but he was referring to diving into the deep end of our pool, not walking away from a job like yours."

"I *am* diving into the deep end, Liv. Metaphorically, anyway," he added with another hearty laugh.

He sounded so happy, she didn't know what to say. Happy and whole and, good heavens, she couldn't remember the last time she'd heard Dane laugh like that. Maybe before Dad died, before he got sick. Her younger brother was a solemn man and losing his father only intensified that. Dane needed to laugh like people needed to breathe.

And as that realization hit her, she leaned against the railing of the boardwalk and decided not to fight him. He needed her support, and she was going to give it whole-heartedly.

"So, what's your next move, maestro?" she asked.

"I have no idea. My lease is up next month and I don't want to deplete my savings by paying astronomical Silicon Valley prices."

As he talked, she turned to the group she'd just left and stared at them, bits and pieces of her little speech still echoing in her head.

"I'll probably look for a smaller place in—"

"Sanibel Island," she interjected.

"What? Nah, that's your thing, Liv."

She could hear the echo of her own words. *They want inside jokes and sandcastles made by two siblings who aren't fighting. They want game night on the deck and new memories every morning. They want the best of each other. A family, united and supportive and appreciative and loving and...and...*

"Come on, now, Dave," she teased, using his hated name to butter him up with one of those inside jokes. "Listen to me. I have a two-bedroom house that's very empty with just me." Even as she made the offer, she could feel her heart filling with hope. "Please."

"What about the piano?"

Yes! He was considering it! "Put it in storage, or ship it here and I'll make room for it. Pack up as little as possible, sell the rest, and come to where..." She let out a sigh. "Come to where your family is. Nothing could make me happier, Dane."

She squeezed the wooden railing, digging her nails in, waiting and wishing to hear one word.

"Okay," he said, making her want to jump for joy. "I think I will."

When they finished the conversation, she turned and ran over the sand, feeling light and happy for the first time in what felt like so long.

"Guess what, everyone?" she called, holding up the phone. "That was my brother, Dane. We're about to have one more story for *The Last Resort!*"

Chapter Twenty-one

Claire

"You nervous?" DJ came up behind Claire at her bathroom vanity and threaded strong and callused fingers into the hair she was about to brush.

"Should I be?"

"Day of reckoning," he said, coming around to lean on the counter and look down at her. "You're even putting on some makeup for the video call with your boss."

"A lot less than I used to wear when I went into the New York offices of Wills, Sears and Killian."

"You're beautiful without it." He lifted her chin, tipping it from one side to the other, examining her face like she was a work of art up for auction. Then he smiled like he wanted to make a bid. "And beautiful with it."

"Thank you. What are you and the kids going to do while I'm on the call?"

He crossed his arms and leaned against the counter again, looking past her. "Me and the kids. That sounds..."

She waited for him to finish. Nice? Homey? Familiar?

"Permanent," he finished.

Her heart dropped a little. "Not a place you like to be, is it?"

He waved off the comment and narrowed his eyes at her. "Are you going to join the Quitter Club today, Claire?"

"The Quitter Club? That doesn't sound like something I want on my resume."

"Exactly. But just think about it. I quit to pursue my passion, and Sophia is quitting high school."

"She's going to get her diploma, though it'll take some time," Claire said, happy that Rachel agreed to let her daughter move to Shellseeker Beach. Maybe a little too easily, but they were working things out. Rachel had even agreed to sell Sophia's car so she could buy one to have on Sanibel.

"She's doing so well." He glanced out the window toward the pool, where they could hear Noah and Sophia laughing about something. "So? Quitter Club?" he urged.

"I don't know what I'm going to do, but, you know, there does seem to be something in the air. Livvie left her job to move here, and now her brother is doing the same thing. Poor Eliza is a little out of sorts, but trying to understand it. I'm sure you certainly do."

He regarded her through those thick lashes, his intense concentration always making her feel just a little off-kilter. "All right, I'm going to ask straight out. What do you think is going to happen on this call?" he asked. "Will you quit if they force your hand?"

God, she hoped it wouldn't come to that. "I'm praying they say yes to the Southwest Florida office. I'm bringing some clients to the table, thanks to Miles, and I'm willing to put the time in to take the bar and run the place."

He nodded, considering that. "Is that what you want?"

"Very much," she answered without a moment's hesitation. "I have no desire to walk away from practicing law, which a lot of people think is boring beyond belief—"

"Beyond," he teased.

"But I happen to love my work," she insisted. "I respect what you did, Deej, and Olivia and Dane and anyone else who follows their passions. But law *is* my passion. As much as I've loved every minute of these last few months when I was able to work remote and put it on the back burner, I miss the job."

"I understand," he assured her. "And I'm sorry if it seems like I belittle it. I don't mean to, I swear."

She smiled, and knew the apology—like everything he did—was truly genuine.

"So what if they say no, your job is in New York?" he asked. "Then what?"

She looked at him long and hard, hating the cold feeling that thought gave her.

"Then I'll have a very big decision to make," she whispered, reaching for his hand. "I don't want to go back. I don't want to leave...this family or this life we've cobbled together. You know how I love Noah, and Sophia, for all her big personality, is quite soft on the inside and I like her."

"And what about me?"

"I like you, too," she teased, going for light, because they never got serious. It just wasn't the nature of their relationship, and she chalked that up to DJ's "live in the moment and follow the stars" philosophy. That meant he could leave, too, at any time. And it would hurt if she'd had too many intimate conversations about their relationship and it all blew up in her face.

"Enough to stay if they want you to go back to New York?"

She just looked at him, considering how to answer that. Noah was enough for her to stay, and he knew it. So what was he really asking?

"I hate to go all lawyer on you and answer a question with a question," she said. "But what about you?"

"No one's asking me to go back to New York," he said.

Did she need to spell it out? "Are you going to stay?"

His dark eyes flickered in response, but he didn't say a word.

"I mean, it's only fair that I know that, right? You are a man who follows his passions. Your passions could change or Sophia could beg you to go back to California with her—she's certainly capricious enough—or you could go off to conquer new pizza worlds." As she said the words, her chest tightened, and she knew that this had been bothering her from...well, from the very first time they'd kissed. "You, Dante Joseph Fortunato, are not a sure thing."

He let out a breath she suspected he'd been holding for that whole speech. "Guilty, counselor."

"Oh." She didn't meant to let her disappointment be heard in that one syllable, but there it was.

"I don't want to be disingenuous, Claire. I'm very happy here, very connected to this place, and very content to have two of my three kids around."

But what about her? She searched his face, waiting.

Without a word, he lowered himself to one knee, and for a moment, her heart stopped. Was he—

"I ruined my first family," he said. "I take full responsibility for that mess. And because of that, I'm scared to death—and I mean to *death*—of making the same mistake again. I am holding back from letting myself fall completely in love with you."

She nodded, letting the words fold in her heart. "That's very...honest."

"It's all I can be, Claire." His eyes filled, which didn't even faze her anymore. DJ was emotional and didn't fight tears the way other men did. "And all I can ask of you is to...wait? Trust? Be patient? Give me a chance?"

She smiled. "That's a lot of things to ask, Deej."

"I know. But I'm here now, and I want to be here tomorrow. Each day is a learning experience for me."

She put a hand on his cheek, letting his whiskers rub her palm. "You're certainly not like any man I've ever met," she admitted. "But if we're being honest, I will say that I...wouldn't want you to change. I guess complicated and unpredictable people are my comfort zone, considering Dutch Vanderveen and Camille Durant are my parents."

She felt his whole body relax. "Thank you, Claire."

He put his hand over hers and slid her palm to his lips, kissing it. "Now, go get what you want from your boss."

As he walked out, she stared at her own face in the mirror, replaying the conversation. He was scared to death...and holding back.

No, DJ Fortunato still wasn't a sure thing. But that didn't stop her from caring more for him every day.

IT DIDN'T TAKE five minutes on the video call with Douglas Killian for Claire to know that she was not getting what she wanted.

A Southwest Florida office was shot down so fast, she was kind of stunned it took any time at all for them to get back to her. With offices in Jacksonville and Miami, the partners didn't see the need to rack up that kind of expense for small clients. Period. *Fini.*

With disappointment choking her, she accepted that, because her boss rarely went back on a decision. He hadn't gotten his name on the door at a firm that big and well-regarded by second-guessing decisions.

Now she'd either have to beg to continue working remotely or head back to New York or—

"But I have a different plan, Claire."

She looked into the two-dimensional face on her screen, catching the very serious note in his voice. Very serious.

Was he about to fire her? Was this it? The decision made for her? What if she worked part-time remote? Her mind whirred with various ways of negotiating that. Maybe three months of the year in New York? Six? Would that give her what she wanted from family and career?

Before she put her cards on the table, she watched him align his—well, some notes in front of him—and waited to let him speak first.

"I'm looking at a senior partner letter." He lifted his gaze to meet hers. "And it has your name on it."

She frowned, not sure she understood. "A senior partner..."

"Congratulations, Claire. You are being invited to join the innermost circle of partners at Wills, Sears and Killian."

All she could do was blink in shock. *Senior partner?* She had been worried she was getting fired and would have to negotiate part-time remote and he was...

Senior partner? She hadn't expected that for four or five more years. The only tier higher would put her name on the door.

"Doug..." She didn't even know what to say, other than, *Are you kidding me?* She'd been working remote for months, her billing was way down, she hadn't taken a new case in ages, and she'd missed every partner meeting since she left for Sanibel. They were rewarding that?

"Don't look so shocked," he said on a laugh. "You were on track for this before you left."

"Not that fast," she said on a soft laugh. "And I am shocked, I have to admit."

"Shocked and pleased, I hope. Isn't this everything

you've been working for since you got out of law school, Claire? Well, now it's yours. A fantastic opportunity that we hope is all you need to get back to your office...or a new one in the corner." He leaned closer to the screen. "This, Claire Sutherland, is a big deal and—"

"You actually have a letter?" She still couldn't believe the other senior partners agreed on this.

He waved a paper. "Right here. Senior partner is a sure thing."

A sure thing.

Exactly what DJ wasn't.

Outside her window, she heard a scream of laughter and a splash, pulling her attention to the pool. There, Noah and Sophia were enjoying the gorgeous day and playing some kind of game that made them sound like kids, not young adults.

"It shouldn't be that complicated," Doug added with a bit of an edge in his voice.

"It's not," she said.

But that scene outside? That was complicated. A son she only recently met. A daughter who wasn't hers and filled the house with color. A man who could disappear like smoke at any minute. Not one of them "needed" her —but she *so* needed them. She so needed this family that life and work and time and decisions made when she was not much older than Sophia had taken from her.

Now she had this family...but she also had a *senior partnership.* Another lifelong dream.

"Claire?"

She nodded, shifting her gaze back to the man on the monitor.

"The stipulation, obviously, is that you are back here full-time. We need you on several cases and new business development, and leading at least a dozen new associates coming in this year. We've got a whole new antitrust department and I would very much like you to head that operation and build it up to a major force in the legal world."

"Antitrust..." She was good at that. Great, even. And it would be a high-profile department to run.

Noah made a loud whoop before a cannonball splash, snagging her attention.

"The truth is, Claire, we don't have anyone else quite like you. You've always been willing to stay in the background, do the hard work no one else wanted, and bring in huge payoffs. That kind of work is going to be rewarded. The money is, well, you know. Seven figures with the bonuses—"

A girlish shriek of "I won!" and Sophia's musical laughter came through the closed window. What were they laughing about? What game were they playing? And why wasn't she out there enjoying this precious moment in the sunshine *with her family*—the one she'd always wanted and never dreamed she could have.

"Of course, there is room for negotiation, Claire," Doug added, his voice a little taut with frustration. "Although we didn't think that would be necessary."

She let a few seconds tick by. Long enough to let

peace settle over her. Long enough to find the right words. Long enough to make her boss scowl.

"Thank you so much, Doug, but I'm going to have to pass."

Even through the monitor screen, she could see him pale. "You have *got* to be kidding me."

She gave a tight smile. "I'm not leaving Sanibel Island," she said.

"Get a winter home there, for crying out loud, Claire. Because if you don't take this position, there isn't one for you at this firm. You need to be present and in the office. Period."

"Noah! *Staaahhhhp!*" Sophia's squawk had to be loud enough for Doug to hear, followed by a noisy splash and peals of laughter.

"What's going on there?" Doug asked, not making any effort to hide his impatience and frustration.

Claire just smiled. "That's my family, Doug."

"Your...*what?*" He drew back, confused. "I thought you were single and childless. Not that it matters," he added quickly. "But your, uh, lifestyle was a big part of our decision."

In other words, she could bill eighty-hour weeks because no one needed her at home.

Well, that just wasn't true anymore and hallelujah for that.

"I have a family," she announced, getting a little thrill from the words. A family as unconventional as all get out, but it was hers. "My son, Noah, who is twenty-six years old."

"You have a twenty-six-year-old? How could we not know that?"

"Because he didn't find me until a few months ago. And his father is here, and he has a daughter named Sophia. We're all a...family." She couldn't wipe the smile from her face. "And I'm staying here with them."

He just stared at her for a moment. "I didn't realize you had, uh, other commitments down there. I thought you were straightening out your late father's affairs and helping your mother."

"I was," she said. "But now I'm home, Doug. And I'm not leaving. So, about the new Florida office—"

"No. It's off the table."

She cocked her head in concession. "Understood. Then I'll open one on my own." The very second the words were out, she knew that was the right thing to do. The absolute right thing. The only thing. She wouldn't be in the Quitter Club. She'd be in the Business Owner's Club. "Again, thank you for the offer," she added. "I'll get my resignation letter drafted and have my admin clear out my office."

The minute she said the words, the whole world felt lighter and better and filled with everything good.

"Oh. Okay." He nodded, and she saw the minute he was done with her. "Thank you, Claire. Good luck to you."

Within seconds, the call was over, leaving her staring at a blank screen. The yells and giggles were still audible in the background, along with the view of some people she either already loved, could love, or would love.

Life, she was learning, wasn't always a sure thing, but it was worth taking a risk to find out.

With a sense of peace in her heart that she hadn't felt in a long time—maybe ever—she went to her room, grabbed her bathing suit, and changed in a flash. Then she hustled out to the backyard, ran to the pool, and jumped in right between Noah and Sophia.

When she popped up, they were all staring at her. She swiped the water out of her eyes and looked at DJ with a secret smile. Not that secret, though. She could tell by his look that he knew exactly what she'd just done.

Instantly, he leaped out of his chair, launched himself at the pool, and joined them with an epic splash.

When he came up, he wrapped his arms around her and kissed her on the mouth, the first time in front of Sophia...who let out a whooping cheer that no one saw coming.

And right that moment, happiness felt like a sure thing.

Chapter Twenty-two

Camille

It was hard not to get caught up in the infectious enthusiasm of what they were all playfully referring to as Operation Found Family. Everyone around Camille seemed to hum with anticipation as they gathered at Teddy's on a Sunday morning after a week of lively discussions and hilarious "meetings" before *The Last Resort* contingent showed up.

Everyone but Camille. The only thing she was humming with was a frustrating ache for more sleep. She'd battled insomnia all week, and chalked it up to one too many exciting dates with Abner, who was utterly convinced this was love.

And he might be right. Something seemed to have her whole body on edge lately.

She missed him deeply today, but it was Davis's birthday and he was expected at Penny's house, of all places. He promised to come over later for the "event" and would add color to the story she would be sharing with...but...but...

She sighed as a fog of confusion pressed on her brain. Was she supposed to talk to the guests while in the gazebo with Olivia or down at the cabana with Claire, Noah, and DJ?

Her chest tightened with the stress of knowing how important this was, but she couldn't muster the energy to do her part. And it was definitely going to cut into her nap time, which she desperately needed.

She raised her hand with the obedience of a school-girl, making Eliza laugh. Well, she was the one who was standing in the middle of the room like a teacher, trying to get everyone's attention for one last walk-through before they all headed off for their various tasks.

"Will you go over the names of the people coming and who is supposed to pair off with who again?" Camille asked.

"I'm trying to," Eliza told her, then clapped, but the room was still full of chatter and noise. "Everyone!"

Miles stood next to her and put two fingers in his mouth and let out a whistle that brought a sudden and complete silence.

"Thank you," Eliza whispered, leaning into him with a laugh. "And now that I have all of your attention, can we just go over everything one more time? It's really important that everyone know their roles and what's expected. Please?"

Everyone settled down and finally paid attention.

"Okay. As you all know, four representatives from *The Last Resort* are going to arrive at approximately three o'clock this afternoon. We have them all afternoon and evening, which will include a cocktail party on the beach and a private pizza dinner at the tea hut. Before that, we'll take them on a well-orchestrated tour that will include every single person in the room."

"And me!" Harper stood and squeaked, raising her hand like the real schoolgirl in the room.

"Of course you, Harper! You're our most important ambassador."

Her eyes flashed with joy and she straightened with self-importance, leaning closer to her mother. "I'm an am*ass*idor."

And it took thirty seconds to stop the laughter.

"Do you want me to take the visitors to my daycare center?" Jadyn asked. "It's a bit of a walk."

"Make that a game-time decision," Eliza said. "We'll start with the garden, where Teddy, Camille, and I will greet them and plant the seeds—" She gave a wink to Miles. "See what I did there? We'll *plant the seeds* for the grand group of stories they will be hearing during the tour."

He grinned back at her, as smitten as a man could be. Camille knew what smitten looked like, because she saw it every time she looked into Abner's eyes.

Pushing the thought from her head, which was over-loaded enough, she concentrated on what Eliza was saying.

"During that conversation and with the help of..." She glanced at Teddy.

"Oolong and cypress tea I've been steeping since last night," Teddy answered. "And a whole lot of crystals placed all over the place."

Eliza smiled. "With a little of Teddy's special tea

formula and happy crystals, we'll start to weave the tale of what brought us here, and how we are all connected through one man."

A few of them gave surprised looks, but Eliza appeared to expect that.

"Yes," she continued. "We are going to be open about Dutch, his marriages, and his...complicated life. Camille and Teddy and I have discussed this and agree that he's central to so many of us being here. Plus, his story with Teddy? Our message is Shellseeker means family, in all its iterations. This place is a living, breathing entity that brings people together."

"You should just write this Hidden Gems feature for her," Miles teased.

"Or I will," Noah chimed in. "Nicely put, Eliza."

"Thank you. Okay, so when we're done, we'll hand the group over to Katie and Jadyn and Harper," she added with a grin to the girl. "They'll tour Junonia, walk the path along the beach and, while they do, Katie will share her story about coming here. Right?" She visually checked with the always uber-private Katie, but now that her family had found her, she seemed much more open about her past.

"Absolutely," Katie said. "And Jadyn's got a story to tell, too."

"Great. You'll take them to Sanibel Treasures." She gestured to Roz and George.

"And we will be ready!" Roz assured her. "I'll tell her how we walked in as customers and met Teddy and ended up moving here to manage the store. And George will do the whole Teddy Roosevelt message-in-a-bottle schtick—"

"Excuse me," George interjected, sending a teasing glare to his wife. "It's history, not a schtick."

"You're right, George," Eliza assured him.

"From there," George said, "I take them to the cabana." He gestured to Noah, who picked up the thread.

"And I will get them on paddleboard and kayak rides, share my story, and I promise there won't be a dry eye in the house."

"That's my boy," DJ joked.

Noah laughed. "Then I'll take them to the gazebo for champagne with Livvie, who will finish the job—"

"With a surprise," Eliza said.

"A surprise?" Olivia frowned. "What is it?"

"We're not a hundred percent sure it's happening, so I'll tell you in a bit," Eliza said. "But let's finish this itinerary. While all that is happening, we'll be setting up for the pizza party at the tea hut around three o'clock. But first, they'll talk to Camille."

Camille pushed up, needing some effort to get out of her chair. "So I just need to be in the garden with you and Teddy at three o'clock?" she asked. "Is that correct?"

"Ready to share from your heart, Camille. Your story of how you had ownership of this property and gave it to Teddy will be the backbone of everything."

She felt like she didn't *have* a backbone right then, but managed to nod and find her bag. "Then I'll be here at two-thirty. I'm going home to catch a nap."

Claire instantly came close to her. "Are you all right,

Maman? You look pale."

Teddy appeared at her side. "I can give you some of that oolong to take with you."

She shook her head and put a hand on her chest, the very idea of hot tea making her a little nauseous. "No. I'm fine. Just haven't been sleeping. So let me have my beauty rest and a chance to dress to impress and I'll be back."

With quick air kisses and a flutter of her fingertips to say goodbye to the group, she escaped, but not before her daughter snagged her arm.

"Let me drive you. Or Noah can."

"I can drive, Claire. I'm simply tired. You stay here where you're needed to set up. Noah, too." She sighed and put a hand on Claire's cheek, feeling a sudden rush of love for her daughter. "I'm so pleased to see you look so radiant, *cherie.*"

Claire pressed her palm over Camille's hand. "I'm so happy right now, *Maman.*"

"Stay that way," she whispered with a kiss to her cheek. "And don't worry about me. I'll be back right on time, looking gorgeous and ready to wow the crowd."

"God, I love you." Claire gave her a spontaneous hug, and finally let go so Camille could make her way to her car and the short drive to Bowman's Beach.

But somewhere after Rabbit Road and before the turnoff to her complex, the smile Camille wore from the exchange with Claire disappeared. In its place, she flinched because the low-grade nausea that had been plaguing her intensified into stabbing heartburn.

And she hadn't eaten all morning!

As she parked, she heaved a sigh of utter fatigue, using all her energy to get out of the car. She grabbed her bag and walked toward her unit, turning the corner and coming to a dead stop at the sight of the very last person she ever wanted to see.

"Penny?" she choked the name. "Aren't you supposed to be hosting a birthday lunch?"

It was a silly question, but her brain froze and just didn't feel like it was functioning. A question like, "What the hell are you doing at my front door?" would have made more sense, but she was too tired to make sense.

"Of course you know my family's every move, you gold-digging vixen."

The tone, not the words, were so hot that Camille's head felt light. Reaching for the railing that surrounded her small porch, she steadied herself and refused to show an ounce of weakness to this woman.

"Not every move," she said. "How can I help you?" But as she said the words, she suddenly realized that something could be wrong with Abner. Why else would Penny be here? "Is Abner all right?" she asked, tamping down a wave of worry.

"No," she barked the word. "He's not all right."

"Is he—"

"He's in *loooove*." She dragged out the word with disgust and a curled lip.

For a moment, Camille just stared at her, thinking of all the ways to respond. But the only thing she wanted at that moment was a soft bed and a cold cloth on her head. She marched to the door, keys already in hand.

"Excuse me, Penny, but I don't—"

Penny snatched her arm. "You will not blow me off."

"Really? Watch me." Shaking off the woman's touch, she stuck the key in the lock and turned, pushing the door open and stepping inside. She twirled fast to slam the door in Penny's face, but that move...whoa. Bad idea.

The whole world spun and it looked like there were two, no *three* Pennys glaring at her.

One was bad enough.

She slapped her hand on the door jamb to steady herself, and Penny used the excuse to muscle her way in. Camille simply wasn't strong enough to fight her.

"Fine! You win!" Camille exclaimed. "I don't feel well. Please."

"You'll feel better in a minute," she said, getting right into Camille's face.

Camille blinked, certain she didn't understand.

"Threats don't work with a woman like you, obviously."

That was a small victory, and Camille tried to smile but her vision was still playing tricks on her. Penny's face looked distorted and she was so close, Camille could smell a sickening, cloying perfume.

Bile threatened to rise up, making her whimper in fear of throwing up right in front of this woman. It would serve her—

"How much do you want?" Penny demanded. "Be reasonable, nothing ridiculous. We're prepared to do business, however."

What in God's name was she talking about? "I'm sorry, but I'm not able to—"

"Get able. You're a problem—a big, fat, major problem—and my husband and I say anything that can be solved with money isn't a problem anymore. How much will it take to make you go away? And I mean far and for good. Twenty thousand? Thirty? I can go up to—"

Camille stumbled backwards, the screaming in her ears not caused by this shrew spitting dollar amounts at her. It was in her head, like someone was in it with a foghorn. Her stomach clutched again, but the real pain was in her chest.

Like a hot, searing poker was being stabbed between her breasts.

"Oh my God, Penny..." She flailed again, reaching out for help, but the other woman backed away in surprise and Camille lost her footing, not strong enough to stay standing. "Help me."

She collapsed to the ground like a ragdoll, her knee slamming to the hard floor with an agonizing smack. With a groan, she clutched her chest, falling backwards as a sharp pain shot down her left arm.

Her left arm. Her *left* arm. Did that mean she was having a...

"What is wrong with you?" Penny demanded. "Is this some kind of act to get me up to six figures? Because we—"

"Heart," she groaned pressing her chest. "My...heart."

From her collarbone to the tips of her fingers, fiery sparks of pain radiated over her body, so intense she couldn't speak or move. She managed to lift her face to look at Penny, who stood in abject shock, staring at her, white as a ghost.

"Please," she mouthed, unable to get any sound from her chest. The one that was breaking...for real.

"You're having a heart attack." It wasn't a question. It was...an answer. "Just...like...Polly."

"Please...help...me." Wouldn't she? Wouldn't she help Camille get up or call an ambulance or...

Mon Dieu. No. This horrible woman was capable of walking out that door and leaving Camille to die.

Was it that important that Camille leave Abner alone? Important enough that she'd *kill* for it? Because if she didn't—

Another spasm rocked her chest, gripping her like a vise was smashing her ribs, making her drop her head to the floor as the agony took ownership of her body.

"*Aidez-moi!*" she cried out for help, falling into French as the parts of her brain that knew English seemed to shut down. "*Aidez-moi, s'il vous plait!*"

Tears streamed down her face as she rocked with the next wave, blinding her. But somehow, she managed to open her eyes and look up at Penny Conway, who stood frozen.

She wasn't going to help?

Blackness came from her peripheral vision, closing like a curtain, slowly drawing over Camille's vision and dragging her away from the pain.

Away from this monster. Away...from life.

Chapter Twenty-three

Eliza

"Moonstone." Teddy placed a smooth white stone against Eliza's chest, determination in the older woman's gaze. "You need this."

"For luck?"

"For stress. Eliza, you need to calm down."

"I am calm," she said, easing the stone away and smiling at Teddy. "I thrive on a little controlled chaos. Tea all ready down at the hut? No word from the special guests? Do you think they'll make it in time?"

Teddy suddenly searched Eliza's face as if something other than this whole event was on her mind. "This really matters to you, doesn't it?"

"Of course! We want to get that feature and..." She let her voice fade out as she studied the woman who'd become as close as any friend, mother, or sister. "It's not about the feature," she admitted softly. "It's about the family. So many people depend on Shellseeker Cottages now."

A slow smile pulled. "I'm so happy to hear you say that, because that means you truly and genuinely understand the magic of this little place."

"There's so much magic. Found families. New families. Returning families. But all those planets circle around one sun." She put her hands on Teddy's slightly weathered cheeks. "You. They are here because you are here, because of your warmth and light, Teddy."

"Oh. That's so sweet. But I won't be here forever."

"Hush. I expect thirty more years out of you, Theodora."

"And you may get them," she said with a wry smile. "Why do you think I drink so much lavender and lemon tea? It's like the fountain of youth."

"Then maybe we should bathe in it," Eliza teased, making them both laugh.

"Oh, Eliza." Teddy wrapped her arms around her friend and squeezed. "We're quite a team, aren't we?"

As Eliza laugh-cried, she wiped under her eye. "Dang. Now I wish I'd worn waterproof mascara."

Teddy laughed. "No tears. It's a happy day, no matter what happens with *The Last Resort*."

"Oh, I know what's going to happen. We're going to —" She gasped. "The gift bags! Did you—"

"Yes, yes. Katie and Jadyn finished stuffing them and George added personalized messages in bottles, with a collection of shells and gifts from the store. They're down at the tea hut, with everyone else who have gathered for one last hug and a high-five. Except for Claire and DJ, because they were worried about Camille."

Eliza drew back. "Why?"

"She wasn't answering her phone, and not feeling well when she left. I think Claire was worried she took a nap and slept through an alarm."

"Oh, dear. We have time, but..." She looked at the kitchen clock. "I hope she's okay. I'm going to call Claire and check—"

"Eliza! Eliza and Teddy!" Claire's voice came through the open sliding glass doors, a note of deep panic threading through it.

"Or talk to her," Eliza muttered, rushing toward the doors to the patio. There she saw Claire below, holding her phone, turning from one side to the other as if desperate to find help.

"Claire! I'm here!" Without waiting for an answer, Eliza ran to the stairs, her heart rate kicking up. She spotted Noah jogging toward the gardens with purpose. "What's wrong?"

"My mother! It's my mother!" Her voice cracked with a sob just as Eliza reached her, shocked to see her sister's face ravaged with tears.

"What happened?"

She couldn't quite catch her breath. "Hospital. Heart attack."

Teddy rushed to reach them, and so did Katie and Noah, with Roz, George, Asia, and Olivia not far behind.

"We went to check on her," Claire managed, panting. "I was worried about her and she didn't answer her phone."

"Come on, Mom," Noah said, nudging her with a gentle hand on her shoulders. "We gotta go. DJ's got the car right there to take us."

"I have to tell them," Claire said, finally catching her

breath. "She wasn't home, but her car was there and her door was unlocked."

"How do you know she's in the hospital?" Eliza asked.

"Penny called me." She held up her phone.

"*What*?" All of them asked the question together.

"It's...a long story. But she called to tell me Camille is in ICU and the hospital needed to talk to me so I can approve open heart surgery!" Over their gasps, she cried out, "I have to go!"

"We all do," Eliza said.

"Absolutely," Teddy agreed. "She needs us there."

Claire looked like she'd collapse with relief. "But the...thing. *The Last Resort* will be here any minute. You can't—"

"Oh, yes we can," Eliza said. "Nothing is more important than supporting you and Camille."

She meant it, too, looking around to see that everyone was in agreement. Only Jadyn hung back, with Harper in her arms, listening but protecting the child from hearing something upsetting.

"I love you," Claire whispered on one more hug to Eliza. "And, yes, I need you. I need you all so much."

"Just go. We'll be right behind you," Eliza promised.

"It's Lee Memorial. Cardiac Care Unit." She squeezed her eyes shut. "I can't believe I'm even saying that. I thought she was so healthy, but—"

"Shhh." Eliza calmed her, pressing the moonstone she still held into Claire's hand. "Go with Noah and

Katie. You are not alone, Claire. Your family's here. All day, all night, whatever it takes."

"Thank you," she mouthed, pressing her clenched fist and the stone to her chest, and leaning in to kiss Teddy. "I'm so sorry," she muttered. "This ruins everything."

"Stop that right now," Teddy said, adding her own tearful hug. "We'll be there soon."

With a burst of goodbyes and last-second logistics, Claire and Noah and Katie ran off to the parking lot where DJ was waiting with the car.

In their wake, the rest of them stood in stunned silence as the magnitude of what had happened settled on them.

Emergency heart surgery meant...Camille might not make it.

They all knew that, but no one could actually say the words.

Taking a breath, Eliza looked from one face to the next, and zeroed in on Jadyn, who'd just put Harper down, but held her hand as they walked closer.

"I'll handle everyone coming," she said with confidence. "With Harper."

"Yes, Aunt Eliza!" Harper danced a little, obviously unaware of what was unfolding. "I'm your am*ass*ador!"

Eliza reached down to give her an impulsive hug. "And such a beautiful one." She straightened and looked at Jadyn. "Are you sure? There are four people and—"

"I'll help." Asia hustled closer, one hand on the baby strapped to her belly in a colorful carrier. "I'll stay and help Jadyn. We don't want the kids in the hospital."

"Amen to that," Roz added.

"What can I do?" Sophia stepped into the group. "I honestly don't know Camille well and I'm happy to stay here and represent the Fortunato family and help."

Jadyn was already nodding. "I'll do the gardens, beach, and cottage."

Eliza hugged her, too, swamped with appreciation.

With one more flurry of instructions and hugs and hopes and silent prayers, they headed off. Eliza put her arm around Olivia, so grateful to have her daughter there. If only Miles—

"I just texted Miles," Olivia whispered. "He's meeting us there."

Eliza exhaled with relief and hustled with the others, giving one last glance over her shoulder. She could kiss *The Last Resort* feature goodbye, but who cared? As long as they didn't have to kiss Camille goodbye.

THE FIRST PERSON Eliza saw when she walked into the main lobby of Lee Memorial was, well, the last person she expected.

In a corner, on a chair by herself, Penny Conway sat with her arms crossed, her face set in an expression of pure misery as she watched the door. As soon as she saw Eliza, she popped up.

"Can I talk to you, please?" Penny asked.

Eliza nodded. "Of course, but we need to see—"

"One minute. It's urgent. I'll be brief."

Eliza glanced at Olivia and Teddy. "You guys go on and find the cardiac unit," Eliza told them. "Text me with a floor number and I'll meet you there."

They both looked a little skeptical, but after a second, they headed off and Eliza turned to Penny. The other woman tipped her head toward the door, indicating they could talk outside.

"I admit I was surprised to hear you were the one who contacted Claire," Eliza said as they walked. "Was Buck with her, and called you?"

She shook her head as they stopped at a low wall surrounding some shrubbery and sat down. "I was with her. Buck...doesn't know yet."

"You were with her? I thought she went home to nap."

Penny stared straight ahead and then pushed some hair out of her eyes, heaving a sigh. "She did. I... ambushed her."

"Excuse me?"

"I think I might have..." Her face crumpled and she shuddered with a sob. "God help me, Eliza, but I think I brought this on. I'm...so sorry."

Eliza just stared at her. "What did you do? Threaten her again? Just because you're worried she wants his money?"

Her eyes flashed. "You...know?"

"I do, but Camille doesn't. She has *no idea* that Buck has a dime. He's never told her and she never cared one way or the other. She liked the way he made her feel, period. And I take it that goes both ways."

Penny's face grew even more sallow and sad as she swiped a tear. "It does, and I feel...so guilty." She fisted a hand against her chest.

"What happened?" Eliza asked.

"I went to her townhouse. I wanted to make her an offer. For money, you know? To make her go away. Not for good!" she added with a flash of her eyes. "Just..."

"Just to get out of the way of his happiness...and his will." Eliza finished for her. "How incredibly selfish, Penny."

"Worse than selfish," she admitted, her voice ragged. "And when she collapsed, it was like Polly all over again. I called 911 right away and got her in the ambulance. The whole time, all I could think about was how I was there when my sister had her heart attack, and in the hospital when Buck promised he'd never marry anyone else."

"And you're holding him to that promise?"

"Not if she lives," she whispered. "I don't care anymore. They can..."

Eliza stood, anxious to be done with this woman's confession and get to Claire. As she did, Penny looked up and reached for her. "What can I do to make it up? I know you're in the final running with *The Last Resort* today. Can I go put in a good—"

"You know what you can do?" Eliza replied. "Tell your former brother-in-law that a woman he cares deeply about is in the hospital facing surgery. He deserves to know. That's all, Penny. Nothing else matters."

With that, she nodded goodbye and headed back into

the hospital, checking her phone for a text from Livvie, and following her instructions to find the fifth floor.

She walked into the small waiting room and took one look around, anxious to see Claire, but there was no sign of her. Just Teddy and Olivia, Katie, DJ, Roz and George.

"Claire's with Camille," Olivia said, practically leaping from her chair when Eliza walked in. "What did that woman want?"

"To apologize for putting Camille in here."

"*Excuse* me?"

Eliza shook her head. "Claire's with Camille, so that's good. She's not in emergency surgery yet?"

"They're prepping her for it, but they are letting immediate family in with her. So Claire and Noah are the only ones who qualify." She pointed to a set of double doors, reading the words Cardiac Surgical Unit embossed on the sign next to them. "They'll be back when they take Camille for surgery. Could be a while."

Eliza felt her shoulders sink. "I can't go in and wait with her?"

"No. Just sit here with us and tell me what Penny wanted." Olivia led her to an open chair next to Teddy. "Tell us everything."

She almost told them about the money, but she'd promised Miles she'd keep it confidential, so she just shrugged. "She'd gone to make one last plea for Camille to leave Buck, and thank God she did. If she hadn't been there, Camille might have taken her nap and..."

They all exchanged sickened looks.

It was enough to make them huddle together, whispering, praying, supporting each other as they waited for any kind of news.

"Where is she?"

Startled by the man's loud voice from the hall, they all whipped around when Abner powered into the waiting room. Eliza and Olivia stood, but he barreled right by them to the nurses' station.

"I need to see Cami Durant," he said, making them share a quick look of surprise at the nickname and his attitude.

A nurse looked up and lifted a brow. "Immediate family only. Her daughter's in—"

"Miss," he said, leaning his tall frame over the countertop. "You see that flashing light right there on your phone?"

She blinked at him, confused.

"I'd pick it up if I were you. It's a man named Peter Dunwitty. Name ring a bell?"

She snorted. "The CEO of the hospital? Yes, the name rings a bell."

"Then answer his."

With a sigh like she was completely over the demands of stressed-out visitors, she picked up the phone and answered with a curt, "Cardiac Care Unit." Silent for a moment, her eyes widened. Then she nodded as if the person on the other end could see. "Uh-huh. Yes, of course, Mr. Dunwitty. Absolutely. Thank you, sir. Yes. You, too. Yes."

She hung up very slowly and looked up at Buck, silent.

"Through those doors?" he asked, pointing at the entrance to the Cardiac Surgical Unit.

"Yes, Waiting Area Two. I'll ring the nurse and tell her you're coming."

As he strode to the doors, Eliza leaped up, rushing to him. "Buck! Abner!"

He spun and looked down at her, the creases in his weathered face deepening as if he didn't want to be stopped right then.

"Claire is my sister."

"Eliza," he said softly. "Cami loves you."

She felt her lips lift. "I think I can say the same for you. Can I, um, go with you? I long to hold my sister's hand through this."

He considered the question, then nodded. "I'd like more witnesses for what I'm about to do."

With that, he put an arm around her and sailed through the double doors like he owned the place.

For all she knew, he did.

Chapter Twenty-four

Camille

She wasn't going to make it.

Camille had known from the moment she'd first come to in the ambulance that this was the end for her. It was funny how she knew, and she wasn't scared. She'd see Dutch again—maybe. No telling where either of them would end up. And her mother and father, and...

It didn't matter what was on the other side. This was the end for her on *this* side.

"*Maman?* Some water?" Claire's sweet voice traveled through her head like a silky tendril, soft to the touch but so thin, she couldn't get ahold of it.

All Camille could do was try to shake her head, but she was foggy from drugs. Opening her eyes or squeezing Claire's hand felt like a staggering, monumental task that she simply couldn't attempt.

So she stayed very still on the bed, listening to Claire and Noah whisper to each other, the beep of the machines, and her thoughts.

Thoughts about her life, her behavior, her decisions, and the end that she was facing.

"Everyone's here," Claire whispered, stroking

Camille's hand. "You should know that everyone left Shellseeker Beach to be here with you."

She tried to frown, but it was so much effort. Why would they do that? All she'd done was snap at people, judge them for the most mundane things, and use her sharp sense of humor to hide real barbs.

"They all love you so much, *Maman*. After what you did giving Teddy the property back, and bringing Olivia in as a partner in your store, and how you've loved Noah from the moment you met him..."

"I'm right here, *Grandmère*."

Camille took a slow breath, but the slightest movement stabbed her chest with the pain that had become weirdly familiar.

Had she done all that? Yes, she had. But had it been enough? When she died on the operating table—something she sensed was inevitable—how would she be remembered by these people? By anyone?

Beautiful, well-dressed, elegantly French, yes. But also caustic, judgmental, unforgiving.

"They all care so much about you. Eliza and Teddy led the charge, giving up the chance to meet with *The Last Resort* to be here with you."

She managed a groan at that, which hurt, but she could feel Claire lean closer.

"No, no, it's fine. They know what's important, *Maman*. Family. And they've become ours, haven't they?"

Yes, she thought, but wasn't strong enough to speak.

They had, and that meant Claire would be surrounded by love when Camille was gone. That made her—

"Ms. Durant?" The nurse's voice cut through her foggy thoughts. "This man is—"

"Cami!"

Abner? She felt her whole body rise an inch at the sound of his voice and the use of his pet name. It was like they'd put something in the IV, instantly giving her...that magical something that Abner seemed to emanate. Hope and happiness and light and life.

Oh, she hadn't expected this!

"My sweet, beautiful Cami." She felt the grip on her hand transfer from Claire's light touch to the callused palm and fingers of her bait salesman.

"Buck," Claire whispered. "I'm so glad you're here. And Eliza! They let you in."

She sensed Claire stepping away from the hospital bed and imagined her floating to her sister, and another wave of gratitude washed over her. Claire was well-loved, and well taken care of.

So when this was over and she was...wherever she was going...hopefully, looking down on all this, she'd see Claire surrounded by family.

She forgot Claire for a moment, suddenly able to smell that masculine scent of Abner she'd come to adore.

"Don't you leave me, darlin'." His Southern drawl was like music to her. "I need you on this Earth next to me, Cami."

She tried to smile and open her eyes, but she just

couldn't. Her heart, though, as malfunctioning as it was, kicked up a beat.

Ouch. That hurt. But she couldn't stop it any more than she could stop the true and genuine feelings she had for this man.

"I'm not kidding, Cami," he continued, so close to her that she could feel his warm breath on her cheek. "I don't throw my weight around this old world very often, but I did today, 'cause I had to see you. I had to talk to you. I had to tell you something, Cami."

She managed the softest whimper.

"She's awake," he announced, as if he were telling the others in the room. She heard a murmured response, recognizing Claire's voice and Eliza's.

"And that's good," Abner said. "Because a woman ought to be awake when a man tells her he loves her."

He loved her? Once again, her heart felt like it shifted in her chest and...oh. That poor broken valve or whatever it was squeezed hard, nearly taking her breath away with the pain.

But she didn't care. It was worth it to hear what he said.

"I do," he insisted in a soft voice. "I love you, sweet woman."

Sweet? She was anything but.

"I love your spunk and sass and them darn high heels that make me dizzy."

Oh, that was nice. The words made her a little dizzy, too, but she didn't care.

"I love your accent and the colorful life you've lived

and how much you love your makeup and clothes and girlie things."

He waited a beat, and wow. That beat hurt. Her heart was screaming in pain, but it didn't matter. These were her last minutes alive and they were good ones.

"Now, you know I'm not a man who waits for things. Life's short, as you have heard me say."

Yes, it was. Today, in fact, hers was reaching the end. She tried so hard to squeeze his hand, but all she managed to do was flutter her fingers a bit.

"Yep, she hears me all right." He leaned even closer, the weight of the bed dipping a little. "So she's going to hear this. Camille Durant, I am here on bended knee."

He was?

"I'm a humble man who doesn't have all that many years ahead. But what I have left, and what you have left, could be spent together. Would you be a darlin' and make me the happiest man alive? Would you marry me, Cami?"

The gasps she heard from the others in the room matched the one she wanted to make.

"You don't have to say yes now, my love. Just when they wheel you out of that operatin' room, and you come to? You tell me then. Until that moment, you got somethin' to fight for, honey. Somethin' to hold on to when they go in and fix that heart that belongs to me. That's when you can tell me if you want to be my wife. Nothing could make me happier, and I know I could make you happy."

Suddenly, she heard a thud and more voices, including a nurse she'd come to recognize.

"The OR is open!" someone announced. "The team is ready. Please, you need to leave this room. You can wait in the hall and say goodbye as we wheel her out."

Say goodbye. Say goodbye. *Say goodbye.*

The words screamed in her head, louder than anything around her. Louder than the instructions the nurses were firing at each other, than the beep from the machine attached to her, than the screaming pain in her chest.

She didn't want to say goodbye.

She felt a jolt and started to roll, vaguely aware of the people around her.

"We've given you a little cocktail in that IV, Camille," a nurse said in a sing-song voice as they rolled her along. "You'll be asleep soon and when you wake up, it'll all be over."

Yes, she knew that. Like she knew her name, she knew she wouldn't survive this.

But...Abner wanted to marry her!

"Godspeed, Camille," Eliza said softly.

"Be strong, *Grandmère*," Noah whispered.

"I love you, *Maman*." She felt Claire's lips brush her cheek.

"Marry me, Cami." It wasn't a question, but he had asked a moment ago...and she hadn't given him an answer. Because she knew there wasn't going to be a wedding or a marriage or a life after this. He'd just be sad and...

She felt her soul stir and that burst of something that only Abner could give her. Energy. Youth. Hope.

Digging for it, she took a painful breath and finally felt her eyes flutter open, just a slit. But it was enough to see his loving gaze, his weathered face, his genuine smile.

She looked right at him and whispered the only word she could possibly say as the end loomed over her. Why not? She wanted to die happy.

"Yes."

Chapter Twenty-five

Olivia

When Eliza, Claire, Noah, and Buck came back through the double doors, they looked...well, not dancing on air, but lighter. Hopeful.

Olivia's mother and aunt held hands, saying something to Buck, who just gave a slow smile, and a tip of that invisible hat.

"I'll be back, ladies." As he passed Olivia on his way out of the waiting room, he winked. "She's going to be fine," he whispered.

She was? He knew that? Olivia popped up to get more information from her mother, not totally surprised to see her eyes were red and her cheeks were wet.

"Buck said she's going to be okay," she said. "Is that true?"

The other two women looked at each other and shared a secret laugh and a headshake.

"This is funny?" Olivia asked as Roz and George and the others looked on, waiting for some kind of report.

"She said yes," Mom said with another laugh. "I can't believe it."

"Wait. What?" Olivia frowned. "Yes to...Buck *proposed?*"

"He sure did," Noah said, shaking his head. "Asked like a total boss, too."

Claire pressed her hands to her mouth in disbelief. "He got down on one knee and popped the question!"

As everyone hooted around them—including Olivia—a thread of something sickeningly close to envy wound its way around her heart. Which was so shameful she didn't want to think about it. The woman was literally knocking on death's door and Olivia couldn't be happier for her.

Claire held her hands up to fend off the avalanche of questions coming at her. "All that matters is that she has a reason to fight her way through this."

"I think what matters is old Buck is going ring shopping," Olivia joked. "I should tell him not to get pear-shaped. She says pears are for brie."

Everyone laughed with a giddy, optimistic ride on the hospital waiting room rollercoaster, loud enough to get a scowl from the nurse at the desk.

"Sorry," Olivia said. "We're a noisy bunch."

"And well-connected," the nurse added wryly. "But just so you know, this can be a four-hour operation, or more. Someone should stay here, because you will be alerted by law when she is put on perfusion, but it's going to be a long wait."

At their confused look, she added, "That's when she's technically being kept alive by a machine. But don't worry. Our doctors are the best."

They clung to the words, and each other, as they realized just what they were facing today.

"I'm not leaving," Claire said. "I will be right here until they come out and tell us she's in recovery."

"Then I'm with you," Eliza told her.

"I'll get coffee and food," Miles offered. "And will stay with you day and night. Tink's with a dogsitter, and I'm not going anywhere."

"Mom, do you want me to go back to Shellseeker Beach and help Asia and Jadyn with *The Last Resort* people?" Olivia asked. "I'm happy to check on things."

Her mother thought about that, then glanced at her phone, and at Teddy. "You can if you like, Liv. But the reports I'm getting are pretty positive, so..."

"So you'd prefer I stay?"

Her mother nodded. "I'd like you close, Livvie Bug."

"Of course."

After a while, they assumed their waiting positions, talking, texting, coming, going, and always watching the surgical board for the moment it changed from "in surgery" to "in recovery."

At the two-hour point, a nurse came out, asked for Claire, and announced that Camille was officially on the perfusion machine.

"How's she doing?" Claire asked, her voice taut with concern.

The nurse took a slow breath and nodded. "It's a little more complicated than expected, but Dr. Greene is the best thoracic surgeon in the state. Stay strong. And if you're a praying family, it would be a good time. The next hour or two are very...tricky."

With that, she headed back and Claire threaded her fingers through DJ's, dropping her head on his shoulder.

"I'm going to hit the bathroom," Olivia said, realizing she'd been waiting for that nurse to come out. "Come with, Mom? Maybe get some air."

"Go with her, Eliza," Claire said, giving her a nudge. "Nothing's going to happen for a while. Take a walk with Livvie."

It didn't take a lot of encouragement and a minute later, they left the waiting room for the first time in what felt like days, not hours. After stopping in the ladies' room, they headed to the elevator to go outside into what was now the early evening.

"I need to hear every word old Buck said," Olivia urged. "Although, true confession: I can't believe my business partner is going to get married before I do, even with the in-laws from hell."

"His hundred million will ease the pain," her mother said.

Olivia whipped around. "Excuse me?"

"Miles told me it was okay to tell you now."

"He's worth a hundred—"

The elevator door opened and Olivia snapped her mouth closed, stepping back to let a woman off the elevator.

"Mia?" Her mother held out both hands. "What are you doing here?"

"Oh, I found you!" A woman who looked to be in her late thirties, with light brown hair escaping from a casual ponytail and a narrow build, stepped out and reached both hands out, giving Olivia's mother a surprising hug. "I really hope I'm not intruding."

"Did you finish at Shellseeker Beach?"

Oh, that Mia. *The Last Resort* lady. She'd come to the hospital?

"We did finish, but I heard what happened and since I was passing the hospital on my way out, I just had to stop by to give you my best wishes. I really don't mean to intrude on private time."

"Stop, no apologies. This is my daughter, Olivia Whitney. Liv, this is Mia Watson, from—"

"*The Last Resort*," Olivia finished, shaking her hand. "I'm taking it as a good sign you're here."

Mia gave a self-conscious laugh, and then asked, "How is the patient? Camille, right? Your...sister's mother?" She seemed uncertain of the relationship, making them all chuckle.

"Yes, that's exactly who she is. A testament to the complicated Shellseeker Beach family." Her mother gave a genuine smile. "She's still in surgery, and it could be a few hours before we know anything. But so sweet of you to come, really."

"Well, I had to after..." A soft flush deepened her cheeks. "After that conversation I had with the Dornenbergs. How did you swing that?"

"They made it?" Her mother gave a soft clap. "They were driving from Georgia, and weren't sure they'd be here in time to see you."

"They came just to talk to me." Mia shook her head

and looked at Olivia. "Wow. Talk about pulling out all the stops."

Olivia frowned, not having a single clue who the Dorn-whatevers were. "I'm in the dark," she confessed.

Mia sighed and slid into a wide smile. "Your mother and Teddy worked some magic," she explained. "They persuaded one of Shellseeker's longest returning couples to drive down and tell me about their family's lifetime of memory-making at your resort."

Well, that made sense. "Great idea, Mom." It fit perfectly with their theme.

"And Mia *is* one of their family memories," her mother added. "You know, they remembered you and that's why they wanted to come. Also, I gave them one free week for this winter's vacation." She wrinkled her nose playfully. "Hope that's not cheating."

"Not at all. It was a lovely reunion, and apparently I became an inside family joke as 'Alec's beach crush.'" She rolled her eyes. "Embarrassing, but so fun."

"Lost again," Olivia whispered.

"It's a long story," Mia said.

"And Alec?" Her mother lifted her brows. "I understand he's single."

More color rose in her cheeks. "That's the word from Mr. and Mrs. D." She pointed at Eliza. "You get him here and that *would* be cheating. And you'd win."

"So...you haven't made a decision yet?" her mother asked tentatively.

Mia inhaled slowly. "Not yet. It appears I'm the tie-breaker, too. There are three other reviewers, and they have each voted for one of the properties. One vote for Sunset Palms—"

"I've heard it's gorgeous," Mom said.

"It was spectacular, but a tad over the top. And another voted for Tarpon Villas."

"A fan of the ghosts," Olivia joked.

"And the overall historical richness of the place," Mia said. "And the third absolutely loved Shellseeker Cottages. Which leaves the final decision to me and...it's a very difficult one."

"The Dornenbergs weren't enough," her mother guessed.

"They nearly were, because their testimony was so rich and genuine. Mrs. Dornenberg wears a locket with pictures of her children on Shellseeker, and her grand-children. There's a depth to the family aspect, and I can tell you know that, because Asia and Jadyn shared a lot."

"I'm glad they did, but there's so much more," her mother said, pressing her hands together like she was bursting with all she wanted to say. "You can't even imagine how many lives have been changed by Shellseeker Beach. Many of them are here, in this hospital. And..." She sighed in soft defeat. "We had so many stories to share with you."

Mia's brows rose with interest. "Really? That's...no. I can't interview people here. That is far too intrusive."

"When do you have to make a decision?" Olivia asked.

"By tonight," Mia said. "But honestly, I don't want to talk to anyone, or take more of your family time. I just wanted to see you, give you my thoughts and prayers for Camille, and thank you personally for the Dornenbergs. That was an incredibly sweet touch."

As she spoke, Olivia had an idea. "Mom, why don't you go back with Claire and give me a minute with Mia?"

Her mother almost said no, but she must have seen the spark in Olivia's eyes. The spark of someone who didn't want to give up yet.

"I think that's a good idea. And Mia..." She offered a spontaneous hug. "Whatever you decide, it's been a pleasure."

"It really has," Mia agreed.

Olivia waited a beat until her mother had disappeared around the corner and then she looked at Mia, thinking how to slide into all that she wanted to say.

"You know, I wanted to meet with you at the resort today," she started. "Because I think it's important that you know from someone who uprooted her whole life to be here that Shellseeker Beach is not...ordinary."

"Oh, I can tell," Mia said. "But whatever makes it so special, we, as journalists, have to be able to communicate that in a review. And to be honest? The other two resorts do have a certain...something."

"But we have a certain some*one*," Olivia said, sliding her hand into Mia's arm. "Can you come with me? You won't talk to anyone, I promise. I just want to tell you...something."

Mia nodded and they walked through the hushed hall in silence, slowing down when they reached the long glass window that looked into the waiting room. Teddy and Eliza's heads were close as they exchanged quiet conversation. Claire, Noah, DJ, and Katie sat in a family-like cluster, holding hands. Roz and George were napping, their heads close to each other.

It wasn't everyone, but it was a good group.

"Mia," Olivia whispered. "Let's start with that little family of four. The young woman, Katie? She showed up in Shellseeker Beach as a pregnant nineteen-year-old."

"Oh, is that Harper's mom? I met that little angel today."

"Who is healthy, happy, and thriving because of Shellseeker Beach and Teddy."

Olivia put a hand on Mia's back and started to recount Katie's story, then Noah's and DJ's, even Sophia's, who wasn't here but who Mia had met.

She told her how Roz and George came and stayed to work for Teddy, and Claire, too. And, of course, she shared her mother's story, and her own. Lastly, she told Mia about Camille, and the proposal from a man who now sat by himself in the corner, reading a magazine.

"That particular love story," she said, "wouldn't have happened if Camille hadn't stayed here after she transferred the property and was made to feel like family by Teddy."

Like so many others, her heart and life was changed by one place, and one woman.

"We're not related by blood, but by—"

"Teddy," Mia supplied, her gaze shifting to the wavy white curls that managed to look like a halo around the older woman's head. "She's the glue that holds the whole thing together."

"Yes, she is. No other resort, large, small, fancy, or haunted, has Teddy Blessing."

For a long moment, Mia just looked at Teddy, quiet and thinking.

"The Cottages were homesteaded by her grandfather," Olivia whispered. "They were built by her father, and worked by her family for well over fifty years. She has never lived anywhere else in her entire life. In that time, there are, I'm sure, a hundred more stories of families who have been changed and formed and found and saved by time spent at the oasis she's created in Shellseeker Beach."

Olivia blinked as she stared at Teddy, realizing that her eyes were filled, but she didn't care. This wasn't a pitch to get a feature in a magazine—these were the real stories of a very special place.

When she looked away from the window to get Mia's reaction, she was only a little surprised to see a tear rolling down her cheek, too.

"Olivia," she said softly, wiping it away. "Thank you for sharing all that. It's astounding how much influence one woman, and her little grouping of cottages and people, can have."

"Truly astounding," Olivia agreed. "And there's more."

"I know," Mia said, laughing. "You didn't even mention the guy with the long hair, the former Navy SEAL. He told me Teddy saved him when he was—"

"*Deeley?*" Her heart leaped. "Who told you about him?"

"He did. Well, as best he could with his little boy running after a kite on the beach and asking about... someone named Wibbie?"

Olivia just stared at her. "He was...there? Today? In Shellseeker Beach?" How was that possible? Unless... unless...*he came back.*

"He was on his way here, too," she said, glancing around. "Hasn't he come in yet?"

"He's coming here?" Her voice rose and cracked as every cell in her body stood up and wanted to dance. "Why would he..." She looked at the hall, her whole body aching to run to that elevator and rush out and find him.

Mia smiled. "Why don't you go look for him?" she suggested on a tease. "I'm pretty sure you're more excited about talking to him than to me."

Her breath caught as she nodded. "I mean, you're great, but...he's coming here?"

"He said as soon as the little boy got the kite up once, he'd be here." Mia gave her a gentle prod. "Go."

"Yes! Thank you. I will!" She practically kissed the woman, but decided to pivot instead and head—okay, fly —to the elevators.

She banged on the Down button with a shaky hand, holding her breath when it opened and was...empty.

Still, he was coming here?

Downstairs, she rushed out, dodged a couple holding a bouquet of flowers and darted toward the doors, not caring if she looked like a lunatic. Deeley was back?

The instant the automatic sliders opened, she stepped outside, looking left and right, but not seeing—

"Wibbbieeeeeeeee!"

She whipped around toward that beautiful, beautiful sound, arms out as Bash raced toward her, his mouth wide open, his eyes wild, his hair—who cut his hair?

"Bash, baby!" She scooped him up and squeezed him to her body, nearly crying out with joy. And over his little shoulder, she saw the man she loved, sitting on a half-wall planter, a sly smile on his face, that incredible look in his eyes. And, thank God, no one had cut his hair.

"Hi." He pushed up and ambled over, holding her gaze with one that was just so full of...intention.

"What are you doing here?" she whispered, vaguely aware that Bash had just dropped his head into her neck and stuck his thumb in his mouth with a sigh that sounded like he'd been holding it for...a month.

Deeley just looked at her, his golden eyes filled with so much emotion she couldn't quite absorb it. "I am standing here in all my idiotic glory. We are just two guys. A man who made the dumbest, most ridiculous decision, and his kid, who hasn't stopped reminding him of it since we pulled off Sanibel Island."

She blinked at him, not sure if she wanted to laugh, cry, or smother Bash with kisses. "He has?"

"He's missed you so much. Wibbie this. Wibbie that. Wibbie, Wibbie, Wibbie. And every time..." He put his hand over his heart. "This thing broke even more."

"Aww." She stroked what was left of his blond curls. "Thanks, Bash. I missed you, too."

Deeley took one step closer and inched his head toward hers, placing a hand on her cheek, his eyes misty.

"I love you, Liv. I can't live without you and I don't know what I was thinking, because I wasn't thinking. I made a huge mistake."

"No kidding."

He laughed. "I'm sorry. I'm so sorry. I just had to come home and hold you again and be a family and—"

She silenced him with a kiss, unable to wait one more second. He wrapped them both in his arms, pressing his lips to hers with a whimper of pure relief and joy.

"Wait." She tried to catch her breath. "Your dad. He needs you. He—"

"He sent me back. Pop has a healthy respect for true love and wanted me to have it."

True love.

Dizzy, lost, and wonderfully out of control, all she could do was kiss him, and tell him over and over again that she missed him and loved him, too. She loved them both.

Just then, someone cleared her throat and they finally separated.

Mia stood a few feet away, smiling and looking from one to the other. "Well, looks like you found each other."

"And we're never losing each other again," Deeley said, tightening his arm around Olivia and Bash.

"Good for you," she said, reaching over to tap Bash's nose. "You got your Wibbie back. And you," she added, looking at Olivia. "Have good news waiting upstairs. Camille is out of surgery and in recovery."

"Oh!" Olivia squeezed Bash with a joyous shriek. "That's fantastic!"

Deeley threw his head back, looking at the sky like the prayers he'd sent there had been answered.

On a laugh, Mia backed away, holding up two hands to say goodbye. "I guess I'll see you when I come to write the Hidden Gems feature."

"Really? We got it?" Olivia asked.

"You closed the deal, Olivia." She blew a kiss and backed away to the parking lot, her hands still raised as she pointed from Olivia to Deeley and back again. "And please tell me there will be a wedding on the beach while I'm there!"

With that, she turned and took off, leaving the three of them holding on to each other, and Olivia felt more hope than she thought was possible.

"Well, there is going to be a wedding," she whispered. "Cami and Abner."

Deeley just smiled. "Maybe...there will be two."

*Don't miss **Sanibel Sunsets,** the next book in the Shellseeker Beach series! Once again, this found family unites to overcome adversity, support each other, encourage true love, and ensure that every sunset on Shellseeker Beach is joyous and beautiful.*

The Coconut Key Series

If you're enjoying Shellseeker Beach, you'll love Coconut Key, Hope Holloway's first, now completed, series set on the sun-kissed sands of the Florida Keys!

The Shellseeker Beach Series

Come to Shellseeker Beach and fall in love with a cast of unforgettable characters who face life's challenges with humor, heart, and hope. For lovers of riveting and inspirational sagas about sisters, secrets, romance, mothers, and daughters...and the moments that make life worth living.

About the Author

Hope Holloway is the author of charming, heartwarming women's fiction featuring unforgettable families and friends, and the emotional challenges they conquer. After more than twenty years in marketing, she launched a new career as an author of beach reads and feel-good fiction. A mother of two adult children, Hope and her husband of thirty years live in Florida. When not writing, she can be found walking the beach with her two rescue dogs, who beg her to include animals in every book. Visit her site at www.hopeholloway.com.

Made in the USA
Las Vegas, NV
21 November 2022